She lay face down _____ ____ _____
submerged. The wat_____ _____ _____ent
basin, pelting her body ___ _____ cascade.

I stared at the grim sight, willing it to turn into balloons or blossoms. Anything but my neighbor. Then instinct propelled me into motion. Libby might still be alive, if this had just happened. She might live—if I acted quickly.

I knelt on the rocky ledge that bordered the fountain and pulled her hand out of the water. It was cold and slick. She had no pulse, and her hair streamed down her back in seaweed strands.

For the first time since discovering Libby's body I looked up at the satyr. His hand with the long, curving fingers seemed to be beckoning to her. Or to me?

★

DOROTHY BODOIN
SECRET *for a* SATYR

W●RLDWIDE®

TORONTO • NEW YORK • LONDON
AMSTERDAM • PARIS • SYDNEY • HAMBURG
STOCKHOLM • ATHENS • TOKYO • MILAN
MADRID • WARSAW • BUDAPEST • AUCKLAND

To my nephew, Maximillian James Bodoin.

Recycling programs
for this product may
not exist in your area.

SECRET FOR A SATYR

A Worldwide Mystery/May 2009

First published by Hilliard & Harris.

ISBN-13: 978-0-373-26671-5
ISBN-10:   0-373-26671-5

Printed in U.S.A.

Acknowledgments

The author wishes to thank Marja McGraw, Shirley Schenkel, and Susan Shaw, my good friends and critique partners who followed *Secret for a Satyr* from the first glimmer of an idea to the final draft, offering advice and encouragement. Also thanks to my sister-in-law, Karen Bodoin, who shared her expertise on spinets and themes.

ONE

Someone was watching me.

I stood still in my vast, sunny backyard. My hand tightened on the rake, and I looked around. No one was there. I was alone, except for the ultra-realistic satyr statue next door, surely the most decadent piece of art ever crafted.

Horns poking up through marble white curls, gaze frozen in a perpetual leer, he stood in the center of my neighbor's fountain, trapped in a circle of falling water. His eyes burned in the morning sunshine, and he held his left hand out in an unmistakable invitation. If it weren't for his goat legs and long tail, he would have been quite handsome.

It—not he—I corrected myself. It's a stone carving of a satyr, more suitable for a Roman villa than a backyard in Maple Creek, Michigan. Sensuous and wicked, but only a pricey decoration that contrasted sharply with the wood-cut daffodils and bunnies in front.

Why would a sedate piano teacher like Libby Dorset keep such a monstrosity on her property?

Still, the fountain was a fixture on Beechnut Street, as old as the elegant white Victorian that towered over my modest ranch-style house. Although it couldn't be seen from the sidewalk, passersby knew it was there because of the constant splash of water.

I looked away and tried to concentrate on raking last fall's dried leaves out of the tulip bed. The warmth and high humidity had dampened my enthusiasm for spring clean-up, and I felt uncomfortable with the statue so near.

He was disconcerting, a little disturbing, almost disgusting.

Don't be silly, I thought. *It's a slightly risqué hunk of stone. Nothing more.*

My unease was an ongoing state with clear causes that had nothing to do with the satyr fountain. Not making the cut on the Texas Starfall Project. Starting over at the age of twenty-nine in my hometown. The porch renovation I'd set into motion. No job. Dwindling savings. Too many changes, too little diversion.

In truth, I didn't feel settled in my new house yet. Maybe that would never happen.

You can't go home again. Why did you think you could?

Having no answer, I guided the garden debris carefully into a lawn bag. Neatening my slice of the environment was something I could do.

A screen door squeaked open, and the fountain's owner, Libby Dorset, glided down the steps of her porch. Dressed in a bright floral print for her afternoon piano recital, she carried an enormous basket filled with spring flowers.

"How pretty," I said.

"Good morning, Cressa." Libby set the arrangement down on a long table set up under the yard's lone maple tree. "They came from the Farmers' Market. Everything has to be perfect today. My students worked so hard. They deserve the best."

Her face was flushed. Her voice and hands were fluttery, and a few blonde strands had wandered away from her neat chignon. "I ordered individual strawberry tortes from the Bakery on Main. We'd love to have you join us for refreshments."

"I'd like that," I said. "Thank you."

"Around three-thirty, then? I'm wrapping up the program with one of my own compositions."

"The piece you were practicing this morning?"

"Yes, *Fountain Music.*" Libby pulled the yard's other fixture, a white wicker rocker, over to the table to join a collection of mismatched lawn chairs. "Now if the storm holds off…"

She glanced at the sky, a spring-blue expanse with clouds floating above the treetops and not a sign of rain.

"It should stay dry until tonight," I said.

Two slender girls with streaming yellow hair burst through the screen door, trailing bunches of multi-colored balloons. They'd traded their traditional denim for long sheer dresses and chandelier earrings that sparkled in the sunlight. They were Libby's oldest students, Aleta and Linda, soon to be high school graduates.

"Where do you want these, Miss Dorset?" Linda asked.

"Around the table. Then in the maple if you can reach that low branch."

"I'll give one to the satyr." Aleta stood on the fountain's narrow edge and tied a purple balloon to the statue's hand. I noticed that his fingers were long and curving. Like talons.

"Be careful," Libby said.

"Oh, Miss Dorset. You worry too much."

Libby fussed with the flower basket while the girls decorated the table and tree. The statue cast a long, odd-shaped shadow on the grass, but nobody seemed to notice it. The sound of splashing water blended easily with light chatter and laughter. The festive air was contagious, and soon the day would be filled with music.

Since the weather had turned warm, Libby left her windows open. If I was working outside, I could hear the scales and sonatas and sweet airs that evoked the graciousness of a bygone age. Libby practically lived at her piano. She had a special fondness for the songs of Stephen Foster and often played them in the evening, after her last student had gone home.

In many ways, I was fortunate in my choice of neighborhood, even though I'd imagined myself renting a cottage on Marble Lake for the summer. Instead, I was renovating the smallest house on a street known as Victorian Row.

For the rest of my life? I sent that thought away. Nothing in my life was certain anymore. Nothing was forever. Like the seasons, the best laid plans had a way of changing. The secret to survival was to change with them. I suspected that I was suffering from a delayed case of buyer's remorse.

Or perhaps envy. I'd like to have been able to purchase a grand old mansion with gables, gingerbread trim, and a charming storybook turret. The house I could afford was a plain white frame with bright green shutters, two porches, and a balcony. It looked as if it had been set down on the lot long after the block was complete, but it had a bountiful spring garden. A magnificent weeping cherry tree grew in the front yard. Its blossom-laden branches swept down to the ground like a pink waterfall, brushing the tops of the purple violets that bloomed in the grass.

I leaned the rake against the tree and gazed at the soft mix of color that surrounded me. After a chilly, rainy April, nature was working overtime. The flowers appeared to be growing even as I watched them. They were familiar plants in happy Easter colors: showy hyacinths and several varieties of golden daffodils, all planted by the house's previous owner.

Now to enjoy the fruits of my labors.

I picked up the shears and cut a large bouquet of tulips for myself. Red and deep pink, purple with fringed petals, orange, and bright yellow, their colors formed a rainbow in my hands. They matched the balloons and the splashy florals in Libby Dorset's dress.

Fresh flowers always made a house more cheerful. Feeling almost happy, I climbed the wooden steps to the back porch and went inside.

LATER THAT AFTERNOON, I changed into beige slacks and an ivory blouse, clasped my star pendant around my neck, and joined the small group of piano students and guests who had gathered in Libby's backyard to celebrate a successful recital. The strawberry tortes rested on paper plates, but the tablecloth was linen and the punch bowl made of antique cranberry glass. Libby's refreshment table was as elegant as her house.

Throughout the day the temperature had climbed steadily, but a light breeze and deep shade transformed the yard into a cool oasis. No one ventured near the fountain. Still, nobody could escape the statue. It was at least six feet tall, and its shadow seemed taller. The purple balloon moved frantically in the falling water as if trying to free itself from the stony grasp.

I didn't see Libby, but several people had remained in the house where it was still undoubtedly cooler. In a far corner of the yard, some distance from the statue, the children clustered around a smaller table of their own. Like bright little birds, they chattered about the recital and decorated their ice cream with chocolate syrup, crushed nuts, and maraschino cherries.

Helping myself to a torte and punch, I found a vacant lawn chair and settled back to listen to the soothing splash of water. Snatches of conversation swirled around me. Nearby, three women talked about the fountain in subdued tones. One quiet exchange caught my attention:

"They say that as long as the water runs, the satyr will protect the family."

"Who are they?"

"It's something I heard a long time ago, a neighborhood legend."

"What happens in the winter?"

"It keeps going. There's a heater inside."

"That fountain must cost a fortune in energy bills."

"Consider it a propitiatory offering. Anyway, Libby Dorset has plenty of money. She only buys the best."

As I sampled the torte, I had to agree. The strawberries in the batter were fresh, and real whipped cream topped the little squares. I finished the last bite and glanced at the table. Libby had set out at least four dozen servings for about twenty-five people. Should I take another one? They were smaller than cupcakes. Miniatures, actually. If they stayed out too long in the sun, they would spoil.

Apparently someone else had the same idea. A woman emerged from the overgrown area between the houses and made her way up to the refreshment table. Her gaudy patchwork skirt and the blue bandana tied around her hair suggested that she wasn't one of the guests.

But she must be. How else would she know about the recital?

As I watched, she grabbed six tortes, squishing them together on a single paper plate. She trailed her finger through whipped cream and licked it clean. Then, with a furtive glance behind her, she slipped into the woods that arced around the house. In her wake, twigs snapped and leaves rustled.

No one had taken any notice of her. Or so I thought.

"Who was that person?" The voice was loud, the tone angry. A hush fell over the yard. "Does anybody know her?"

The woman fixed me with a belligerent glare, obviously waiting for an answer.

"I've never seen her before," I said.

My mind registered stray details. The angry woman might have stepped out of the seventies with a stiff, sculptured hairdo in a glossy brown shade. Her dress had a high waist and short, youthful hemline.

Her companion, who was plump, fair-haired, and pretty, had squeezed her ample form into a hot pink sundress and applied matching lipstick with a heavy hand. She waved a fan lazily back and forth. "I didn't see her inside," she said.

"She's not one of us, then." The angry woman fixed her gaze on me.

"Libby Dorset invited me," I said quickly. "I live next door."

Her frown rearranged itself into a hint of a smile. "In that little white house? You must be the girl from Texas. I noticed your license plate." In a minute she'd probably add, "You're not one of us, then."

"I was raised in Maple Creek," I said. "My name is Cressa Hannett."

The smile broadened but didn't offer any warmth. "Pleased to meet you. I'm Gwendolyn White. Welcome to the neighborhood, Cressa."

The other woman said, "I'm Patti Graham, sort of a newcomer myself. Gwendolyn and I live right across the street."

"Not together," Gwendolyn said quickly.

Patti giggled. "Good heavens, no. We'd never make it as roommates. Tell me, Cressa, why do you have a Texas license plate on your car?"

"Well…I've been working on the Gulf Coast," I said.

"What do you do?" Patti asked.

I hesitated, uncertain of what else to say. Naturally new acquaintances would be curious about my Texas years, and I couldn't give them any details. I'd better order a Michigan plate as soon as possible and be vague about my past.

"I had a government job, but I can't talk about it," I said.

Gwendolyn's eyes lit up. "Top Secret! How fascinating! Do you mean you were a spy?"

"Nothing so glamorous. I worked in an office."

"Oh. As a secretary?"

"Gwendolyn, she can't talk about it," Patti said.

I shifted in the chair, uncomfortable with the direction of the conversation. I could excuse myself, wander up to the table for a second torte, and find another place to sit. Or I could start an interrogation of my own. Which did I want to do?

"I see you ladies have met." Libby appeared with an enormous bakery box. "I've brought reinforcements. There's a fresh pot of coffee inside and hot tea. Anyone interested?"

"Lord, no," Patti said. "I'm burning up. It's too warm for May."

"Well that's a Michigan spring. Forty degrees one day, a heat wave the next. How about you girls? Gwendolyn? Cressa?"

"The punch is fine," I said. "It's delicious, and I enjoyed the music. You have a talented group of students."

Libby nodded. "We put together a good program, and all the kids did their best."

"My Aleta was amazing," Patti said. "She puts so much sparkle into her performances."

"She certainly does. Aleta can have a career as a concert pianist, if she wishes."

"Did you see that woman with the scarf over her head, Libby?" Gwendolyn asked.

"She looked like she was dressed up for a costume party," Patti added. "Like a gypsy."

Libby frowned and surveyed the gathering. "I didn't notice her. Why?"

"She just stole a bunch of your cakes and took off into the woods."

"That's strange." Libby looked around again, just as another twig snapped. This time the sound was farther away. "I know everyone here."

"Like I said, she's gone."

"I won't worry about it. I have more than enough of every-thing."

"We could follow her." Gwendolyn started to rise. "Bring her back. Call the police."

"No, let her go." Libby walked over to the table and brought the new tortes out of the box. "If she's hungry, I guess she's welcome to what I have."

That was what she said, but a slight tremor in her voice didn't match the words. Quietly, she threw the empty plates in the trash can and glanced once again toward the woods.

They were dark and quiet, the way woods should be, with trees growing too close together, saplings vying for light and space, and weeds taller than I was. They provided a haven for birds and squirrels and no doubt other wild creatures. I'd never seen anyone walking in them before, or even considered the possibility of an intruder on this quiet street.

"That's somebody's property, isn't it?" I asked.

"It belongs to the old Maywood house over on Willow Court," Gwendolyn said. "The owner wants to keep the acreage in its natural state. It's the largest undeveloped tract of land in Maple Creek."

"I always meant to have a privacy fence put up," Libby said. "It's something I never got around to doing."

"Oh you should, Libby," Gwendolyn said. "It's so much safer when people can't see into your backyard."

"I've always felt safe here."

"Times are changing, even in a little town like Maple Creek. A strange woman just crashed your party. Little kids come to your house all the time. Someone could swoop down and carry one of them off into the woods."

"Gwendolyn, you're spouting gloom and doom today," Patti said.

"I like to think of myself as forewarned. Give that cute Lieu-tenant Gray a call, Libby. Have him check out the gypsy woman." She turned to me. "If you're in the market for a man, Cressa, you should meet him," she added. "He's Maple Creek's finest."

LATER STILL, in the last hours of daylight, I heard a familiar melody coming from the street. I couldn't identify it, but the merry notes conjured happy memories from the past. A song from my school days? Square dance music?

Then I had it. Oh, there never was a fiddler like old Zip Coon, he can play all night on the same old tune… Or something like that. The Good Humor man's theme. The music was near and coming closer every minute, growing louder with each repetition.

I thought the ice cream truck had vanished from Michigan's towns, along with soda fountains and street cars, but here was a tiny bit of Americana alive and well in Maple Creek. It had been a lifetime since I'd answered its siren call. Why not do it today to celebrate the first warm day of the year?

As the music ended in mid-refrain, I slipped my key and a few coins into my pocket and hurried outside to the gleaming white truck parked at the corner of Beechnut and Eversleigh. The giant ice cream cones painted on its side were as bright as beacons. If the music didn't draw a crowd, the pictures would.

A gaggle of noisy children had converged on the driver, a person in a clown costume and bright Raggedy Ann wig. A little apart from them stood a tall man in jeans and a plaid shirt. He was stocky and muscular with handsome features and light brown hair. His warm, lazy smile made me feel as if we'd already met in some distant place, perhaps under a hot Texas sun, but, of course, I'd never seen him before.

As the man stepped to one side to make room for me on the sidewalk, I noticed that he walked with a limp and that his eyes were attractive, a blend of green and blue with light flecks that matched the streaks in his hair. "Ginger is the most popular girl in town today," he said.

"Who's Ginger?" I asked.

"The clown. My neighbor's daughter."

"Oh…" I looked again. The Good Humor person had pale hands with four rings on her fingers and long red nails. She handed a cone to a towheaded boy and turned to a little girl waiting patiently beside her tricycle. "What'll you have, honey?"

"Chocolate, please. Double dip."

"That's my favorite flavor," the man said. "Ice cream is a surefire way to beat the heat."

Yes, the heat. It was warmer now than it had been only a few hours ago. Away from the shelter of the maple trees that lined the street, the sun beat down on my head, and my rayon blouse felt as heavy as wool.

"Mine is rocky road," I said. "How long has it been since you patronized an ice cream truck?"

"A long, long time." He laughed, and his eyes seemed to grow lighter. "One day last August."

"Just a minute, young man." Ginger held a fudgsicle in mid-air, well out of the grasp of a sandy-haired little boy. "You don't have enough pennies. You need five times that many."

"How 'bout if I give you the rest tomorrow?" the boy asked.

"It doesn't work that way." She turned to the man. "What'll you have, Mr. Emmerton?"

"One chocolate cone, and here…" He reached into his pocket and, bringing out a crisp dollar bill, nodded toward the boy. "This should cover it, Miss Ginger." He patted the boy's shoulder roughly.

"Hey, thanks, Mr. Emmerton."

"Okay, then." She took the money, relinquished the fudgsicle, and handed Mr. Emmerton his cone. He gave her a special smile.

"Eat it up before it melts," he said to the boy who scampered away with another mumbled thanks, holding his treat tightly in his grasp as if afraid someone would snatch it away.

"That was a nice thing to do," I said.

"It's called sharing the wealth."

Ginger turned to me. "For you, miss?"

"I'll have an ice cream cone," I said. "Rocky road."

A few seconds later, it was in my hand. I bit into a nut that lay on top of my scoop. "This is absolute perfection."

"So is mine. Enjoy it and stay cool," Mr. Emmerton said and limped away, heading toward Main Street.

The children had already run off in different directions. Ginger cranked on the fiddler song again and moved the truck slowly down Eversleigh, where she made a right turn at the traffic light. As the merry notes faded, I began the short walk home, feeling unaccountably happy as I savored each marshmallow bit and nutty chunk.

This cone was even better than Libby Dorset's strawberry tortes. And why had I never taken the time for a leisurely stroll in my new neighborhood? I really needed to slow down.

Overhead, the leaves moved languidly in a gentle breeze, and blossoming trees scented the air. I breathed deeply and felt instantly lighter, practically rejuvenated. *Oh, to be in Michigan now that May's here!* I was home, and this street where I lived was spectacular.

The houses were vintage Victorians set on wide, shady lots. Each one was slightly different from its neighbors in color, style, or degree of gingerbread trim, but all had spacious front porches and graceful gables reaching up to the sky. Atmosphere and nostalgia hung in the air with the fragrance of lilacs.

Although I walked on a paved sidewalk past twenty-first century vehicles parked in the street, I felt as if I were traveling backwards through the years. Each step seemed to bring me closer to a distant era when life was easier. For the first time in days, I felt calm and optimistic about my choices.

In spite of the dozen concerns that chipped away at my sense of well-being, I had to admit that my world was stable, reasonably satisfactory, and, at the moment, blessed with the magic of this wondrous season of rebirth. I had new people to meet, a host of career opportunities, and a future in a town to which I had strong ties.

Everything was going to be all right.

Then, like a dark shadow, an image of the woman in the patchwork skirt slipped into my mind: the gypsy, scooping up six strawberry tortes and disappearing into the darkness of the woods. She was someone whom Libby didn't know and Gwendolyn White wanted to report to the police, a person who might pose a danger to me.

The Maywood acres adjoined my property as well as Libby's and every other house on Beechnut Street. Perhaps I should think about installing a high fence to keep unwelcome visitors at bay.

A splash of falling water broke through my thoughts. Soft, insistent, soothing—but not entirely so. Always there. Without realizing it, I had begun to walk faster. Three more houses, and I would be home.

TWO

EVENTUALLY THE HOUSE on Beechnut Street would feel like home to me. I knew this and realized that it would take time. Already I loved my airy second-story bedroom with its skylight and small balcony where I intended to end each summer day.

I sat here now, high above the ground, as close to the sky as I could get, waiting for the stars to appear. On my right, lilac bushes heavy with pale lavender flowers grew up to the rooftop. They brushed against the white wood railing, filling the air with their light fragrance, conjuring images of another spring in my grandmother's garden when I was a child and everything I desired seemed attainable.

I wasn't the only one enjoying the outdoors this evening. Libby Dorset was sitting in her yard reading a book. For some reason she had left the strawberry tortes on the table instead of refrigerating them. She still had on her floral print dress, but after long hours of wear, it seemed limp and shapeless. Viewed from the balcony, she looked as deflated as the balloons flapping in the breeze.

As I listened to the splashing water, I let my thoughts drift back to my broken dream of traveling in space. All I had left was a diamond star on a silver chain, a handful of keepsakes, and a lost romance with a man named Jase Clayborne whose face was fading from my memory as rapidly as the last of the daylight.

How could that be when I'd fallen for him so completely?

Jase was a dashing, dark-haired engineer from Fort Worth with handsome, rugged features and a rough-and-ready charm. Over the years, our connection had deepened and flourished. We might have had a future together, but that wouldn't happen now.

He lives in your past, I told myself. *Leave him there. Look to the present.*

First, I needed to give myself another pep talk.

Earlier today, I'd been optimistic about my prospects. Teaching astronomy or even general science could be rewarding. Possibly. I'd know more tomorrow after my interview at Maple Creek High School. Whatever job I chose, in time I might find new friends, possibly a new love, and I'd always have the stars.

The nostalgic scent of lilacs wrapped around me, invoking memories of Jase and driving home to Michigan, pondering my next career move all the way. Over a thousand miles from the Gulf of Mexico to Marble Lake. Finally breathing fresh, sweet air again. One quick decision and I was a homeowner with a yard to maintain, a porch in pieces, and a construction loan. And all the time in the world to second-guess that decision.

I knew that I'd never return to Texas. Working with Jase on the Starfall Project had been the highlight of my life. Unfortunately, in the end, it wasn't my project.

I could still find another one; I would. Maple Creek had its own attractions. I decided to think of my future as a blank book. On its pages, I'd write a grand adventure, a red-hot romance—whatever I wished.

So everything really would be all right. Lulled by the evening warmth and lilacs, I leaned back in my wicker chair, closed my eyes and let my thoughts slip into slow motion. Before long, I drifted into a dream. Alone, amid strange constellations and eerie lights, I floated in space, which should be vast and cold and above all, silent.

This version of the void crackled with raised voices, distant thunder, and a dog's incessant barking. Like the ice cream truck's music, the sounds came closer and grew louder with every passing minute. The slosh and splash of water increased in intensity, and the ceiling fan in the bedroom beyond the French doors shrieked like an alarm bell.

I struggled to find an exit from this mad, discordant world and woke up abruptly. Something or someone had cried out. Or was the cry part of the dream?

I didn't know. The only sounds were the chirping of crickets and the wind. While I'd dosed, the gentle breeze had strengthened into a full-fledged gale. It tossed lilac branches against the balcony and threatened to send my geranium pots tumbling to the ground.

I'd missed the sunset. The stars, usually glittering in a pitch black sky like the stones in my pendant, were somewhere beyond the encroaching storm clouds. At Libby's Victorian, all of the lights were out with the exception of one in a third-floor room. And something was different.

Of course, something was different. It was nighttime now, and I was sitting alone in the dark.

No. Something else. A quiver of fear borne on the air, blowing with the wind and mixing with the lilacs' perfume.

For heaven's sake!

Since I'd moved back to Michigan, my imagination had been running amok. First a lascivious statue and now a vague feeling. I must have left my rational, scientific side behind in Texas.

Find Venus or Jupiter. Make a wish. Then go to bed.

As I scanned the sky, searching for the one special star powerful enough to restore a dream, a loud snapping sound drew my attention down to the ground.

Relax, I told myself. It's an animal stepping on a fallen branch; a night-roving cat or dog.

I had scarcely completed the thought when a thin figure in a long dark cloak emerged from the darkness beyond the fountain. A voluminous hood concealed its face. Like a shadow come to life or a wraith, it shambled across Libby's yard. As the sensory motion lamp at the back of the white Victorian flashed on, the figure turned away from the beam of light.

I stood up and leaned over the railing, hoping for a better view of the intruder, but whoever it was entered the overgrown section between the houses and melted into the night. Thunder rolled across the sky, directly overhead.

The incident was all very melodramatic and Gothic, like a scene from a nightmare and over in a heartbeat, but it didn't necessarily have to be mysterious. Maybe somebody was taking a shortcut through Libby's yard to the street. But anyone passing this way would have to come through the woods. Who would do that at night? Some young person returning from a romantic tryst? The gypsy woman?

That was pure speculation. Whatever the answer, I couldn't puzzle over it now. Large, cool raindrops began to fall; then a sudden cloudburst, whipped along by the wind gusts.

I had waited too long to find my wishing star. Quickly, I moved the geraniums away from the balcony's edge and went inside, locking the French doors. Trying to ignore the feeling that I had left an important task undone, I switched on my bedside lamp. The blades of the ceiling fan turned, circulating warm air through the room. Now their shriek reminded me of a sob.

THE BLACK JERSEY DRESS was a good choice for an interview with a school superintendent. Simple, classy, and memorable. That was the impression I wanted to convey, and my star pendant was the perfect accessory as well as a good luck charm.

My physical assets were few: dark auburn hair, green eyes accentuated with taupe shadow and a slender, toned figure. I applied lip gloss and stepped back from the dresser mirror, satisfied with my appearance. As soon as I had a light breakfast, I'd be ready for anything, even a dreary Monday morning.

In the kitchen, the tulip bouquet added welcome color to the depressing, outdated décor. I filled the tea kettle with water, pausing to glance out the window at the unpromising view. Last night's rain had left a waterlogged landscape and light mist in its wake. In Libby's yard, the balloons were gone, but the strawberry tortes were still on the table.

That was strange. Most people wouldn't leave food outside during a thunderstorm. Libby must have intended to give the leftover cakes to the birds, but maybe she'd been too tired to finish taking her party apart. I should have offered to help her. I could still do it.

My gaze shifted to the back of the yard where the statue gleamed in the mist, its tall, lean form wreathed in gauzy shreds. Flowers skimmed the surface of the water below. Like the tulips, they provided a splash of color in a dull monochromatic scene. Orange, yellow; and red; purple, blue, and violet on a green background.

There was something familiar about that combination, and here was another strange element. When had I ever seen flowers in the fountain? I must be looking at the balloons, cut loose from the branches. Or… I pushed the curtain aside, trying to see clearly into Libby's backyard. A horrible suspicion closed in on me; another possibility. From here it looked as if something substantial was in the fountain.

The rainbow melt on the water resembled the dress Libby had worn yesterday. *That meant*… Leaving the teakettle on the counter, I rushed through the back porch out to the yard. *That might mean*…

Drops of moisture dripped down from the trees as I plowed through the high wet grass, following the sound of water. I broke into a run, hoping that when I reached the fountain, I'd find a tangle of flat, soggy party balloons after all.

But the colors were the floral pattern on a dress, and the dress covered a body.

"Oh, Libby, no…"

She lay face down in the fountain, completely submerged. The water crashed into the cement basin, pelting her body in an endless cascade.

I stared at the grim sight, willing it to turn into balloons or blossoms. Anything but my neighbor. Then instinct propelled me into motion. Libby might still be alive, if this had just happened. She might live—if I acted quickly.

I knelt on the rocky ledge that bordered the fountain and pulled her hand out of the water. It was cold and slick. She had no pulse, and her hair streamed down her back in seaweed strands. Her right arm lay at an awkward angle as if she had been trying to reach the statue's outstretched arm.

To hold onto it as she lifted herself out of the water?

For the first time since discovering Libby's body I looked up at the satyr. His hand with the long, curving fingers seemed to be beckoning to her. Or to me?

Dear God, lose that thought.

Nausea washed over me. Why was I still holding Libby's wrist? I lowered her hand gently into the water and moved away, taking deep breaths. My sleeve was wet and, for a moment, I couldn't remember why that mattered.

I had only made physical contact with Libby once before, shaking her hand when she welcomed me to the neighborhood. Now I had touched Death, and I felt its presence—peering out from the woods, prowling through the rooms of the old Victorian, and lurking among the boards and tools on my unfinished back porch. Everywhere.

Shivering in the damp air, I corralled my runaway thoughts. Wet clothes and minor discomforts were insignificant. Libby lay dead in her fountain, and all I could do for her now was call the police.

As long as the water runs, the satyr will protect the family.

Gwendolyn White had said that at the reception yesterday. The water still ran, but Libby was dead. So much for sacrificial offerings.

The thought ran crazily through my mind as I watched the police enclose the yard with yellow tape. Little details tugged at me: a chunky pillar candle with a blackened wick; two china teacups filled with an amber tea-rain mix; Libby's book on the ground, its pages and cover ruined by the storm. And no balloons, not even the one Aleta had tied to the statue.

There seemed to be a story here, but pieces were missing. Did Libby plan to read outside by candlelight? Had she served tea to a guest and, at some point, let her book fall to the grass? Then, when the storm broke, what did she do? Or was she already dead while I moved my flowerpots and took shelter inside my house?

If Libby wasn't alone, what happened to the guest—and where were the balloons?

The answers lay somewhere in the lost chunk of time between sunset and night. While I'd dreamed about strange stars and noises, Libby might have uttered the cry I'd heard. I could have saved her life, if only I'd thought to investigate it.

She must have been in the fountain at that time. Otherwise, when the storm came, she would have rushed inside and turned on more lights. Was the Victorian still dark when I left the balcony? I hadn't noticed, which was unfortunate because that information might be important.

Libby hadn't changed clothes, which suggested that she'd been in the water for about ten hours, unless she'd gone inside and come out again when the storm passed. I had to make sure that I didn't forget anything when I talked to the police. Both the cloaked figure and the sounds I'd heard in and out of my dream might help them determine what had happened, in case it wasn't an accident.

"What's going on over there?" Mr. Harrison, the elderly gentleman who lived in the house on the other side of mine, asked the question.

"Miss Dorset drowned in her fountain," I said.

"Oh, no. Not Libby." His hand moved up to the knot in his tie. "How could that happen? Did she have a heart attack?"

"I don't know. I only found her."

He turned away, but not before I saw the glisten of tears in his eyes. I looked for Lieutenant Gray, the tall, dark officer who appeared to be in charge of the investigation. He was in the driveway arguing with Linda who had attempted to cross the yellow tape line. Their voices carried out to the street—his, loud and authoritative; hers, defiant—but I couldn't make out what they were saying.

I would be next on his list. Soon now.

Libby was already inside the ambulance, on her way to…wherever. The morgue, I imagined, or to the hospital for an autopsy. In a few more minutes, my involvement in the sad affair would be over.

Before the police arrived, I'd kept a lonely vigil at the fountain, trying not to look at the satyr. He seemed to have grown to a height of eight feet, and his stone eyes had a triumphant glitter. I could almost hear him say, "I'm going to get you, too."

All deplorable imagination. I couldn't be afraid of a hunk of

stone. Still, I longed to run back into my house and hide from
the horror that had descended on Beechnut Street. I didn't want
to leave Libby alone, though, and being part of a crowd brought
a measure of normalcy to this terrible morning.

The sirens had quickly drawn Libby's neighbors out of their
houses. Children en route to school exchanged gruesome speculations about the tragedy, while a medium-size black dog with
tan and white markings sniffed intently around the bed of
flowers, keeping out of the officers' way.

From across the street, Patti Graham waved to me. I hesitated for a moment, then walked over to join her. Tears filled
her eyes, streaking the pink blush on her face. To my surprise,
she hugged me.

"I just can't believe it. Is it true?" she asked.

"I'm afraid so," I said.

"Maybe they can give her CPR or a shot or something."

"It may be too late."

"But that doesn't make any sense." She mopped her face with
a tissue. "How could Libby just tumble into her own fountain?
She had to know it was there."

I didn't have an answer. Unless Libby had lost her way in the
storm and gone in the wrong direction. On her own property?
For now I'd keep that unlikely theory to myself, along with my
suspicion. "It's a mystery," I said.

Gwendolyn White hurried down the street, tottering on stiletto
heels, and threw herself into the conversation. "Maybe Libby had
too much punch. That was a pretty potent brew she mixed together."

Patti frowned. "You had three glasses yourself, Gwendolyn."

"But I keep my wits about me."

The man I'd seen at the ice cream truck yesterday, Mr.
Emmerton, limped over from a picturesque blue house and
joined us. "It looks like a freak accident." He opened a small
black notebook and took a pen out of his pocket. His summer
tan, certainly not acquired under a Michigan sun, made his eyes
lighter today, and the flag pin on his lapel had a bright shine.

"Morning, Mr. Emmerton," Gwendolyn said. "I suspect
foul play."

"Would you care to elaborate?" he asked.

"I've seen some unsavory people loitering around town this summer."

"She means the homeless population," Patti said.

"Libby owned a lot of antique jewelry," Gwendolyn added.

"Are you suggesting that some vagrant pushed Miss Dorset into the fountain and robbed the house?"

Gwendolyn shrugged, and Mr. Emmerton gave us all a non-committal smile, but his eyes lingered on me, on my square neckline and the star pendant resting on black. Suddenly remembering my interview, I glanced at my watch. I had two hours before my appointment, but I'd have to change my dress if the sleeve didn't dry by then, and I needed something to eat, maybe a piece of toast.

"Try this scenario instead," he said. "Miss Dorset dropped something in the fountain, tried to retrieve it, and lost her balance. Then she hit her head and lost consciousness."

"That would do it," Gwendolyn said. "If she let herself get overly tired, she might have felt faint."

"What could she have dropped?" Patti asked.

"Anything."

His explanation seemed plausible—to a point. "I wonder why she would have been so close to the fountain," I said.

"Trying to cool off? Remember how hot it was yesterday."

"Or maybe a wounded bird fell in the water," Patti said. "Did you see anything in the fountain that shouldn't be there, Cressa?"

"Only Libby."

"Were you at the scene, Miss…?" Mr. Emmerton asked.

"Cressa Hannett. I saw something in the fountain from my kitchen window and walked over to see what it was."

"And it's a good thing you did," Patti said. "She could have stayed there for days decomposing in the water."

Mr. Emmerton jotted down a few sentences in his notebook. "My name is Matt, Cressa. You must live in that white house next to the Dorset place, then?"

As I nodded, he wrote another line.

"I just remembered," Gwendolyn said. "Something similar

happened a long time ago. They say a child drowned in that very fountain."

Patti gasped. "It's a death trap."

"For a little kid maybe. Not for a grown woman."

I tried to absorb the relevancy of Gwendolyn's recollection. If the story was true, the fountain had claimed two lives. That might explain my aversion to the statue—which was the most irrational thought I'd had in hours.

Matt made another notation in his book. "There should be a record of it. I'll see what I can find out."

Patti said, "I never liked that goat-man creature. An angel or fairy would have brought better karma."

"Miss Dorset inherited the fountain with the house," Gwendolyn pointed out. "A large statue isn't something you toss out like a birdbath."

"Aleta is going to be devastated when she hears the news." Patti fumbled in her pocket and brought out another tissue. "The girls cleaned house for her, you know. And I'm going to miss her, too."

"Libby Dorset was a fixture on Beechnut Street," Gwendolyn said. "A real lady."

I felt a cold nudge against my knee and looked down to see the black dog wagging its tail, eyes fixed hopefully on me.

"Hello, pooch," I said. "I don't have anything for you." But I offered my palm to sniff, and his tail wagged more rapidly.

"That's Pepper," Matt said, giving her a quick pat on the head. "She's always running free. Go home if you have one, girl, before you get in trouble."

That seemed like good advice for me, too. My house waited across the street, only a minute's walk away, but I couldn't go anywhere until I talked to Lieutenant Gray. I was growing impatient for the interview to happen and be over. Then I had another one at the school board office. Suddenly the day seemed too busy.

"Here comes the sun," Gwendolyn said, as ray of light broke through the overcast sky.

"It's already warm," I added.

While we'd been occupied with Libby's death, the morning mist had dissipated. The air smelled of freshly mowed grass and lilacs. I took a deep breath and felt a little better. *Thank God I'm alive,* I thought.

Libby had loved May flowers, especially the short-lived wild violets and delicate grape hyacinths. How sad to leave the earth in the springtime. But people died in every month, and Libby's years had run out.

"I'll let you know what I find out about the child," Matt said, and he limped down the street, moving with determination and purpose.

Patti yawned. "Life goes on, I guess, but I feel like going back to bed."

"I for one am out of the mood to work," Gwendolyn announced. "I think I'll call in sick today."

"We need a transition," Patti said. "Come on over for coffee and doughnuts. You too, Cressa."

"I'd like to, but…"

Again I looked for Lieutenant Gray. He must have dealt with Linda, for she swept past me, hair bouncing on her shoulders, anger in every stride. I couldn't imagine why she'd challenged him. No one with a modicum of sense would defy an armed policeman.

He moved out to the sidewalk, surveying the crowd, obviously looking for someone. The noise level dropped perceptibly as his gaze came to rest on me.

"I have to talk to the lieutenant," I said.

"Lucky you." Gwendolyn gave me a conspiratorial wink. "See if you can wrangle a date with him."

"I don't think so," I said but couldn't suppress a smile. Life *did* go on. In spite of the circumstances that had brought us together, I'd noticed that Lieutenant Gray was an extremely attractive man with movie-star good looks and a commanding presence.

He's even more handsome than Jase, I thought as I crossed the street to meet him. This was the last ordeal of a traumatic morning, and I'd welcome anything that made it bearable.

The white Victorian already had the bleak, deserted look of a house whose owner has gone to another place. The gingerbread trim on the gables resembled lovingly crafted teardrops, and one of the wood-cut daffodils had fallen over. Its yellow petals were as pale as if they had been bleached by the fountain's water all night.

At this time, on a typical Monday morning, Libby would have been giving piano lessons to one of her adult students, perhaps the thin, white-faced young woman clutching a large brown folder who gazed blankly at the house.

Often I'd hear music wafting through the air. Scales that rippled across the keyboard like water over river rocks; stumbling, slow exercises; artfully performed sonatas; and sentimental songs by Stephen Foster were suddenly part of the past, all gone like Jase and my previous life. I felt like crying for all lovely, lost things.

"Looks like that statue got her." The husky young voice rang out into the midmorning stillness.

Lieutenant Gray snapped to attention. "Who said that?" he demanded.

He waited for an answer that no one offered. But a red-haired boy began to pedal his bike furiously down the sidewalk in the direction of Main Street. Unfazed by the lack of response to his query, the lieutenant directed his next comment to me. "I'm ready for you, Ms. Hannett."

THREE

RAYS OF SUN beat down on the cruiser's window, turning the interior into a giant oven. Lieutenant Gray moved the air conditioner fan to the right, and cool air gushed out from the vents. At close range, he was still an extremely attractive man with an air of quiet authority and cornflower blue eyes. An intriguing combination. But his brusque, official manner made me nervous.

I'd told him about my dream and how the cloaked figure had materialized in Libby Dorset's backyard. For good measure, I added the unknown woman who had crashed the party and disappeared in the woods with a stash of strawberry tortes.

Apparently the only part of my narrative that interested him was the figure.

"Why do you say cloak?" he asked. "Why not simply coat?"

Why indeed? I'd never wondered about that. Now I had to come up with a plausible answer.

"Cloak was the first word that came to my mind," I said. "It was long and full, like a cape, and dark. Navy blue or brown. I couldn't tell in the dark."

"Do they sell them in department stores?" he asked.

What kind of question was that? "I've never shopped for one," I said.

"My guess is they don't."

"But you might find them in costume shops or little theatre groups."

He hooked his hand together. "Tell me, who wears a garment like that in eighty-five degrees?"

"Anyone who listens to the weather report," I said.

The fan hummed in the stillness, chilling the car. Lieutenant

Gray fixed his blue eyes on me and waited. They were sharp, missing nothing, giving nothing away.

I shifted uneasily on the hard seat, wishing I were outside. Most of the onlookers had vanished, but a few lingered, their eyes riveted on the patrol car, which suddenly didn't seem so private. Ignoring my craving for fresh air, I added, "Somebody who didn't want to get wet. There was a storm watch yesterday."

I ran my hand over my sleeve. It was still damp.

"Let's run through your statement again," he said. "This figure activated the sensory motion light and took off into those saplings between your property and the Dorset house."

"That's right. A few minutes later, it started to rain."

"You said you didn't get a good look at her face?"

"I couldn't tell if the figure was male or female," I said.

"Did this person know you were there?" he asked.

Again, that hadn't occurred to me until now. "I don't think so. No."

"So, with the possible exception of the individual in the cloak, you were the last one to see Miss Dorset alive."

I nodded. "So far as I know. From my balcony, I have a clear view of Libby's yard. She was reading."

The Collected Poems of Sara Teasdale. I'd glanced at the title during my vigil at the fountain. Nobody I knew read poetry during their leisure time. Then, I'd never known anyone quite like Libby Dorset. Libby once mentioned that she cherished her books. She would have regretted the extensive water damage to the slender volume.

"When was this?" he asked.

"Around nine or nine-thirty. Then I dozed off."

A sardonic gleam danced in his eyes. "Do you usually take a nap before bedtime?"

"This one just happened. When I woke up, it was dark and windy. That cry could have been Libby calling out for help."

"Or a bird or animal," he said. "Maybe you dreamed it."

"Yes, and everything that happened in between is a blank screen. I guess I'm not a good witness, falling asleep at a crucial time."

"You'll have to do, Ms. Hannett. So far, you're the only one we have." He jotted down a note and said, "I think this about wraps it up, unless there's something you'd like to add."

"Only a few details. They may be relevant."

He listened politely but didn't make any additions to his report.

The two teacups, suggesting the presence of a visitor, didn't seem significant to him. He pointed out that Libby had provided coffee and tea for her guests, as well as punch, a fact I'd overlooked. The candle might have been on the table all along, but the vanishing balloons grabbed his attention.

"There were about two dozen of them hanging from the branches last evening," I said. "They were all colors."

Lieutenant Gray closed his book and laid down his pen; looked up and frowned. "We'll look for a cache of deflated balloons. They'll probably turn up in the trash."

"Libby didn't have enough time to take them down before the storm came."

"Are you suggesting that someone else did? In the dark? Before the rain?"

"I only know that it's strange," I said. "They have to be somewhere. Libby's death appears to be accidental, but maybe it wasn't."

"That's right." He opened the door and walked around the cruiser to the curbside where he held out his hand to assist me. "Thanks for your cooperation, Ms. Hannett. We'll try to find out exactly what happened."

How could he do that when I was the only witness and my information was so skimpy?

"Will you look for the cloaked figure?" I asked.

His mouth arranged itself into a half smile. "Slight form, height unknown. Features obscured by hood of—cloak. Yes, ma'am. She should be easy to find."

"She or he," I said, as I made my escape.

BY ELEVEN O'CLOCK the temperature had risen into the high eighties again, taking my spirits along with it. My job interview had gone well. Maple Creek High School was a sunny, newly-landscaped building on a hilly half acre a few miles south of Main Street. The halls teemed with youthful energy and chatter; posters advertising the Memory Dance decorated the halls.

Working in this happy environment might yield its own rewards. It might even be fun.

The superintendent had an unappealing pompous streak, but Mr. Gorman, the principal, was friendly and enthusiastic about his staff and students. My credentials impressed both of them. I left the school feeling that, as long as I renewed my teaching certificate, the tenth grade science position was mine, if I wanted it.

Did I want it? I wasn't sure.

Over a late breakfast at the Country Kitchen, I weighed the advantages and disadvantages of making the leap from space engineer to high school teacher. It would be like falling from a brilliant star down to earth. If I felt that way, I shouldn't even consider their offer—if they made one.

Still, I had to pay my bills. I had to eat. Perhaps not banana-nut pancakes and bacon every morning, but something, and the next generation had to learn to appreciate the mysteries of the universe.

How about a compromise? I could teach for a year, sell the house next spring, and start searching for a new job in the space field where I belonged. Perhaps in time I'd climb my way up to the stars again. I drank my coffee slowly and allowed myself a few minutes of delicious fantasy. I'd relocate to Florida or California or maybe go back to Texas.

Slow down, I told myself. *You're home in Michigan, where you wanted to be.*

Where a bizarre death had shattered the comfortable old-time ambience of the neighborhood.

The moment of euphoria burst into fragments of still-vivid images: Libby lying in the fountain with her hair streaming down her back. My hand holding her lifeless, dripping wrist. The sinister satyr statue watching us. The dress with its rainbow colors bleeding together under the relentless cascade.

Was there any blood on Libby's body? There must have been, if she'd landed on her face, but I couldn't recall seeing a red cast in the water.

Because I happened to be on the balcony yesterday and looked out my kitchen window this morning, I was part of her tragedy. Maybe my strange dream reflected actual events unfolding in Libby's backyard while I slept.

Raised voices, a dog barking at a nocturnal disturbance, and an intruder fleeing into the night might point the way to the truth, but apparently Lieutenant Gray had rejected them as dream happenings or figments of my imagination. Even the mysterious figure.

He probably thought I'd fabricated it and used a melodramatic word for an added touch. But I had seen a cloaked figure and assumed that the person, whoever it was, had played a part in last night's events.

All of a sudden I wasn't certain that I'd been unobserved. Suppose this person had looked up and seen me on my balcony with an unobstructed view of the fountain, a witness to whatever happened there. If Libby's death wasn't an accident, my involvement in the case might be only beginning. I could be in danger myself.

THE HULKING WHITE E Z Construction truck was parked in my driveway behind a Dumpster that had been a permanent fixture for three weeks. The workers were unloading large terra-cotta paving stones. Encouraged by any sign of progress from the pokey crew, I left my car in the street in front of Libby's house and walked around to the back.

They halted their good-natured banter to greet me, and Tim, the burly, gregarious boss, turned down the volume of a radio, dousing a heated political rant. "We're going to work on the patio today." He gestured toward the crime scene tape. "What happened next door?"

"A terrible accident. My neighbor drowned in the fountain this morning."

"Not Miss Dorset!" He shook his head. "I don't trust those

man-made water contraptions. None of 'em are one hundred percent safe."

"No one knows the details," I said.

"That's a shame. Miss Dorset was such a nice lady. She brought us lemonade once when you were away."

His gaze traveled from the house to the fountain and back to me. Back to business again. "We'll have the stones set in by the end of the day. As soon as Jeff and Toby level off the area. That uneven ground is another accident waiting to happen."

A linden tree grew about three yards from the porch, surrounded by a wide band of bare ground. No grass could survive in the dense shade, and several years of rain and snow had eroded the soil, bringing a tangle of high roots to the surface.

"Don't hurt the tree," I said.

Tim wiped his forehead with a bandana. "We'll be careful, Ms. Hannett."

I glanced down at the stones. They had a pattern of interlocking ovals that reminded me of four-pointed stars.

"Unless we hit a snag, you can barbeque chicken for Memorial Day," he added.

"If someone else does the cooking," I said.

I had no plans to buy an outdoor grill. My vision involved a round table with an umbrella and sandwiches on paper plates. Nothing elaborate. Just a shady place to sit on long summer days.

"Go see what you think of your porch," Tim said.

I wove my way around a load of fresh dirt to the door and peered inside. The screens were in place and the new wood floor swept clean of construction debris. Finally the skeletal shape had evolved into a proper outdoors room with spacious dimensions and a wraparound ledge, all ready for furniture and plants. Perhaps the seemingly interminable project was truly winding up.

Before long, they'd take the Dumpster away. The annoying radio would be gone, too, along with the workers' running commentaries. Today, though, I didn't mind the noise. Without the men milling around, Beechnut Street would be too quiet. The heavy silence that had descended on the white Victorian unnerved me. With its locked doors and closed windows, it was as if the house were in mourning for a fallen mistress. As if Libby was already a ghost, flitting through the halls.

She was a spirit now.

If Libby were alive, I imagined she'd play a trio of sad songs suitable for the occasion, and the music would drift through the air over to my house. I could almost hear it.

Toll the bell for lovely Nell... Why should the beautiful die? Massa's in the cold, cold ground.

Libby wasn't buried, not yet, but the graveyard atmosphere seemed to thicken by the minute. Then I realized what was wrong. The fountain was dead, too. For the first time since moving to Maple Creek, I couldn't hear splashing water. The police must have unplugged the pump before removing Libby's body.

With a quick glance around to make sure that no police lurked on the street, I crossed the yellow tape and made my way over the grass to Libby's yard, as I had this morning.

Every single festive trace was gone, along with the evidence of the morning's death. The officers had cleared the table and taken away the trash can. The folded lawn chairs leaned against the side of the house, and Libby's rocker had been moved to the porch. It was hard to believe that only yesterday we had feasted on cake and punch and basked in the afterglow of a spring recital.

At the fountain, I gazed down into the basin, searching for a sign of blood. There was none, no indication that a woman had died here. Only drying concrete and a few stray leaves and twigs.

The satyr's hand reached out to me in a perpetual unspoken invitation. His long curved fingers froze my heart. I stood in his shadow, looking up at him, trying to figure out why this insentient creature bothered me so.

His body glistened in the sun, and every artfully carved angle radiated with light. Being a piece of art crafted in the image of evil, his leer would never fade. The pointed ears, lower goat body, and curling tail would always set him apart from the rest of mankind. As long as he existed, that is.

For I had the absurd notion that, without water, he would soon die. That would be a blessing.

"You know what happened," I said and stopped myself, aghast that I'd just spoken to a statue. Luckily the rock music blaring from my own property drowned out the outrageous comment.

If I were so impressionable, I'd better leave Libby's yard and never come back. Even then, the satyr would be too close.

Heels tapping on concrete drew my attention to the driveway. Patti crossed the yellow tape and came silently up the ribbon drive. She had changed into a plain black sleeveless dress, and the only color in her pale face was her dark red lipstick. She held a yellow daffodil with delicate ruffled petals and a soft apricot center.

"I know we shouldn't be behind the tape, but there aren't any cops around," she said. "Are you all right, Cressa?"

"I'm just terribly sad."

"Well, I'm still shaking. I don't know how I'm going to tell Aleta." Patti dropped the flower into the fountain. "For Libby. She loved yellow."

"And spring flowers," I said, close to tears again.

"The neighbors left three bouquets on the front porch. I thought Libby would be more likely to see this one, since she died here." Her voice broke as she added, "It would be even worse if she did this to herself."

"You mean—killed herself?"

"That's what Gwendolyn heard through the grapevine."

"I don't believe it. She was so happy yesterday, so excited about the recital, so…"

So fragile in a limp party dress, sitting in her rocker, as deflated as the missing balloons.

"Libby died in a strange way," I said. "There's bound to be gossip."

"Nobody knows what's really going on in people's lives. They show you the face they want you to see."

"But Libby was always so serene. I thought people who killed themselves were depressed or confused. Out of other options."

They didn't practice the piano all morning, host an elegant

reception and read old poetry at twilight. Unless Libby had decided to indulge in her favorite activities one last time. The suicide theory seemed wrong, but how well did I know Libby? Only as a neighbor; only for a little over a month.

"The police should be able to uncover the truth," I said.

Patti sighed. "Suicide or murder, anyway you look at it, Libby is gone. What does it matter now?"

I was about to say that it *did* matter when Tim's voice boomed out over the rock beat. "Hey, Ms. Hannett. Over here! Come see what we found under your tree."

FOUR

"JEFF! TURN THAT BLASTED radio off," Tim shouted. The rock music died in mid-verse. With Patti trailing behind me, I walked quickly over to the linden tree where the men stood in a semi-circle looking down at the ground.

What now?

They had unearthed a skeleton in a shallow depression between two gnarled roots. In the light of the sun, it had an eerie grayish-green glow. For a moment, I wondered if it was real or some grotesque Halloween decoration.

Toby handed me a narrow leather collar, gritty and stiff with age. "We found this, too, and some stray bones."

"It was a dog," I said.

Patti peered over my shoulder. "Are you sure it isn't a child?"

I ran my fingers over the dirt-encrusted buckle and swallowed the lump in my throat. "I'm sure. That's a canine skull."

The remains suggested an animal a little larger than Pepper. My imagination added soft fur, bright eyes, and a wagging tail. At one time, someone's best friend.

"Ugh," Patti said. "Imagine having a cemetery at your doorstep."

Tim picked up the shovel. "I'll give it the old heave-ho. Straight to the Dumpster."

"No," I said. "You can't do that."

He looked at me, dark brows furrowed, hands frozen on the handle. "Why not?"

"This was a pet—buried with love and tears. You can't just toss him away with scraps of old wood."

"Do you want to build your patio over it?" he asked.

"No…" I glanced toward the invisible line where my property joined the Maywood acres. "I'll move him. Maybe back there."

Not too far from the original grave where daffodils struggled to bloom in the shade of dark encroaching trees. I'd dig another hole directly opposite the Maywoods' old red canoe that appeared to be permanently anchored in a lake of vegetation. Then, if I ever changed the landscaping, I'd always know where the skeleton was.

"In the woods," Patti said. "That's a good idea, if you insist on keeping it."

"Alongside them. I can't bury a dog on land that doesn't belong to me."

"They'll never know."

"Oh, but *I* will. Besides it's illegal."

"When you decide on a spot, the boys will take care of it," Tim said.

"Thanks, but I can do that. If you get the bones together for me, I'll find a sheet to wrap them in."

"You must like dogs, Ms. Hannett," Toby said.

"I do. Even the ones I never knew."

Patti shivered. "This is too creepy. Death is all around us today."

"In the strangest places," I added.

She took one last look at the skeleton and turned away. "I'd better be going. I want to tell Aleta about Libby before somebody else does. Unless Linda already did. Linda was upset because she left her purse at Libby's yesterday. They wouldn't let her in to get it."

With a hasty wave, she hurried down the drive to the street.

"I'll be right back, Tim," I said.

In the linen closet I found a new flannel sheet that smelled of lavender. It was too nice to bury in the ground, but the unknown dog deserved this small measure of respect. As I changed into jeans and a tank top, I tried to figure out how long it took for a canine body to decompose. A few years or a few decades? I had no idea but could find the information in one of my college textbooks. Perhaps the dog's owner was dead, too. At one time he must have lived in my house.

By the time I rejoined the men, Jeff and Toby had laid the first row of stones. The skeleton lay on a crumpled blanket a short distance from the tree. Tim nudged the bones onto the sheet with a rake, and I wrapped them securely for what I hoped would be the last time. Then I carried the small bundle to the back of the yard, well out of the satyr's line of vision, and began to dig a hole.

Beneath the hard top layer, the soil was laced with roots. I cut through them with the shovel's edge and soon had a deep and roomy space. As I worked, I remembered how my collie had died on the veterinarian's table. They took her body away to be cremated, while I held her leash and collar and wept for my own best friend. Out of my sight, she was never out of my memory, even after fifteen years.

Burial in the ground was better, and I wouldn't have to think that the dog lay beneath the patio whenever I walked across it. But I couldn't so easily forget Libby, and the satyr still languished in the middle of the empty fountain without sustenance, burning in the noonday sun. Patti was right. Death was all around us today, casting a dark shadow on the soft pastels of spring.

Don't give It that power.

Still, every time I looked at the white Victorian, I thought about Libby and sadness overwhelmed me. If I happened to glance at the satyr statue, the emotion shifted to apprehension. Libby's house would always tower over mine, but a grape arbor on the property line or, better still, a privacy fence would hide the lower portion of the satyr's body. The goat part.

Out of sight, out of mind?

I suspected that no barrier was high enough to keep the abomination at bay, so I'd better learn to live with it. Maybe the next owners would demolish the fountain and reduce the statue to chunks of concrete and nightmares. On that hopeful note, I lowered the sheet into the hole and covered it with dirt.

For a final touch, I gathered an assortment of rocks from the tulip bed and arranged them on top of the fresh earth. Now no curious animal could disturb the site, and the daffodils would lend their bright color to the grave until they, too, died.

The scene blurred as I stepped back to survey my work. *There are tears of things.* I'd heard the line in a college literature course and never understood it. Today it made sense.

Sadness dragged down the air. It was as heavy as the silence that hung over Libby's house, all around me and growing constantly stronger.

"Go back to sleep, pooch," I said.

AT FOUR O'CLOCK, the men went home. Soon afterward, Beechnut Street began to buzz with activity. A stream of mourners on foot or in cars paraded past the white Victorian. Floral tributes filled the front porch and overflowed onto the lawn. As I opened the door to bring in the Tribune, two little girls stopped their tricycles on the sidewalk in front of my house. I paused to listen to their conversation.

"That old statue pulled her into the fountain, and she drowned."

"No way."

"He did so!"

That was the version of Libby's death as filtered through the juvenile grapevine. Thank heavens they hadn't heard the suicide gossip.

This day seemed interminable. I dropped the paper on the kitchen table without unfolding it and opened the refrigerator to an uninspiring selection: eggs, carrots and celery; root beer and ginger ale in cans. I had bread and wraps for a sandwich, but no lunch meat.

The Blue Lion on Main Street was within walking distance. In ten minutes, I could make myself presentable for the dinner hour. I brushed my hair, touched up my lip gloss, and slipped into my black dress again. The only way to make this ghastly day better was to have a hot meal cooked by somebody else.

One of the oldest and most picturesque restaurants in Lapeer County, the Blue Lion boasted distinctive medieval décor and the best food in town. More importantly, it was a storehouse of happy memories for me. When I was a child, my mother and I used to come here for fish and chips every Friday. We'd sit among the lions and unicorns painted on the walls, and I imagined that I was dining in a fairy-tale castle.

I always ordered lemonade and chocolate peppermint pie, and ate the meringue first. If those items were still on the menu, I could recreate that cherished childhood meal. Now, being an adult, I'd eat my dessert the proper way, topping, filling and crust together.

I stepped into the dim, cool interior, eager to reconnect with my past. Everything was exactly as it had always been, storybook magical, except for the number of people waiting to be seated. As I took my place at the end of the line, I realized that I'd finally found the familiarity that had eluded me. To add a dollop of icing to the cake, someone I knew stood in front of me. A third chance encounter with Matt Emmerton was an incredible coincidence, but here he was, tall and husky, leaning against the railing.

Then I recalled that he lived nearby, in the showy blue Victorian down the street. He must have walked to the restaurant or, because of his limp, more than likely driven. And why did his mode of transportation matter?

He greeted me with a warm smile that held the light of morning sunshine. "Hello, Cressa. We meet again."

"So we do, at the most popular place in town. I love the Blue Lion."

His friendly manner made me feel as if I had known him years ago in those distant yesterdays that I longed to recapture, when all my dreams were ahead of me.

Matt said, "I had the impression that you just moved to Maple Creek."

I was surprised and pleased that he'd given me a second thought.

"I noticed your Texas license plate," he added.

"I've been working on the Gulf Coast, but Maple Creek is my hometown. I came back last month."

"To stay?"

"Maybe. I think so."

"There's no state like Michigan, is there?"

"Not for me," I said. "You have the prettiest house on the block."

"Thanks, but I just rent it during the week. My real home is out in the country." He paused and checked the line. "There's always a longer wait for single tables. Would you like to share one with me? We'll be served faster."

I suppressed a smile at this blatant pick-up line. But why shouldn't we sit together? I was growing hungrier by the minute, and Matt was easy to talk to.

"That makes sense," I said. "We're now a group of two."

He smiled again. "With thirteen people in front of us."

An unlucky number, I thought, but then the hostess led a party of six away to a double table, and we moved forward to stand alongside a panel of knights forever frozen in hunting gear with their ladies and faithful hounds in the background.

An image of the canine skeleton jumped into my mind. Hastily I turned away from it. For the first time in weeks I had an attractive male dinner companion, a wholesome man with sunny glints in his eyes and a patriotic flag pin on his lapel. I could entertain all the gruesome thoughts I desired when I was alone.

"I don't remember the restaurant being so crowded," I said.

"The Blue Lion had a Five-Star write up in the *Free Press* last week. That's bringing a flock of new out-of-town customers in."

"You'd think Mondays would be slow, though."

"Usually they are. With this spell of nice weather we're having, people are in the mood to go out."

Two elderly women followed the hostess to a booth, and we moved away from the entrance, closer to a hundred delectable smells, near enough to catch a glimpse of trays loaded with servings of prime ribs and steaks and French dip sandwiches. All the glorious comfort foods I tended to avoid in the pursuit of a healthy lifestyle. Dinner at the Blue Lion was infinitely better than carrots and celery at home.

"Did you find out anything about the child who drowned in Libby's fountain?" I asked.

"Not a thing. It's probably an urban legend."

"I wonder how a story like that gets started."

"That's no mystery. A little kid falls in the fountain twenty or thirty years ago. The details get garbled and embellished with each retelling. Over the years, a close call turns into an actual fatality. That fountain is a natural for bad vibes."

"Have you felt it, too?"

"I think everybody on the block has."

"There's already been talk about Libby's death," I said. "Who knows what they'll be saying a hundred years from now?"

"It won't matter. The real version will be in the *Tribune* archives."

He was so earnest that I couldn't resist teasing him. "And that makes a story true? Because it's in the newspaper?"

"At the *Tribune,* yes. We report facts and always present them accurately. Or we print a correction the next day."

"Are you a reporter?" I asked.

"Sometimes. I'm also the editor-in-chief."

That explained his note-taking this morning. He'd been covering the story of Libby's demise for his paper, and I'd told him that I was the one who found her. I wished I hadn't. It would serve no useful purpose for me to be connected to Libby's death in the local paper.

"I hope you didn't mention me in your article," I said.

"No ma'am, I didn't." A glint appeared among the light flecks in his eyes. "Are you running away from something in Texas? Like the law or an irate husband?"

"Not really. I'm a private person who doesn't usually stumble over dead bodies."

For a moment, it seemed as if all sound around us ceased. The hum of conversation, the waiters' footfalls, and the clink of silverware faded to silence. But I was overreacting. People were engrossed in their own conversations. No one except Matt had paid any attention to my comment.

"I don't want to be notorious," I added.

"You won't," he said. "Not if I can help it."

At the head of the line, the smiling young hostess cast an inquisitive glance at Matt. "Good evening, Mr. Emmerton. Table for one tonight?"

Matt laid his hand lightly on my arm. "Table for two, Mary."

Her smile widened to include me. "Follow me."

She seated us in a cozy nook decorated with murals depicting medieval hunting scenes. There were dogs all around us, with lean, sleek bodies, caramel-colored coats, and jewel-studded collars. The background greens were intense, reminiscent of the leaves shading the new grave in my yard.

"Do you know the legend of the yellow lion?" Matt asked.

"They're all blue except one?"

"That's right. And if you find it, your wish will come true."

"I think that's a fable made up to lure the kindergarten set."

"Consider it a bit of local color," he said.

Our waiter set tall glasses of ice water down on the table and oversize menus printed in Old English script. I scanned the Day's Specials and Entrées, looking for fish and chips, and found seven variations on my childhood favorite. Breaded scrod with cottage fries, and cole slaw? That would do. Now for the desserts. There it was—chocolate peppermint pie. One of life's most extravagant indulgences.

"Would you like a glass of wine?" Matt asked. "Beer? Something stronger?"

"Just lemonade, and we'll have separate checks."

"Of course," he said. "Except for the drink. That's on me."

He looked enormously pleased with himself. Our unplanned meeting had the look and feel of a date. My black dress and diamond star pendant could take me straight into a festive evening, but as soon as we'd placed our order, he turned into a reporter, quizzing me on my impressions of the accident scene. Imagining an expanded version of the Libby Dorset story splashed across the front page of tomorrow's *Tribune,* I said, "I'll tell you—but off the record. Okay?"

"Whatever you say."

He listened quietly as I described the rainbow colors in the fountain that I thought were flowers, my first inkling that something was wrong.

"While I waited for the police, I noticed two teacups and a candle. I thought that Libby might have been entertaining a visitor. Lieutenant Gray doesn't agree, mostly because she left all the dishes and cakes on the table."

"Someone else on the scene? Hmm. Interesting."

"One more thing. The yard was full of balloons yesterday for the recital. They all disappeared."

"That is strange, but the police will sort it out. The lieutenant is a thorough investigator who doesn't trade speculations with civilians." He closed the menu and reached for the water. "Libby Dorset was a kind, caring lady who would do anything to help a neighbor. She didn't deserve such an ignoble death."

"Did you know her well?" I asked.

"She was my friend. Once, when I was laid up, she brought me dinner on a tray every evening. Then, when her life took a troublesome turn, I couldn't help her. I always regretted it."

"That sounds ominous," I said. "What happened?"

"Last winter, Libby was involved in an automobile accident. The other driver blamed her for causing the collision and all sorts of unrelated misfortunes."

"Was it Libby's fault?"

"Technically, but the roads were snow covered and slippery. She lost control of her car. I don't see how she could have done anything to avoid it, except not go out in the first place."

"Was anyone seriously hurt?" I asked.

"Miraculously no. Just cuts and bruises. Libby had a few cracked ribs, but a few days later, the other driver showed up at Libby's house, claiming that Libby had ruined her relationship with her boyfriend. She started following Libby around, wanting to rehash the accident and talk about personal problems."

"In other words, stalking her. They have laws against that."

"Yes, but this particular stalker was elusive. She even found out Libby's phone number and called her during the night. Libby was terrified."

"That's outrageous," I said. "Usually after you exchange insurance information, you never see the other driver again."

"Not in this case. It turned out that the woman had a history of mental illness. She'd been in and out of institutions."

"What did Libby do?"

"She ended up taking out a restraining order against her. Eventually the woman left town."

That would account for the air of serenity that set Libby apart from every other person I knew. When I moved into the house next door, the incident was long in the past, and she could concentrate on music and quiet pursuits.

"Do you remember the stalker's name?" I asked.

"Not off hand. I can check the back issues and let you know. Why?"

"Just in case Libby's death wasn't an accident," I said.

Anyone who left town could always come back, as I had. To move in secrecy, what disguise would be better than a long full cloak with a hood? But that explanation was too obvious. And if I could make the connection between an unbalanced stalker and a bizarre accident, why couldn't Matt? But maybe he had.

"If the police suspect murder, I'm sure they'll track the woman down," he said. "So far as I know, she was Libby's only enemy."

"Unless it was a random crime," I said. "A killer looking for a victim, and Libby was there."

"I'm beginning to rethink my theory that Libby dropped something in the water," Matt said. "She grew up with that fountain."

"So why would it turn on her at this late date?"

Matt glanced up at me. "That's a novel way to express it," he said.

"I've been listening to the younger set's version of the accident."

"The living statue? I've heard it. Well—I'm tempted to do a little investigating myself."

The waiter returned to take our order, and Matt launched a discussion about changes in Maple Creek. Since there weren't very many, we talked about Texas and West Virginia, where Matt had been raised. He had a third home in that state, a farm that he'd inherited from his grandparents.

He was indeed easy to converse with. From our first meeting at the ice cream truck, that had been true. Maybe too easy?

Remember he's a reporter, I told myself. *He may not be writing down what you say, but I'll bet he can repeat every word.*

In the lull before dessert and coffee, I was tempted to tell him about the mysterious cloaked figure but decided against it. I didn't know Matt Emmerton that well yet. It only seemed that I did.

FIVE

A GHOST OF A MELODY floated through the air, each note like a drop of water dipped in gold before it evaporated in the deep afternoon silence. I knew the lyrics: *Ah! The voice of bygone days will come back again; Whispering to the weary hearted many a soothing strain...*

Who besides Libby Dorset had a piano? And who else would play an old Stephen Foster song?

I stood at my dining room window looking at the old Victorian with its classic lines and soft white color. The gables glowed in the sunlight, and the teardrop trim glittered. Its windows were closed. Mine were open to catch a stray breeze—not a phantom tune.

Ghost and phantom? I'd tossed those words out of my vocabulary years ago. But I *had* heard something.

The ice cream truck cruising the streets of Maple Creek? Not likely, as the driver favored livelier tunes. Besides, her best customers, the children, were still in school. A CD player in a passing convertible, then? Or a radio on a nearby porch?

No, whatever I'd heard had come from somewhere inside the house next door. I was certain of it.

When Libby was alive, she filled her rooms with music: waltzes and sonatas, her own composition that captured the ripple of water over rocks, and her favorite Stephen Foster selections. Imagine decades of sound absorbed by the walls. Wasn't it possible that a fragment of a refrain lingered behind?

No, it isn't, I told myself. *Nor is Libby's Baby Grand playing itself.*

Perhaps the answer was simpler. I'd heard this sentimental piece so often that it had become an echo in my mind.

Since Libby's death, life had returned to normal on Beechnut Street. More accurately, it went on. The mourners no longer stopped by to gawk or leave their memorial tributes, but the bouquets were still on the porch, withering in the heat. The yellow tape was gone, and the grass grew high, invading the flowerbeds where wood-cut tulips overshadowed grape hyacinths.

The house looked as if it had been abandoned for years rather than days. Somebody had drawn the shades on the second and third floors. That puzzled me. Why advertise that nobody lived there? But then Libby's fate was hardly a secret.

Matt Emmerton had published two additional stories about her in the *Tribune*. Neither of them contained new information. From time to time I glanced at his blue Victorian, across the street and half a block away, wondering if he ever stayed home. The house was almost as quiet as Libby's place, but this morning, a bright American flag waved in the breeze, and red geraniums bracketed the entrance.

I wanted to see Matt again. That is, I hoped by now he knew the name of Libby's stalker. But after our dinner at the Blue Lion, we parted company with no plans for a future meeting. He must be busy. Maybe during the long holiday weekend, I'd have a chance to talk to him, but maybe not since his real home was in the country.

I pushed the stack of bills to one side of the table and closed my planner. Next week I had another job interview at a community college. Until then my days and nights were free, but as a new homeowner, I had a full schedule of domestic chores. This was the best time to plant annuals, and the yard needed mowing. Later I had to give the basement a thorough cleaning, even though that was a waste of perfect spring weather.

Wait for a rainy day then, I thought. Do something for the sheer fun of it. Get dressed up and go out to dinner again. A little diversion has more restorative power than a tonic.

The chime notes of the doorbell rang through my thoughts. Welcoming an interruption of any sort, I opened the door to find Gwendolyn White brandishing a brown envelope as if it were a weapon. Her hair was a different color today, glossy black with a blue sheen, but the style still looked dated.

"Hi, Cressa," she said. "Some of Libby's friends are going together on an arrangement for her wake. Would you be interested in contributing?"

"Yes, definitely," I said. "Come in."

She followed me into the dining room where my purse lay on the table. As I reached for my wallet, I said, "Did you hear music a few minutes ago?"

"Where?"

"I'm not sure. In one of the neighbors' houses?"

She turned the envelope around in her hands, and the coins inside jingled. "Not a thing. No one's home next door and poor Libby is gone."

The melody must have been in my mind then, as I'd thought.

Gwendolyn said, "We're going to order a wildflower basket from the Enchanted Forest. After the funeral, the flowers can be planted outside."

I resisted the impulse to smile. "Who's going to do that, Gwendolyn?"

"Libby's niece, Kady, I guess. She's the heir. Did you hear the latest news about Libby?"

"That she killed herself?"

"No, that she was going to retire, effective immediately. She sent letters to all of her students. I read the one Aleta got."

Gwendolyn laid the envelope on the table and added my name to a long zigzagging list. "Now that I look back on it, the whole recital was like a farewell."

"Why do you think that?" I asked.

"Just a feeling. Libby went all out for the reception and made a point of saying something special to each child. Then she played her own work. She never did that before."

"Maybe she was just being a good hostess," I said.

"Why didn't she announce her plans when she had everyone together?"

"I'm sure Libby intended to see them one last time."

"She didn't say that."

"I don't know, then."

Still, I didn't think that Libby had intended to dismiss her students forever with only a few written words. To me, those letters were a strong indication that death had taken her by surprise. She was looking to the future, not an ending.

"Didn't you say you suspected foul play?" I asked.

"At first I did because of that gypsy woman, but when Mrs. Keyes mentioned suicide, it made sense. With this new development, I'm not so sure."

"Maybe the police will turn something up." I handed Gwendolyn a ten dollar bill. "Let me know if you need more for the basket. It's a good idea to buy something that will live on."

"That's what we thought. The children are taking up a collection of their own." She slipped my money into the envelope. "A gypsy, a drowning and a letter from the dead! Don't you wish that Libby could write another one and tell us what happened to her?"

"If only that were possible." I returned my wallet to my purse and snapped it shut. "I'll see you at the funeral parlor."

"Or before." Gwendolyn tucked the envelope under her arm. "Thanks, Cressa. I'll say goodbye now. I have the rest of the block to cover."

As I walked her to the door, she added, "What a sad way to start the summer."

THE BASEMENT WAS the gloomiest part of the house with weak lighting and grotesque shadows that lay motionless on the floor. Even with white walls, birch paneling and stone gray tiles, it still managed to look dark and forbidding.

Eager to be back upstairs, or better still, outside, I leaned the mop against the wall of the furnace room and wound the vacuum cord. While I wasn't finished yet and my work was far from thorough, I'd lost enthusiasm for this subterranean cleaning project. That was understandable since I could look up through the narrow windows and see grass bathed in sunshine.

An old workbench and a maple chair scarred with scratches

filled the northeast corner of the basement, directly under a boarded-up opening that had served as a coal chute in the early decades of the last century. Streaks of ancient paint and dents marred the surface, and two of the lower drawers were gnawed—by a puppy, I hoped.

Because it was too large to move, the former owners had left it behind. I might ask Tim to dismantle it as I had only a few tools and no intention of building or repairing anything. But for someone who did, this would be an ideal place to work.

Some enterprising organizer had attached a circle of wood to the ceiling above the bench and nailed jars to its surface by their lids. They appeared to contain the kind of small bric-a-brac that gathers in any household. Judging from the sweep of cobwebs that festooned the makeshift turntable, I'd guess that nobody had touched it in years.

The idea of keeping little things in their own compartments appealed to me. If I emptied the contents, I'd have a ready made sorting system for my own collectibles. First, I wanted to see what my predecessors had kept.

Standing on the chair, I twisted open the nearest jar, once filled with instant coffee, now a holder for buttons of all sizes and shapes. I set it on the workbench and reached for another. Maybe one of the containers held something more interesting. Finding a treasure trove in my own basement or a relic from a bygone time would make these past dreary hours worthwhile.

Naturally the other jars held dull everyday items like drapery hooks, thumbtacks, rubber bands and screws, and those farther back were empty. But something rested on the ledge formed where the top of the cinder block wall connected to a border of wood.

This might be my treasure! Reaching through a drift of cobwebs, I pulled down a medium-size package, apparently overlooked by one of the previous occupants when moving out of the house.

The brittle brown paper felt cold and gritty—and strange. A little like the dog skeleton's collar. For a moment I felt like letting it slip out of my hand but instead carried it to the window in the laundry room and read the smeared green line scrawled across the front: "For Minta—Do Not Open until December 24, 2000."

I shook the package lightly, sending dust motes flying through the air. It felt like a book. Maybe I'd discovered a Christmas present that someone had hidden and subsequently forgotten. But why stand here and wonder when I could know in a minute?

You're not Minta, I told myself. *This belongs to her, whoever she is.*

Nonetheless, I tugged at the loosely tied string and it fell off—surely a sign that I was meant to open the package. Because I was curious and a little bored and owned everything in the house. Anyone from Pandora on down would do the same thing. Besides, December 24, 2000 had come and gone a long time ago.

Bringing this pointless stream of justification to an end, I laid the package on the dryer where the light was better and tore away the outer wrappings.

I'd guessed right. It was a book, or rather a handmade booklet consisting of sheets of manila construction paper cut in half. A collage of roses, probably taken from a flower catalog, decorated the cover, and yellow curling ribbon strung through heart-shaped holes held the pages together.

Why had Minta's gift languished in this dark corner of the basement for so long? I wondered if she was the one who had left it there and why she hadn't opened it on the designated date.

I did so now, expecting to find a batch of childish crayon drawings or something equally bland, but the first page contained a lovely watercolor picture of a road winding through woods with a lake in the distance. The legend read *Come travel with me back to 1975.*

As I leafed through the booklet, I realized that I'd found a kind of time capsule, not buried in the house's foundation but stashed in an out-of-the-way area where no one would be likely to see it. A jumble of colorful memorabilia covered every inch of the pages: clippings from magazines and newspapers, postcards, color prints with handwritten captions, verses and even ribbons and swatches of fabric.

This project must have taken days to assemble, but the person for whom the memory pages were intended had apparently never seen them. Why was that?

In the kitchen, I drank a glass of iced tea and went through the scrapbook again, more slowly. The bits and pieces brought the long-passed era to life. It was strange, though. All of the snapshots were of places like Maple Creek High School, a dime store on Main Street that no longer existed, and the beach at Marble Lake.

Where were the people? Minta, for example, and the person who had put the booklet together. Feeling that I must have missed something, I scanned the pictures again, but the only humans were fuzzy and faraway, like extras at the back of a movie set. Most likely, the scrapbook maker's purpose had been to create a sense of place, in which case, faces were extraneous.

Now, what was I supposed to do with this homespun treasure? The obvious next step was to locate the owner, Minta, and if I decided to embark on a search, I had a clue. At one time, she must have lived in this very house. Maybe she was still in Maple Creek. Matt might know.

Yes, Matt. In fact… I turned the pages slowly again, noting that the last item was a handwritten story. Matt might want to write an article on my unusual find for the *Tribune*. "Basement Yields Mystery Scrapbook." Something on that order. Now I'd have a good excuse to visit him and ask about the woman who had stalked Libby.

ALETA GRAHAM STOOD at the satyr fountain, silent and alone, gazing down into the empty basin. As the screen door slammed shut behind me, she whirled around and pushed a strand of long yellow hair out of her face.

"Oh, Ms. Hannett—hello," she said. "You scared me. Is it okay for me to be here?"

"I don't know who would object." I walked over to join her, moving reluctantly into the thickening sadness that surrounded Libby's house, and we stood together in the statue's shadow, like two lost souls meeting in a time of darkness.

Aleta dabbed at the tears on her cheeks. "Miss Dorset shouldn't have died this way. She should be in her house, right now, with music…"

"I know." Impulsively I laid my hand on her shoulder.

The week's breezes and winds had littered the fountain with a thin layer of dried leaves and twigs. Patti's daffodil lay where she'd dropped it, pale and shriveled, its short life already spent, and there was a wide red stain beside it. Not a pool of blood but a deflated balloon.

I almost reached down to retrieve it but stopped as I imagined myself losing my balance and falling, crashing to the cement below. Like Libby. Unnerved, I took a step back.

That would never happen. I was young and healthy and wasn't subject to vertigo. But I'd better leave everything where it was. Let Lieutenant Gray find the newly- revealed evidence.

"That looks like one of the party balloons," I said. "Do you have any idea who took them down?"

"Probably the police."

"No, when I found Libby there wasn't a single balloon in the yard."

"Who, then?"

"That's part of the mystery," I said. "But here's one accounted for."

"We had twenty-four of them, for all the years Miss Dorset had been teaching piano." Aleta bit her lower lip. "I guess it was true. She was going to bail on us."

"Maybe not," I said. "Think of them as a symbol of twenty-four wonderful recitals."

"I can do that," she said. "Thursday was my lesson day. Right after school and before dinner. That hour with her and the piano was the highlight of my week."

"Are you going to continue studying music?" I asked.

"Oh, yes. I'm already accepted at the University of Michigan." Her enthusiasm bubbled up to the surface, past the sorrow. I remembered when I'd felt that way, so exuberant and confident in my success that I was ready to soar into the clouds.

"It's what I love most in the world," she added.

"Then it should be your career."

"Miss Dorset used to say, 'Those who are blessed with the gift of making music have a duty to keep it flowing into the world.'"

"She would be proud of you," I said.

Aleta smiled. "Well, I *am* more serious than most of the others. I'll tell you a secret. I really came to check out the satyr. Since Miss Dorset died, he's changing, at least I think so. Haven't you noticed it?"

"I haven't been here in days," I said as I studied the statue's marble features. Comely, sensuous, sinister and crackling with evil vibrations, the satyr was the one unlovely element in the unfolding spring background. Only the gushing water had redeemed him. Now that was gone.

"Do you see that little crack around his mouth? That wrinkle?" Aleta pointed up to a slanted line above the statue's full lips. "It wasn't there yesterday."

"It must have been." But now that she'd called my attention to it, I wasn't so sure. Of course, anything made of stone would eventually crumble. Little pieces would break off and, over time, whole body parts could vanish. Considering his age, it was a wonder that the satyr was still intact.

Still, a brief cold wind seemed to swirl around the fountain. I didn't remember seeing that particular crack before.

"He looks like he's in pain," Aleta said.

"He's dehydrated. We could give him a drink."

"Yes! Break a bottle of wine over his head. That's fitting for a satyr."

"You're thinking of christening a ship. Maybe the next rain will revive him."

"I hope not," she said. "He killed my teacher. It's only fair that he should die, too."

SIX

Morning sunshine poured into the kitchen, washing the faded tulips in pure light. A few limp petals lay on the table. Since I'd picked the flowers the day of Libby's death, they were nearing the end of their lifespan. Fortunately, there were more in the garden, several of them ready to open.

It promised to be another perfect spring day, the last one for a while, according to the forecast. Rain was supposed to arrive for the holiday weekend with a possibility of severe thunderstorms on Monday. In all, a wet, dreary spell was on the way, but the price of every good weather day was a bad one—or two or three.

As I filled the teakettle, I looked out the kitchen window, remembering rainbow colors in the fountain and the red balloon that lay there now. Or I hoped it was still there. Maybe I shouldn't have left it amidst the fallen leaves at the mercy of wind and wildlife.

Then I recalled yesterday's image of myself tumbling into the fountain. I could almost feel the sickening sensation of my heart flipping over in my chest as I fell the short but lethal distance to the bottom. How could an incident that hadn't happened be so vivid? There was something strange about Libby's backyard. If I didn't know better, I'd think that it was haunted.

Cressa, listen to yourself.

I gave the kettle an impatient swipe with a paper towel and set it on the stove to boil. Years of scientific training had fine-tuned my rational antenna. If I couldn't touch something, it wasn't real; and whatever closed in on me when I approached the statue had no substance and, therefore, no power. Obviously the horror of finding Libby's body was still with me, causing my imagination to run amok.

Aleta's allusion to the satyr as Libby's killer had shocked me, especially since I realized that she was speaking literally. She appeared to be an intelligent young woman, not a babbling child. But as soon as she'd uttered the words, she practically flew out of the yard, claiming that she was going to be late for dinner. That was strange, too.

But I knew the difference between reality and illusion, and the satyr was a stone garden sculpture that didn't deserve a second more of my time.

Then stop thinking about it.

I hurried through a breakfast of toast and strawberry jam while jotting down notes in my planner. This afternoon, I planned to take advantage of the nice weather to plant annuals. What else? I had to call Lieutenant Gray to let him know that the balloon had turned up in the fountain, and today I wanted to visit Matt.

Although I was a little curious to see the inside of the blue Victorian, I'd decided to visit him at the *Tribune.* After all, my business with him concerned a story for the paper. His car, a sleek red convertible, was rarely in the driveway except very early in the morning.

Maybe he spent time with a girlfriend. I shook my head, feeling a bit like a stalker myself. Where Matt Emmerton went was none of my concern, even though I had a clear view of his house whenever I opened my front door.

That being settled, I made a few more notes, marveling that with so many items on my agenda, I felt as if I were drifting through my life. I could feel my youth slipping away in an endless stream of humdrum days. The sooner I decided on a permanent job, the better. Maybe I'd look for part-time work this summer, as well.

After clearing the table of china and dying tulips, I checked the view from the window again. Everything was as it should be, sunny and still. Gathering my purse and the scrapbook, I stepped out on the front porch. The sun felt wondrously warm, the air smelled of lilacs, and the day was young. What could go wrong?

"CRESSA!"

The voice was low, almost a whisper, but at the same time clear and bell-like in tone.

I looked to my right just in time to see a slight form round the eastern corner of the white Victorian. But that was wrong. I hadn't actually seen anything. Like a video fast-forwarding at an impossible speed, it was too rapid and fleeting for my vision to catch.

Why would someone call my name and run away?

I crossed in front of Libby's front porch and walked quickly through tall, damp grass to the back. Although I was in excellent physical condition, the light-in-motion person had outdistanced me before the image had fully imprinted itself on my mind. All I had was my impression that the form was female.

No one was here now.

I must have seen another bereft piano student who, like Aleta, wished to visit the death site. Then why didn't she stay and where did she go? The only way she could have vanished so quickly was if she had gone into the woods.

And how did she know who I was?

Libby's yard and the acres of woodland behind our houses might be turning into a macabre tourist attraction for those drawn to the scene of a violent death. If so, I might expect strangers to cross over to my own property at some future time, a prospect that didn't please me.

I stood near the folded lawn chairs and surveyed the area but couldn't see anyone or anything out of place. The satyr glowered down at me from an imposing height. His haughty expression seemed to say, "I know who you saw! It's not what you think." The line above his mouth seemed deeper today, more pronounced.

Not again!

Whenever I came near the fountain, my imagination began to spiral out of control. I was close to thinking of this as a haunted place again. That didn't please me, either.

As I turned to leave, something nudged my leg. Startled, I

looked down to find Pepper, the wandering dog. She stood at my side, tail wagging, dark eyes begging for attention.

"Where did she go, girl?" I asked.

A little whimper was my only reply. I offered her my hand; she sniffed it intently and let me pet her. A canine was a good companion in any situation, and in this spooky yard, practically a necessity, but I had no intention of lingering. Taking my keys out of my purse, I walked back to the front, noting how desolate Libby's porch looked now that someone had removed the mountain of flowers.

Pepper padded lazily along behind me, springing to life when a wild rabbit hopped across our path. With a happy yelp, she set out in pursuit of the small creature, and both of them vanished in the overgrown shrubbery on the western side of my house.

Across the street, Patti Graham was unloading flats of flowers from her trunk. She waved to me and I walked over to admire them. They were impatiens in various shades of pink, all in full bloom.

"I bought them up north," she said. "They're two dollars cheaper there."

"Did you notice anyone out here just now?" I asked.

"Only the mailman. He's early today."

"I thought I saw somebody at Libby's house. A young girl, I think. She ran into the backyard and I lost her."

"That wouldn't surprise me." Patti laid one of the flats down in front of a young Scotch pine. "Except all the kids should be in school. She must be a truant."

"I wish the police had left the yellow tape up."

"Ha! That never stopped anyone. People have been coming from all over to take pictures of the place where Libby Dorset drowned. It's positively morbid."

"Speaking of morbid behavior, do you know anything about that woman who stalked Libby last winter?" I asked.

"A little. She followed Libby home from a movie one afternoon. Libby came to my house instead of pulling in her own driveway and called the police. While we were waiting, she told me about her car crash and the crazy lady."

Patti's account of the events was identical to Matt's with one exception.

"While they were waiting for the police, this woman— Jacqueline something or other—kept screaming at Libby that the accident was all Libby's fault. That she had her wedding dress in the backseat."

"Which must have made everything worse."

"Libby was pretty banged up, and it was snowing and getting dark. Later she told me that was the worst night of her life, and it didn't end there. When Jacqueline's fiancé broke up with her, she claimed Libby had jinxed the wedding and she was going to make her pay."

"How did she know where Libby lived?" I asked.

"I'm not sure how she found out. Anyway, that lady used to follow Libby to restaurants and stores, making scenes and yelling at her. For a while Libby was afraid for her life."

"Then the harassment just stopped?"

"Not until Libby got a personal protection order, around the end of February. After that, Jacqueline dropped off the radar. Libby never saw her again."

"If this woman was so obsessive, why would she give up and go away?"

"A restraining order is enough to discourage some people, even the nutty ones. But I've been thinking. What if she came back? Remember that gypsy woman at the reception?"

During Patti's story, I'd thought about her myself. Sly and secretive, so out of place, she made an ideal suspect. She could easily have slipped a hooded cloak over her gaudy attire and come back after everyone had gone home.

Only one element didn't fit. "Libby would have recognized her," I said.

"Sure, but Libby was inside when the woman took off with the cakes."

"I wonder what Jacqueline looks like," I said. "If she was in all these places stalking Libby, somebody must have seen her."

"You'd think so."

"I remember what the cake thief was wearing but not her

features," I said. "Matt Emmerton might have a picture of the stalker at the *Tribune*."

"This Jacqueline had straight brown hair and high cheekbones. That's all I noticed. We should put our heads together and offer our services to the police."

I smiled at the unbidden image of Lieutenant Gray's sardonic expression. "I don't think they'd accept."

The lieutenant knew about the gypsy, the cloaked figure and obviously the stalker, as well. What if all three were the same woman? No doubt he had made connections and was already on the trail of Jacqueline who appeared to have a strong, albeit demented, motive for wishing Libby dead. For now, the investigation was in capable hands, so all was well.

"Anyway, I'd rather concentrate on ordinary activities like planting spring flowers," I said.

MATT OPENED THE BOOKLET, and a sprinkle of glitter spilled out onto his desk. Small valentine cards filled the page, the kind with comical animal characters and sappy sentiments that young friends have exchanged for ages.

"Nice selection." He brushed the mess to one side. "I'm not sure I understand, Cressa. What do you want me to do with this?"

Suddenly I wished I'd left Minta's scrapbook at home. Why did I think my discovery was newsworthy?

Matt was waiting for an answer and most likely stealing glances at the wall clock behind me. His blue shirt was open at the neck, the sleeves rolled up to his elbows, and those looked like ink stains on his fingers. I was an interruption in his busy day, but he'd never let me know that. He'd brought me a cup of coffee.

I picked up the mug with the *Tribune*'s maple leaf logo and took a long sip, gathering my reasons. "It's a time capsule, only about thirty years old, but it still might interest your readers. If you're running low on material," I added.

"I see. An artifact. All right…"

"There are some pictures of Maple Creek inside. 'The Way

We Were in '75' should make a better story than the one you ran last weekend about that man who carves his own totem poles."

He chuckled and flipped through the pages, pausing to look closely at the street scenes. "It's been a slow month for features. The best angle here is your finding a hidden package in your basement behind a—turntable, was it? I love a good mystery."

I relaxed. My idea wasn't so far out in left field after all. Matt was going to use it. "Maybe Minta will read the article and come back to claim her property," I said.

"That's a name you don't hear very often. I've never met a Minta."

"She sounds like a heroine in a Regency novel."

"I'm not familiar with the genre," he said with a teasing smile that brought out the light flecks in his eyes. "But Minta… Araminta…that rings a bell. Excuse me while I check on something." He gestured toward a table where the coffeemaker bubbled away alongside a bakery box. "Have some more coffee and help yourself to the doughnuts. I'll be right back."

With these words, he left me alone in his sunny office with its view of a drowsy section of Main Street. No one was passing by at the moment; nothing was happening. I refilled my mug and regarded the chocolate-iced fried cakes with keen interest. I'd waited in the lobby for an hour for Matt to come out of a meeting, wishing I'd called ahead for an appointment. It was past noon now, and I was waiting again and growing hungry.

I ate two doughnuts, finished the coffee and leafed through the booklet, pausing to read the poetry. The verses were romantic, drizzling with emotion, and illustrated with little red hearts.

Scrapbooking was suddenly in vogue again, but people had always preserved tokens of their memories on blank pages. Anything was grist for the collection as long as it mattered to the collector. My own mementoes had a celestial theme and included articles about space travel, interspersed with science-fiction memorabilia and pictures of the sky.

This book was different though. The memories had been gathered for another, and they celebrated a specific year.

Finally Matt appeared in the doorway. "I found Minta. That is, I have her history right here." He set a manila folder down in front of me and opened it. Inside were neatly clipped articles and about a dozen black and white prints.

"From the *Tribune* files, circa 1975," he said. "This system predates the microfiche age."

"What did you find out?" I asked.

He handed me a folded page of fragile paper tinged with yellow. It read *Girl and Dog Walk off the Earth*.

"Our Minta vanished into that old thin air in the spring of 1975," he said.

"How do you know she's the right Minta—except how could two girls have that same, unusual name?"

"Because she lived at 714 Beechnut. In your house." He rifled through the papers and drew out a large photograph of a girl with long, dark hair brushed back from her face. She wore a blue school uniform and had a shy half smile.

"This was Araminta Bransford, known to her friends as Minta," Matt said. "She went for a walk with her dog one afternoon and never came back home."

The story reminded me of the canine skeleton that Tim had unearthed. There was no reason to assume that the bones belonged to Minta's dog, but the feeling of a connection was too strong and compelling to ignore. Still, I told myself not to overreact. Many people buried dead pets in their backyards.

"Did her dog disappear, too?" I asked.

"I don't know." He flipped through the file, skimming the articles and frowning. "I'll have to read these more carefully."

"So this happened in 1975, the same year that's written on the scrapbook's first page. That explains why the package wasn't opened. I'll bet nobody else knew it was there."

"I wonder why no one noticed it when the walls were painted," Matt said.

"No one else was curious? Finding a package wasn't in the job description? But wouldn't the police have searched a missing girl's house?"

"I'd assume so."

"What else do you know about Minta Bransford?" I asked.

"She was an all-A student, always on the Honor Roll, and looking forward to graduation. She'd been accepted at Maplegrove College. Minta loved animals and wanted to be a veterinarian. Then one day she was gone." He closed the folder and laid his hand on it. "The story ended."

"Can I borrow the file?" I asked.

"Sure thing…and you'll let me hold on to the scrapbook?"

"Yes, that's why I brought it to you. I hoped you'd see its human interest potential. And who knows? Maybe Minta will read it and come forward."

"Stranger things have happened, but I won't count on it. Her family must have given her up for dead years ago."

He slipped the file in a larger folder and handed it to me. "Be careful," he said with a wink. "You're holding the revered *Tribune* archives in your hand."

"And you have a treasure out of time. Thanks, Matt."

"If you have any questions, just give me a call," he added.

"You, too."

He stood up and clasped my hand warmly, and then he walked around the desk to escort me to the door.

Yes, Matt Emmerton had a talent for making a person feel like an old friend. It must serve him well in his profession.

"Look for this to appear on Tuesday in the Maple Creek Life section," he said.

I paused with my hand on the doorknob. "Before I leave, I wanted to ask you about that other strange story, Libby Dorset's stalker."

"Oh—you wanted to know her name. I didn't forget. It's Jacqueline Doran."

"Do you have a picture of her somewhere in those files?" I asked.

"I only know her name. Why?"

"For a little theory Patti Graham and I cooked up."

Matt's eyes lit up again. "Would you care to elaborate?"

"Not just yet. I'd say that I love a mystery, too, but it sounds too flippant when I'm talking about Libby Dorset."

SEVEN

THE MORN OF LIFE is past; And evening comes at last; It brings me a dream of a once happy day...

Music moved with me through the dream, then faded away. As soft as silk, as sweet as a cherished memory, the luminous old strains seemed to echo, just beyond hearing.

The magical notes erased the events of the past week. Libby was alive again. She'd been playing "Old Dog Tray" on her piano. The recital hadn't happened yet, and the statue in the fountain was decadent but not deadly.

Still I wept for Libby.

I WOKE, SURPRISED TO FIND that my eyes were dry. The poignant melody echoed in my mind, and a trace of sadness stayed with me, even after I'd taken a shower and had breakfast. Libby could only be alive in a dream.

Gray, soggy days fostered gloomy thoughts. True to the forecast, rain fell all weekend, draining the bright new colors out of the landscape and dampening the Memorial Day spirit. Picnics moved indoors, while flags drooped and hardy souls viewed the parade on Main Street under umbrellas. Only the newly planted flowers and the statue could possibly be happy with the deluge.

For the satyr, the inclement weather was a reprieve, giving him a chance to live longer and do more damage. I didn't bother to chide myself for this latest foray into fantasy. I'd be back to normal, or what passed for normal, as soon as it stopped raining and the earth dried out.

In the meantime, deep holiday quiet descended on my house. I took a quick trip to the drug store on Main Street. When I returned, the answering machine showed zero new messages, but what did I expect? Matt Emmerton was the only person in Maple Creek who knew my number, and he wouldn't be likely to call me. As for my friends in Texas, they were celebrating the day under a hot western sun. For them, I was the past.

I wandered through the rooms searching out-of-the-way places in the hope of discovering another one of Minta's secret possessions. Not finding anything else, I finally settled down in front of the television to watch a stack of rented DVD's as the rain continued.

MONDAY'S SEVERE THUNDERSTORMS didn't materialize, and on Tuesday, the sun came out again. Light and warmth always made life easier. Feeling invigorated, I lingered in the kitchen over morning coffee and cinnamon toast, reading Matt's scrapbook story in the Tribune and the sidebar on Minta Bransford's disappearance. He had found a reference to Minta's dog in his sources.

Officer Jack Silvern of the Maple Creek Police Department found the puppy, a seven-month old collie named Sunny, in Wyndemere Park the next morning, still wearing her collar but without her leash. A classmate of Miss Bransford said, "Minta would never let Sunny run free."

What happened to separate Minta Bransford from Sunny, then? Three decades later, it was still a mystery.

I wished I'd told Matt that the remains of an unknown dog lay buried in my yard. He seemed to be an energetic investigator and was already interested in the case.

I could still do it, but why puzzle over the identity of a long dead pet? There was no way I could know anything more about it, and the chance that it connected to Minta was remote. The dog in the grave had been smaller than a purebred collie. Still, at seven months, Sunny wasn't fully grown.

I turned the page and found another story with Matt's byline. Apparently Maple Creek had a surplus of canines abandoned by soldiers being deployed overseas. Some had to fend for themselves; the luckier ones found temporary havens. Lila and Letty

Woodville, the sisters who ran the Caroline Meilland Animal Shelter in nearby Foxglove Corners, had several young, healthy dogs ready for adoption.

The Pet of the Week was a pretty Australian sheepdog mix named Gracie. She looked back at me from the page, blue eyes holding a silent plea: *I'm friendly and obedient, and I need a home. Please.*

Well, why not? I needed a companion.

I clipped Matt's articles and Gracie's picture, as well. If I stayed in Maple Creek, and even if I left, a four-legged friend would enrich my life. I made a mental note to stop at the shelter and meet Gracie, and it had better be soon. A handsome animal like an Australian sheepdog wouldn't remain available for long.

A WOMAN PASSED THROUGH Libby's dining room, stopped at the table for a moment, then moved on. She didn't reappear in the kitchen, which meant that she'd gone up the stairway. I stepped closer to my window, scrutinizing the supposedly empty house. How could this be?

There was no car in the driveway, no light in any of the rooms that I could see, and no sign of anyone there now. Still, I was certain I'd seen someone, as I had on the morning when the fast-as-light person had called my name and vanished into Libby's backyard. That is, I was pretty certain, but I wouldn't swear to it.

Maybe the woman was a maid dropped off at the door by a cleaning service van. Or a shadow? Or, most likely, a figment of my rain-saturated, inactivity-fueled imagination? In other words, nothing.

But just to be on the safe side… For a moment my hand hovered over the cell phone. Then I reconsidered. Calling the police wasn't a good idea. If the white Victorian was empty, I'd look like a jittery fool. Besides, there was another, quicker way to find out if anyone was inside.

Throwing a cardigan over my shoulders, I walked over to Libby's house, rang the bell, and waited. No one came to the door. Still, I peered through the front window at dark antique furniture steeped in silence, ornate lamps, and oil paintings in heavy frames. Without Libby in residence, the room resembled a museum.

But someone could well be on the other side, hiding in the darkness, hoping that I'd go away. What a creepy thought! Who would do that and why?

All I needed to set my wild imagination in motion was to hear music again. Fortunately, there was no sound whatsoever. Now I thought I'd better go back home. With Libby's memorial service scheduled for tomorrow, I was standing on her porch, as if I expected her to materialize at any minute. Anyone seeing me here would doubt my sanity—or my motive.

But there was nobody outside, either.

As I turned to leave, I almost stepped on a blue delphinium left behind when the floral bouquets were removed. The bell-shaped petals resembled crushed butterflies.

I shuddered at the image my mind had given me. The old Victorian was a place of death. I vowed never to come here again chasing a phantom form. Furthermore, I ordered myself to forget about the non-incident. But an hour later, when the police cruiser pulled up in front of Libby's house, I changed my mind.

Through the living room window I watched Lieutenant Gray tramp through the high grass to the backyard. Moments later, he returned with the red balloon in his gloved hand. He moved quickly, rather like light himself, but I could be quick, too. Before he reached the sidewalk, I was on my front porch.

"Good morning, Lieutenant," I said, stepping down to intercept him. "Have you found the other balloons yet?"

"Morning, Ms. Hannett. No, just this one. Thanks for the tip. What we need in this town are more concerned citizens."

"The murder affects me since I live next door."

I accompanied him as he walked to his car. He placed his hand on the door handle. In a moment he would be on his way to the station with my evidence.

"I thought I saw a woman in Libby's dining room a while ago," I said. "You might want to check it out. See if anyone broke in."

He secured the balloon inside the cruiser and regarded the Victorian. A frown darkened his blue eyes. "I'll do that. You wait here."

He rang the bell, as I had, turned the knob, and looked through the window. Then he went around the back again, presumably to try the other entrance. When he returned, he stood on the walkway in an isle of sunlight, his gaze fixed on the third story where the rooms hid behind dark shades.

While he was distracted, I let my gaze linger on him. He was exceptionally handsome, tall and rangy, even more attractive in his uniform with its symbols of power and authority. Cornflower blue eyes and the wayward strand of dark hair falling forward from a center part gave him an endearing boyish look that was almost certainly misleading.

I'd known men like Lieutenant Gray before, many of them, with striking movie star features and giant-size egos. They came and went like glimpses of the sun on a cloudy day. Still, I couldn't help staring at him, couldn't seem to take control of my runaway admiration for this man I'd only recently met.

"It's locked up tight," he said. "I'll get in touch with the owner—that's Miss Dorset's niece—and offer to take her on a tour of the place to see if anything's been disturbed."

"That sounds like a good idea."

"Have you noticed any kids hanging around outside?" he asked.

"One, on Friday. Why?"

"Miss Dorset used to be bothered by neighborhood boys messing with the statue. Leaving women's underwear on it—that kind of thing. Just annoying pranks. One Halloween, they tried to kidnap it. Now that she's gone, it's fair game."

"I'll be on the lookout for mischief makers," I said. "Do you know who has a key to the house?"

"Ms. Dorset's niece. One of the neighbors did, but she turned it into the station after Ms. Dorset died. Said she didn't want to be accused of stealing anything."

"There may be another way in," I said. "But where?"

The house was all high gables and closed windows with no

French doors on the upper levels and no convenient tree to tempt a climber.

His eyes swept the exterior again. "I can't see any, but letting the grass grow is a bad idea."

I nodded. "There might as well be a 'Welcome Burglar' sign on the lawn."

"A maintenance service is coming next week. They should have the outside ship shape in no time. Let us know if you see anything else suspicious. The investigation is still ongoing."

"So you don't know anything definite yet?" I said.

"It looks like a freak accident or suicide. It's too soon to tell."

"How about murder?"

"Murder, Ms. Hannett?" He turned his cornflower eyes on me. They veiled his reactions, concealing his thoughts, revealing nothing. "What makes you say that?"

I offered him a capsule version of my enhanced theory about the stalker, the gypsy and the cloaked figure. It sounded melodramatic, more like fiction than life, but Lieutenant Gray appeared to be taking me seriously.

He tipped his hat, gave me a parting smile, and opened the cruiser door. "At this point, anything is possible," he said.

REMEMBER THOSE WORDS. They may prove to be prophetic.

Gathering spring flowers turned my thoughts away from Libby's death to life's beauty but only for a while. I cut a bouquet of white lilacs from the lower branches of the bushes and dropped them into my basket. Their light fragrance was sweeter than any perfume. Just touching them made me feel as if all was well in my small section of the world.

But Libby might have been murdered. Nobody knew how she ended up in the fountain.

A car door slammed in the silence, and heels clicked on the walk, coming closer. Company—or a trespasser? No doubt a curiosity seeker stalking the notorious satyr with a camera. If so, I'd point out that this was private property and hope she'd go away.

Strangely, my heartbeat quickened at the approaching intrusion. I was getting jittery.

Taking the basket and shears with me, I walked around to the front. A slender blond woman stood on my porch with her hand on the doorbell. She wore white slacks with a paisley blouse and gold hoop earrings. Her hair had sunny streaks and elegant waves. I'd never seen her before.

She smiled at me—or at the flowers. "Oh, what gorgeous lilacs!"

I returned the smile. "Can I do something for you?"

"Maybe, if you're Cressa Hannett. I read about the old scrapbook you found. It's mine."

"Oh…is it?" Suddenly I regretted asking Matt to write the story. I should have known that it would make me famous for an hour or two and possibly attract the attention of a different kind of curiosity seeker.

Or possibly Minta Bransford herself? Could my visitor be the mysterious Minta come out of oblivion to claim her property?

Anything might be possible, but this woman seemed too young. Maybe not. It was difficult to estimate her age in the shade of the awning, and I realized that I had been picturing Minta the way she'd looked in her school photograph. She would be nearing fifty now.

The woman said, "I should rephrase that and introduce myself. My name is Annora May. I meant to say that I made the booklet for Minta Bransford way back in 1975. I gave it to her. Minta was my best friend."

Now I understood, but I was glad that Matt still had the scrapbook in his possession. For some reason, I was unwilling to hand it over to a stranger, even though technically it wasn't mine.

"Let me explain," she said. "When Minta and I were high school seniors, we exchanged memory books. We were going to open them together in the year 2000 and reminisce about old times."

"That sounds like fun. I mean, it would have been fun."

"The idea was to include anything that made the year and our lives memorable. When I learned that Minta's book still existed, I was hoping you'd let me look at it."

Annora was older than she appeared then, and something puzzled me. "How did you know where I live?" I asked.

"Why that's simple. This was Minta's house." She glanced toward the door. "Could we go inside, just for a little while?"

I hesitated, not wanting to be rude, but reluctant to let a stranger into my home, even though she appeared to be sincere. On the other hand, I was eager to know more about Minta and the scrapbook. Especially Minta.

"Let's go sit on the back porch," I said. "I just finished setting it up for the summer."

Arranging the white wicker furniture, creating a charming, comfortable outside room, had been the highlight of my day, and, in my view, my efforts were worthy of a write-up in *Cottage Living*. The lilacs from my own yard provided the finishing touch. I laid the basket on an end table and offered my visitor a seat.

"There never used to be a porch out here," Annora said. "Mrs. Bransford had a rose garden outside the kitchen. She was always fussing over it. The balcony is new, too."

"I believe they were added about twenty years ago."

"Ah well, time passes, doesn't it? After a certain point, one year is the same as ten."

Unable to think of an appropriate rejoinder, I asked, "Do you live in Maple Creek?"

"I used to. I came back last week for my class reunion and decided to stay on for a while. I still own a house here, right around the block, so we're neighbors." She leaned forward in the chair, running her hand back and forth along the pillow. "Being back in town has stirred all these memories for me. Minta wanted so much out of life. She was looking forward to graduation and college. We both were. None of that happened for her."

"Do you think she's dead?"

"She must be, or she'd have come home. Would you mind showing me the scrapbook now?"

I took a deep breath. "The editor of the *Tribune* has it," I said. "If you'll leave me your phone number, I'll call you when he returns it."

There. That was gracious, and I wasn't relinquishing my discovery.

"Then I'll have to wait, I guess." Annora bit her lower lip. "I've been trying to recall what all I put in it, but my memories are fuzzy. It was so long ago."

"You mentioned an exchange," I said. "Did Minta make a scrapbook for you, too?"

"Yes, a lovely one, much nicer than mine. I opened it years ago. So much for a friendship pact, but by then Minta was gone. If I broke into it a couple of decades early, what did it matter?"

"Ever since I heard about the disappearance, I've been thinking about it and wondering," I said. "Do you have any details that weren't in the paper?"

"There wasn't much to know, but I remember the last time I saw Minta. We were in the school parking lot. Usually I gave her a ride home, but I had to go back for an Art Club meeting, the last one of the year, so she went on alone. Maybe if I'd skipped the meeting, if we'd gone together, stopped at the Ice Cream Parlor for a Coke…"

"No one can undo the past," I said.

"How true. I remember she was wearing a green dress she'd made in sewing class. Green was her favorite color. Her hair was blowing all over her face in the wind."

"Didn't you used to wear uniforms?" I asked.

"Yes, but we had a fashion show that afternoon. Anyway, around eight that night, Mrs. Bransford called, wanting to know if I'd seen Minta. The dog, Sunny, was gone, too. The next day the 'missing girl' story was splashed over the front page. The police picked up Sunny in the park, but no one ever found Minta."

Basically, Annora was telling me what I already knew, but her powers of description and the tremor in her voice created a clear image of Minta for me. I could visualize the dress and Minta's windblown hair. But I needed more.

"Can you remember anything else?" I asked.

"Let's see…there was a storm that day. It came on suddenly but didn't last long. I stayed in school, waiting for it to blow over.

That was around the time Minta usually took Sunny for her walk, but nobody can say for certain when she left the house. Her mom and dad were at work, and her little sister was off somewhere."

"So she could have gotten caught in the rain."

"Maybe. They never went far—usually down to Wyndemere and back."

"That's a pretty park, but it's so woodsy and isolated," I said. "My mother never wanted me to go there alone."

"It was the same in 1975. After the police found Sunny, they combed the whole area thoroughly and questioned everyone who knew Minta. All her friends from school, the neighbors, practically everyone in town. The only clue they ever had was Sunny, and a dog can't talk."

"Maybe Minta ran away," I said.

"Never. She left everything she treasured behind, even the pearls her parents gave her as an early graduation gift. Somewhere between her home and the park, she walked off the face of the planet, but she didn't take Sunny with her."

"Like in the *Twilight Zone,*" I said.

"Some of the boys in our class started a rumor that she'd been abducted by aliens. That was their idea of a tasteless joke, but I could imagine some pervert forcing her into a car and driving out of town…only things like that didn't go on in Maple Creek."

"What do *you* think happened?" I asked.

"All I know is that when Minta left the house that afternoon, for whatever reason, she had every intention of coming back. Something happened to prevent it. To this day, I've never been able to figure it out."

EIGHT

A GIRL SETS OUT ON an afternoon jaunt with her dog and walks off the face of the planet.

So said Annora May and the headline in the old Tribune. But real life wasn't a *Twilight Zone* episode. There had to be a rational explanation for Minta Bransford's disappearance, even though no one had found it yet.

The next day I drove by Wyndemere Park on my way to Libby's wake. Ash Court was a quiet, winding street bordered by vintage houses on one side and ten acres of wooded parkland on the other. This picturesque section of town flaunted its wilderness with pride, and the swings and slides resting on last fall's leaves had been old when I was a child. It was easy to believe that dark deeds happened here.

No people were about, but two dogs ran along the trail that meandered under the railroad tracks. I slowed down, attempting to reconstruct Minta's last walk, assuming that she'd come this way. If she had been caught in a downpour, what would she do? Race back home with Sunny, making a game of their flight from the rain? Would she accept a ride from someone she knew? Or perhaps take refuge in one of the houses that faced the park? Maybe, if the person who made the offer was an acquaintance.

So Minta entered one of those sedate Dutch colonials with aging landscaping and never came out again? Please, Cressa, lose the melodrama. And what did she do with Sunny?

Bringing the car to a stop, I studied the train tracks. They ran from north to south on a high rise of land overgrown with saplings and tangled vines. A dog could easily scale the slope, as could a young, nimble girl.

Here was a way out of town, except that by 1975, commuter trains in Maple Creek were as obsolete as streetcars. In Minta's time, as today, boxcars carried freight, and the railway station, still vacant and boarded up, was a mile away.

So much about the affair didn't make sense. Minta vanished on a warm, stormy spring day. Surely at least one person between Beechnut Street and Ash Court had noticed a neighborhood girl walking with her dog and would remember the incident when she turned up missing.

Could someone have seen what happened to Minta and kept quiet, not wanting to get involved?

My thoughts turned to Sunny. How could Minta and her dog have become separated? When that happened, couldn't Sunny have made her way back home? Lassie had accomplished a similar feat in Eric Knight's classic story. But Minta's collie had stayed in the park until the police found her the next day.

Home is where your mistress is—or was last seen.

Did Minta have time to worry about Sunny before Fate caught up with her? Possible scenes from that long ago summer seemed as real to me as if I'd experienced them. I imagined Minta's mother weeping inconsolably in her house—my house now—and her father waiting at the telephone for news, hoping that somehow the dog would lead him to his lost daughter. As for Minta, I saw her pulling Sunny into a wall of rain and falling into a great, gaping void.

But the leash slipped out of her hand, and the dog stayed behind. No one heard her frantic barking. I wondered how long Sunny had lived with the Bransford's after Minta disappeared. Until she was old, with graying fur and a secret trapped in her brain?

The collie was an essential part of Minta's story, but not much was known about her. Annora had only mentioned Minta's dog a few times. In any event, something terrible must have happened to Minta, and it might have occurred in Wyndemere Park. That would explain Sunny's reluctance to leave the area.

Having exhausted my store of ideas, I put the car in drive and pulled slowly away. I had to stop thinking about the case. If it hadn't been solved in twenty years, I wasn't going to find any answers today. Already the mystery of Libby's death tugged at me. Why look for another one in a bygone time simply because the meager facts intrigued me?

At the end of Ash Court, I made a left turn and drove three blocks to the funeral parlor. I had planned my activities to utilize the least amount of gas and time. First, a stop to pay my respects to Libby, then a late lunch followed by my next job interview. Finally, the day's only enjoyable errand—a trip to the animal shelter in Foxglove Corners to see if Gracie and I were compatible.

When I had a dog of my own, I wouldn't let anything separate us.

I STOOD IN THE DOORWAY, letting my eyes adjust to the soft lighting, already missing the warmth of the sun. At the other end of the room, Libby lay in a closed casket covered with a blanket of white roses. Heavy, cloying floral odors floated around me, and the air conditioning was too high for comfort. Well, I wasn't going to get comfortable in this place.

Moving quietly through the groups of visitors, I tried to cast off the unease that always dogged me whenever I found myself near a coffin.

You're here for Libby. It's what civilized people do. Focus on the memorial arrangements.

A massive basket filled with wildflowers "from the Neighbors on Beechnut Street" occupied an entire tabletop. Unlike the formal, expensive bouquets that lined the walls, our gift would go on living, if someone thought to take it home.

There were more flowers than mourners, and I didn't see a single familiar face. Not Gwendolyn, not Patti, not Matt. But that was good. I'd do this quickly and without fuss. A silent prayer at the casket and a signature in the guest book, then a walk in the sun to banish the images of mortality.

I walked up to the casket, keeping my pace respectfully slow. Nobody looked my way. Then, a slender young woman who bore a slight resemblance to Libby came up to me. Her gentle smile derailed my plan.

"Hello," she said. "I'm Kady Dorset, and you're…?"

"Cressa Hannett," I said. "I live next door to Libby."

Kady was Libby's closest relative and, therefore, the Victorian's new owner. Libby had mentioned her so often that I felt as if I knew her already. She was still in college, majoring in music.

"Kady is following in my footsteps," Libby had announced proudly. "Only she's going to teach in the public schools."

"I'm sorry for your loss," I said.

"Thank you, Cressa. My aunt was so happy to have a friendly neighbor."

"I miss hearing her piano more than I thought possible," I added.

"Aunt Libby believed that once you send music out into the world, it can never die."

Kady spoke figuratively, but her words held the chill of truth. Through my open windows, I'd heard Libby's favorite music, those sentimental melodies that carried dreams of a simpler time straight into the present. I heard them still in my mind and knew they would be with me for a long time.

"The neighborhood is too quiet now," I said.

"I've been thinking about moving into the house myself with a few of my classmates. It's been in our family since 1900."

"Oh, I hope you do." I tried to think of what to say next, something heartfelt that wasn't trite. My mind gave me nothing. "I guess I'll pay my respects to your aunt now."

"Thank you for coming, Cressa." Kady turned toward another visitor, apparently someone she knew well, while I walked up to the casket and said a prayer for the repose of Libby's soul.

Repose meant rest. In Libby's case, eternal rest. But could that be possible? Wouldn't the vibrations of her violent passing follow her to the grave?

Don't dwell on impossibilities. Uneasy spirits turn into ghosts—which only exist in storybooks. Remember that.

The heat from the candles warmed my face, and the thick scent of funeral roses bombarded me with unsettling thoughts. As I rose from the kneeler, an elderly woman clutching a black rosary took my place.

Prayers would help. They always did.

Rest well, Libby, I thought, looking at the casket one last time. This was final; this was goodbye. But until the mystery of Libby's passing was solved, there couldn't be a real ending.

Somewhere in Maple Creek or beyond its borders, Libby's killer was no doubt congratulating himself. He'd tricked the police into thinking that she had died by accident or her own design. Those of us who subscribed to the foul play theory owed it to Libby to find out what had really happened.

I could leave now, or as soon as I performed one last ritual. At a small candlelit alcove near the entrance, I signed the guest-book. So many people had come to bid farewell to Libby. Her students, neighbors, Matt... My gaze froze on a name in the middle of the page. Annora May had been here recently, perhaps just before I arrived. Yes, obviously—and why was that significant?

An idea flickered like a vigil flame, just beyond my reach. Then I had it. Annora's presence indicated that she had known Libby. Of course. If she was Minta's friend, she must have. But during our visit, she hadn't mentioned Libby once. When we were sitting on the porch, in view of the white Victorian, it would have been natural for her to comment on the tragedy or that perennial conversation piece, the satyr fountain.

But Annora had only talked about Minta and the scrapbook. On the other hand, I hadn't told her about the canine skeleton in my yard. Because I didn't entirely trust her, or didn't think it was relevant? I wasn't sure.

What did this all mean? Perhaps nothing; maybe something significant.

The next time I saw Annora, I'd ask her if she had any special memories of Libby. Her answer might quickly solve this latest little mystery. Now, finally, I was finished here. I chose a holy card and walked to the door, a little faster now, more than ready for sunshine and fresh air.

The next hours were a mixture of disappointment and frustration. My club sandwich fell apart in unappetizing pieces on my plate; several stellar applicants had already interviewed for the community college job; and Gracie's new owner had taken her home this morning. None of the animal orphans at the shelter possessed the appeal of the Australian sheepdog.

You only saw her picture, I reminded myself. Still, I never thought that she wouldn't be mine for the asking and that we'd become friends. As I headed back to Maple Creek, without my longed-for canine companion, I felt as if my short time at the funeral parlor had jinxed the day.

LATE THAT AFTERNOON, I roamed through my yard, watering the beds and noting how fast the flowers were fading. The dull, papery daffodils drooped, and the rapidly growing perennials were still green. A few late blooming tulips gave my garden its only color. They had moss-colored petals with pale pink edges. Suddenly I found myself longing for brightness, for a dash of red.

Spring, like life itself, was racing by, and there was no way to slow it down.

"Hey, Cressa. Are you in the backyard?"

Matt came around the corner and limped over to the porch. He carried the scrapbook and a deflated purple balloon. Dressed in jeans and a red-striped shirt, he looked like a man in a mood for neighborly conversation. Or murder gossip.

"I just saw you in the front," he said.

"I'm inspecting my estate," I said.

"Is everything in order?"

"Pretty much, but I wish I could make the season last." I set the sprinkling can on the ground, under the faucet. "Come sit on the porch with me."

"I think I will. It's been a day from hell." He handed me the scrapbook. "Your story gave our circulation a healthy boost. Thanks again."

"Everybody likes a mystery," I said.

"Especially an old one. After all these years, people are still interested in the Bransford case."

I opened the door, and Matt walked awkwardly up the two steps. The admiration in his eyes as he surveyed the wicker furniture warmed my homeowner's heart. I'd decorated the porch as if it were a room in my house, with white paint and deep pink azaleas as accent color. The cool, gleaming space was perfect for solitude, entertaining guests, or any pleasant summertime pursuit.

"This is nice and homey, Cressa," Matt said. "I'll bet you spend a lot of time out here."

"I do when I can. The front porch is for curb appeal and the balcony for stargazing." I brushed a thin coat of dust off a cushion, wondering how it could have appeared since this morning. "This is the most comfortable chair."

"You have a good view of the infamous satyr," he said.

"Oh—that. Well, I try to look at the woods instead."

But I glanced at the statue now. It seemed as if it was a little closer to the property line, even though the fountain hadn't moved. Dear God, what prompted that ghastly thought? But the satyr's face seemed to be turned a little toward me, and the horns were more pointed.

Absolute nonsense. It was the aftereffects of visiting the dead, or the angle of light, or my physical state. The day had tired me. Still…

"Did you ever hear that old story about keeping the water running?" Matt asked.

"Some people at the recital mentioned it, but what happened to Libby reverses that idea. She died first. Then the police drained the fountain and turned it off."

"Superstitions don't necessarily make sense," Matt said.

Nor did they make for easy conversation. Surely I could talk about something else with an intelligent, congenial man; and I had just the topic. "I met the scrapbook's author yesterday," I said. "She was a friend of Minta's."

Matt's eyes lit up. "I can write a follow-up for next week. What's her name?"

"Annora May."

"You mean Annora Maywood? She owns the land behind your property. That is, she's an absentee owner—in and out of Maple Creek. Mostly out. She prefers New York City."

I should have known that a newspaperman would have the best information in town.

"You sound like you know her," I said.

"We're friends. It's hard to picture a sophisticated woman like Annora writing Chick Lit, circa 1975, for a scrapbook."

Puzzled by the subtle contradiction in his words, I said, "Well she was younger then. Much younger." As he didn't comment on that slightly catty observation, I added, "Where did you get the balloon?"

"Behind the juniper bush under your bay window. You said the party balloons vanished on the night Libby Dorset drowned."

He placed it in my hand, and I recoiled at the slick damp feel of the limp rubber. But its color was still brilliant. How had I missed seeing it? More importantly, was this another clue or a child's lost plaything?

"They disappeared except for one that turned up in the fountain," I said.

"This might have come from somewhere else."

I shrugged. "They all look alike to me. Before the recital, Aleta Graham tied a purple balloon to the statue's hand."

And after Libby cautioned her to be careful, Aleta told her that she worried too much. I'd almost forgotten that ironic exchange.

"Are you going to throw it away?" Matt asked.

"Not at all. It might be important evidence."

"Offhand, I don't see how."

"Neither do I, but that's two found and twenty-two still missing. The mystery goes on."

"You have my interest," Matt said.

"Unfortunately I can't imagine what happened to them."

Matt had settled himself in a wicker chair, thoroughly at ease as if he had visited me before. And I could make him still more comfortable. "Would you like something cold to drink?" I asked. "Ginger ale? Root beer? Real beer?"

"Please. Whatever you're having."

He rolled his shirt sleeves up one more fold while I slipped into the kitchen and poured beer into two frosty mugs. When I returned, Matt said, "Do you still think that Libby was murdered?"

"Yes, but I may be the only one who does."

"Maybe not," he said. "I've been thinking about that stalker, Jacqueline. She had motive and maybe opportunity." He looked toward the woods, beyond the dog's grave where the red canoe appeared to be sinking in a quagmire of giant perennials. "You know—or maybe you don't—we had a murder here last fall. A woman ate a caramel apple laced with poison at the Apple Fair. From the beginning there was no doubt that was foul play. These circumstances are different. They're ambiguous."

"Three shady characters touched Libby's life close to or on the day she died," I said.

"Three? There's the stalker and that woman who stole the cakes at the reception. Who else?"

I told him about the cloaked figure I'd seen in Libby's yard and my theory that the trio might be the same woman.

"It all feels a little contrived," he said.

"I'm not making this up. These people exist."

"Okay. Let's keep them, and don't forget the vanishing balloons. Unless Libby took them all down and then fell in the fountain."

"I'm sure it didn't happen like that. Lieutenant Gray told me he didn't find them. I assume that means they weren't in the house."

"No, they were floating all over the neighborhood, but somebody had to untie them first."

"And it wasn't the satyr," I said.

"What?"

Why had I said that? Seizing a likely explanation, I added, "That's just something the kids were saying."

Matt cast me a teasing smile that creased the finely etched lines around his eyes. I had a feeling that he didn't believe me. Then he said, "Listen, Cressa, do you hear music?"

I didn't at first until in the distance a familiar tune rolled through the air. *Nelly Bly! Nelly Bly! Bring the broom along; We'll sweep the kitchen clean, my dear; And have a little song.*

One of Libby's merry, happy melodies, the ice cream truck's version.

He set the empty mug down on the coffee table. "Let's go meet it, and I'll buy you a cone. What's your favorite flavor again? Heavenly hash? No, rocky road."

"How did you remember?" I asked.

"We newsmen never forget anything important," he said.

Matt was teasing, of course, but for a moment, I allowed myself to think that my preferences mattered to someone. "That sounds good," I said. "Let's do it."

NINE

WE STROLLED TO the corner, down the street called Victorian Row. Sunlight stole through the leaves, creating fanciful patterns of light and shadow on the sidewalk. Matt took awkward steps while I matched his pace and listened to the lilting notes of "Nelly Bly." An ice cream date with a friendly neighbor was exactly what I needed today.

This kind of impromptu excursion would never have happened in Texas. Everything was different there. The sun had a heavier touch, and Lone Star attractions were giant-size, like Texas men, if one subscribed to the natives' myth: *Everything is larger and more powerful in the state of Texas.*

That was certainly true of my lost love, Jase Clayborne. He never walked when he could drive his Porsche or ride his horse. We had gone sailing in the Gulf and driving through the Texas countryside. We'd dined on thick steaks at upscale restaurants, sometimes finishing our dinner with fancy ice cream concoctions. They were our tradition, even though as a rule Jase didn't eat desserts.

By what magical feat had he transported himself to this quiet street in Michigan, insinuating himself between Matt and me? I thought I'd packed the Jase memories away in a box with my snapshots and treasured souvenirs.

Yes, but I'd neglected to close the lid. I had to keep reminding myself that Jase was a shadow from my past. Matt and this glorious June day were real, and I was lucky to have found a new friend so soon after coming home to Michigan.

So delete every golden, sun-drenched picture. Zap Jase out of existence.

We reached the corner just as Ginger, the girl clown, double parked her truck under a leafy maple tree. Children raced past us, shouting their flavors in excited voices, and the music played on, giving the street a carnival atmosphere.

"This sure is a nice way to end the day," Matt said. "We should make it a new tradition."

I nodded, thinking of the long sunny months to come, of having someone to be with. "Let's take advantage of a mobile dessert cart while the summer lasts."

"I see everybody has the same idea." Gwendolyn White sauntered across the street in sling-back high heels. Her lavender suit suggested that she'd recently arrived home from work. "How are you two doing? Hmm?" She looked from Matt to me, obviously anticipating a report on our recent activities and, incidentally, our relationship.

"I'm fine," I said. "Dreaming of frozen delights."

"Aren't we all? It's too early in the season to be this hot." She tugged at the top button of her fussy ruffled blouse. "I saw that gypsy in the library the other day, Cressa. She was sitting on the sofa with a newspaper in her lap, not even looking at it. Just taking up space."

"The librarian has an ongoing problem with the homeless," Matt said. "People don't like being hit up for change when they're looking for a book, but Molly has a soft heart. She never turns anyone away."

"Wouldn't it be hard to prove that a person wasn't a legitimate reader?" I asked.

"Not if they're caught begging or washing up in the restroom," Gwendolyn said. "Not if they show up every single day. That woman gives me the creeps."

"That's not against the law," Matt said quietly.

Gwendolyn's eyes narrowed. "People shouldn't be allowed to use the library as a cheap motel. I'm going to see what I can do about it."

"What could you do?" I asked.

"Call the police. Complain to the mayor. Organize a letter writing campaign. You could print an editorial, Matt."

Ginger turned her painted clown smile on Matt. "Hi, Mr. Emmerton. Chocolate cone for you today?"

"One chocolate, one rocky road. What'll you have, Gwendolyn? My treat."

Gwendolyn blushed. "Why thank you, Matt. Make mine butter pecan. How gallant you are."

And thoughtful and generous. I imagined that Matt would gladly empty his change into the palm of a needy woman, and if he wrote an editorial on the homeless, it would call for compassion. But should people wile away their days in the library simply because it was cool and comfortable and they didn't have any other place to stay?

Now I sounded like Gwendolyn. But loitering was against the law, and libraries should be reserved for readers.

Apparently, while I'd been away, vagrancy had become a live-wire issue in Maple Creek. I'd have to think about it carefully before choosing a side. Meanwhile, maybe I could do something to help at least one person.

We said goodbye to Gwendolyn, and headed back down the street with our cones. I was indeed fortunate, unlike those who never had enough to eat, let alone a decadent double dip treat.

I couldn't stop thinking about the woman at Libby's reception, sweeping up expensive tortes to gobble them alone in the woods. How sad it would be to subsist on stale doughnuts, lukewarm coffee and charity while the ice cream truck drove by, its merry song a mockery. Then one day to come across a glittering array of fancy cakes on an unguarded table, a temptation impossible to resist.

Matt put his arm around my waist as we reached a wide crack in the sidewalk. The gesture felt natural and welcome. "Gwendolyn speaks for a small minority in Maple Creek. This is an unusually hospitable town."

"With its share of intolerant citizens."

"Like every place I've ever lived," he said.

THE NEXT MORNING brought change to the white Victorian. Kady Dorset unlocked the front door and opened the windows. With

Kady inside its walls, the old house radiated with new energy. The shape I saw moving through the rooms belonged to a real person, and the classical music flowed out from a portable CD player in front of the kitchen window.

If the lonely spirits were going to fly away into the fresh air, this was their chance.

In front, overflowing boxes joined stacks of magazines and newspapers at the curb. Empty milk and juice cartons, cereal boxes, and leftovers in plastic containers attracted the attention of Pepper, the dog who didn't seem to have a home, although Matt had told her to go there once. She sniffed at the contents of a discarded cooler while a squirrel eyed the display wistfully from a safe distance.

Around noon, Kady moved a lawn chair near the fountain to the exact location where I'd last seen Libby sitting in her rocker. Too near. The bright blouse she wore with her jeans had the rainbow colors of Libby's print dress, and her hair, tied back in a long pony tail, was pale, shimmering yellow.

I had an irrational urge to tell her to move away from the satyr, but I didn't.

Instead I tended to my own affairs: my next interview at a parochial high school in Spearmint Lake and a trip to the store for milk and fresh produce. When I returned, Kady's car was still in the driveway, and Pepper lay on the front lawn gulping her way through a scavenged sausage ring.

As soon as I opened the car door, I heard the splash of water on concrete. Although the temperature hovered around eighty degrees, a chill appeared out of nowhere, gaining in intensity as it snaked up my body.

But I should have known that the satyr wouldn't die so easily.

I carried the groceries around to my back porch. Kady was sitting in the yard again, sipping a Coke. The fountain was alive. Great falls of water caught the sunlight on their downward journey, and the fresh scent reached me across the expanse of grass. If I were impressionable, I'd swear that the statue's hollow eyes blazed in triumph and his head had a more arrogant tilt.

After a moment's hesitation, I set my bags and purse down on the porch steps. These few minutes on my own property had banished the strange temperature drop, which proved that my mind was trying to deceive me with impossibilities again.

Kady must be finished with her clean-up project, and I wanted to ask her if she'd seen any signs of an intruder in the house—and, all right, I was a snoopy neighbor, curious about her future plans.

She looked my way and waved. "Hi, Cressa." Her soft voice all but vanished in the rush of water.

"Hello." I crossed the property line, once again surprised to find myself moving in warmth. The chill in the air was gone, but the sound of water was louder now. "You've been busy, I see."

She set the Coke can on the ground. "I'm trying to restore the balance. Isn't it beautiful?"

I chose to think that she meant the wide prism that arced from the sky down to the fountain's base. Filled with iridescent tints, so fragile that it would dissolve at any moment, it was truly a thing of beauty. "Exquisite. I wish I had my camera handy."

But the statue… As always, I wanted to turn away or, better still, throw a sheet over it. Newly washed and rejuvenated, it seemed more hideous than ever. From my perspective, the satyr looked as if he was beckoning to Kady, and his long talon fingers had a brighter sheen.

I couldn't possibly warn her to beware of an inanimate horror, but repeating Tim's warning wouldn't sound quite so outlandish. "Be careful. No pond or pool is completely safe."

Her laugh rang out over the sound of water. "Don't worry, Cressa. I've been around this fountain since I was a toddler. The police gave me permission to turn it on, although I don't know why I had to ask them. Everything is mine now."

"Investigation issues, I guess. Have they closed the case?"

She nodded. "Officially my aunt's death was an accident. She's buried and at peace, so I hope those wild stories die with her."

"Do you think she fell and hit her head?"

"That's what must have happened. Lately, Aunt Libby suffered from vertigo and fainting spells, but her doctor couldn't find the cause. Most of the time, she was okay."

"It only took one incident." I gazed down at the clear water, seeing Libby's lifeless body again. "And being in the wrong place when she had it."

As for the statue, it was just there, part of the fountain. Not evil. Not a killer. Absolutely, undeniably insentient. I had to stop obsessing about it.

"Pull up a chair and join me," Kady said.

"Thanks, but I have groceries to unload."

Pepper was sniffing around my bags. Although they held nothing to interest a carnivore, I'd better rescue them. Quickly I added, "Did Lieutenant Gray mention that someone was in the house last week?"

"Yes. We checked everywhere and didn't find anything out of place. I can't imagine what you saw."

"Well…maybe nothing. Is there any other way to get in besides the doors?"

"Through a window, but that didn't happen."

"I might be mistaken."

That was what I said, but I didn't believe it. The intruder—and I wasn't mistaken—had left no telltale signs behind for Lieutenant Gray and the new owner to find. But why debate the matter with a person who believed the evidence, or lack thereof?

"There's something else." I started to tell her about the vanishing balloons but Lieutenant Gray had already done so. "Did you find them in the house?" I asked.

"A few, but they weren't blown up."

"I don't understand what happened to them," I said.

She shook the Coke can. It was empty. "That's something else we'll never know. Anyway, it's over now. All of it."

Kady was willing to drop the matter, along with the possibility of a break-in and rumors of suicide and murder. Her lack of curiosity puzzled me. Knowing what happened wouldn't bring her aunt back to life, but it might affect Kady's fate.

Then I reconsidered. She already knew the police department's version. Since it was so easy to accept, why wasn't I, a mere neighbor, ready to have the case closed?

"Did you decide to keep the house?" I asked.

"For a few years. I'm moving in at the end of the month. Then, in the fall, my three friends will join me. We're all studying music, so you'll be hearing the piano again. We're not as good as Aunt Libby, though."

"You will be someday," I said, glancing at my porch. Pepper had disappeared, and the bags were intact. Apparently Libby's throwaways held more appeal for a dog than my new purchases. "I'd better get my milk out of this heat."

I left Kady sitting in the satyr's shadow and went back to my own house, hoping for a long string of tranquil days and nights free of trauma.

From now on, if I heard music in the Victorian, there would be a reason for it with college students practicing the piano, visiting boyfriends and occasional parties. Furthermore, Kady viewed the statue as part of her heritage. She'd set the water running again, and if the family legend was still in effect, all would be well. Perhaps the aura that had shadowed the house since the fountain disaster was even now dissipating.

That proved to be wishful thinking. Within an hour of Kady's departure, the place seemed more bereft and desolate than ever, even as the sound of water blended seamlessly into the environment.

At the curb, birds and squirrels descended on the mound of trash. Shredded paper and gnawed plastic lay strewn on the grass, with bits of vegetables, the probable remains of a stew that should have gone into the garbage disposal. One era had ended, leaving the new regime in a state of messy transition.

Before dark, I went next door to tidy the mess. Moldy bread had spilled out of a Harvest Wheat wrapper onto the sidewalk. As I tossed it into a box, I recognized the dead flowers that had graced Libby's refreshment table. Every stem was bent as if an angry hand had wrenched them out of the basket.

Except for a lone sprig of lavender.

On an impulse, I pulled it from the bouquet. The petals still held a trace of scent, but their rich purple color had faded to a dull gray. No matter. This was a remembrance of Libby, and, unlike the deflated balloons, it wasn't a clue. I'd keep it with the holy card from the funeral parlor and always remember the happy moments of Libby's last night on earth.

THAT EVENING I sat on the balcony, waiting for the stars to appear and sorting recent events into neat categories. According to the police, Libby's death was an accident. Kady had given the satyr his life back. Minta's scrapbook lay on my kitchen table and somewhere in Maple Creek, Annora May waited for my call.

On the relationship front, Matt was an attractive and congenial friend, Jase was an autograph on a snapshot and I was at a crossroad in my life, which was a good place to be.

I leaned back in my chair and breathed in the scent of June lilies. They grew wild between my house and the white Victorian, strong, stocky plants with pink speckled petals and a light fragrance, richer than any bottled perfume.

With chirruping crickets and splashing water, the night was pure magic, made for dreaming. More accurately, it was made for romance, but the only man on my horizon was Matt. Could we possibly be more than ice cream friends some day?

Maybe. Who can know the future?

And was that what I wanted?

No, not yet. And when I choose a man, I want fireworks again. The entire super nova experience. Matt is…he is nice.

Kady had left a lamp on in a window on the third floor, no doubt to give the impression that someone was inside. As I focused on the circle of brightness, I caught a detail that had slid out of my mind days ago. Libby had left this same lamp on after the reception. At some point, it had been turned off, most likely by the police.

It was a little treasure shaped like a crystal tree with teardrop leaves. Libby had set it on a table in the window so that it would reflect the sunlight. No doubt Kady loved it, too.

Wait a minute.

When Libby had given me a tour of her house, she mentioned that she rarely ventured up to the top floor. "The rooms are all furnished, but I use them mainly for storage," she'd said. "Climbing stairs is too much of an effort for me these days."

Why leave the lovely lamp in such an out-of-the-way place? More importantly, who had turned it on, if not Libby?

The room in which the light shone was the prettiest one in the house, with dainty forget-me-not wallpaper and vintage furniture. Libby had walked over to a quaint Victorian dresser and drawn my attention to an antique vase shaped like a harp.

"One of my school friends gave this to me—oh, years and years ago," she'd said, running her finger lightly across the creamy surface. "I love it, but even in a large house, everything can't be downstairs at the same time."

The lamp was taking its turn in storage, then.

Stop, stop, stop trying to find a mystery in every aspect of Libby Dorset's life. You're not a detective. Even if you were, the case is closed. Think about something else.

I let my thoughts wander aimlessly down a dozen innocuous paths. Steep flights would be no problem for Kady or Aleta and Linda. I wondered if Libby's student-housemaids had dusted every one of those figurines and decorative plates and each picture frame.

One of these days I had to give my own house another cleaning, a thorough one this time. When?

Somewhere a dog began to bark, a persistent don't-leave-me-alone-in-the-dark sound. The animal appeared to be nearby, perhaps on the other side of Libby's house or in the woods. But if no one was around to hear—I was assuming that because I didn't hear a shouted canine name—what was the point of non-stop fussing?

Dogs didn't think like that. They'd whine, even in an empty house whenever they wanted something, trusting that a human would eventually materialize. This canine-in-distress barked on and on. I hoped he settled down before I went inside to bed—which had better be soon, as I had a busy day tomorrow.

But if he's a soldier's abandoned pet, he'll bark forever.

While I'd been pouring trivia and speculation into my mind, the sky had filled with tiny sparkling stars. I made my wish and added a prayer for good measure. Even though my future was still unsettled, my life was running smoothly for the first time in months. I looked forward to the next day.

TEN

I SAW THE GIRL as soon as I opened my balcony doors. She sat on top of the overturned canoe at the edge of the woods, facing the fountain. In her mint green dress, she looked like a figure in a sentimental turn-of-the-century print—a flower fairy or the Spirit of Spring.

I set my coffee cup on the wicker table and looked across two hundred and fifty yards, wishing for a telescope. My eyesight was good, but a light mist blurred the features of the young visitor. She could be another one of Libby's grieving piano students or a neighbor's daughter.

Doing what? Hanging out in the Maywood acres on a Saturday morning?

Technically she wasn't trespassing, at least not on my property, but it felt as if she was, and that something was wrong. Some element amiss. Some strangeness that eluded me for the moment.

I picked up the cup and walked to the railing, taking long sips of coffee and gazing into the misty shreds. As the strong brew slid down my throat, the answer appeared.

While the tall perennials that grew at the back of the yard blew back and forth in the wind, the girl's long dark hair never moved. Either she had exceptionally effective hairspray—or she wasn't real.

That was it. I was looking at a life-size lawn statue placed on the canoe by an unknown person for some unfathomable reason. I must be half asleep to not know the difference between a human being and an inanimate object, but with the deep lot, two stories and rolls of mist separating us, I couldn't be sure.

Still, I called out to her. "Hello…Miss?"

She didn't answer, didn't even turn her head.

I gulped the rest of my coffee on the way downstairs and hurried out to the backyard, needing to see for myself who or what had taken up residence on the Maywood's ancient canoe.

The fog was thicker at ground level, rolling eastward with the wind. It wrapped damp tendrils around my bare arms and seemed to pull me forward across the wet grass, past the dog skeleton's grave, toward the woods. But I could see that it was too late. The girl had vanished.

If the intruder was on a private mission, she must have heard me approach and run away. I'd moved quietly, though. I didn't think she'd noticed me on the balcony or heard my call.

On the other hand, if I'd seen a garden statue, where was it now? I was alone with only the splash of water and a raucous cawing of unseen birds to break the silence.

The peeling underbody of the boat glistened with moisture. If the girl was real, her pretty green dress would be wet. But no one had been sitting on the canoe, and no object had rested there. Just to be sure, I ran my hand along the surface, searching for a dry area. There was none, and now I wasn't certain what I had seen—if anything.

This incident was too weird to absorb, much less comprehend, especially at an early hour.

As I walked around to the sidewalk, I felt the first pinpricks of apprehension, the kind I associated with the satyr, and remembered the other intruder—the fast-as-light person who had called my name and disappeared. What was going on in this town?

I could think of only one answer. Someone in the neighborhood was playing tricks on me. I wasn't amused, not when her antics brought old memories bubbling to the surface.

Impossibilities…shadows springing to life…a remembered face in blowing snow… I shook my head as if to dislodge them. This current episode required an explanation, but I didn't have to travel to *Twilight Zone* territory to find it. I'd simply apply cold, clear logic, which seldom failed me.

People are often drawn to the scene of a tragic happening, even long after the event. Many of Libby's students used to have their lessons on Saturday morning, giving this day of the week and place significance for them. Aleta and the fast-as-light person, as well as this girl—if there was a girl—all could have legitimate reasons for making a pilgrimage to the scene of Libby Dorset's death. Fear of discovery by an irate homeowner might make an intruder run.

But who would set a lawn decoration on an abandoned canoe and whisk it away later?

If only there was somebody to question: a passerby, a neighbor en route to the Farmers' Market or getting an early start on the day's shopping, even the paper boy. I looked around, but I was still alone.

Deep Saturday silence lay heavily on the gracious old Victorians that faced one another through swirls of fog. I could see as far as Matt's driveway. His car was gone. Every other house in my view was dark and quiet, its inhabitants still in bed or away from home. The gables and rooftops gleamed through gauzy white wrapping, but the stacks of discards at the curbside spoiled the effect.

With three days remaining until trash pickup, creatures had pillaged the boxes and bags again. More moldy bread lay on the sidewalk, and a spill of jelly beans made a bright rainbow splash of color on my front lawn.

As I walked across the grass to pick them up, I glanced at the third floor of the old Victorian. Last night's puzzle bounced back into my mind. There was no light in the window today. Ribbons of mist floated past the pane, obscuring the top half of the lamp that was usually visible from the ground.

Set the girl in green aside, then. Try to figure out this mystery. Use logic.

I could rule out a break-in, as intelligent burglars don't turn on lamps, but many houses were equipped with timers. Could that explain the capricious lightshow? Maybe, but Libby had claimed their settings were too complicated for her, and since she usually stayed home, they were extraneous.

What else? Sooner or later, bulbs burn out. Or Kady might have paid a late night visit to her new home and wandered up to the Blue Room. No, that didn't make sense. She wouldn't ascend three flights of stairs before realizing that she needed light.

Everyone needs light except ghostly presences. They favor the dark.

I didn't like the direction of my thoughts. So, where did that leave me? Standing alone on my walkway with a handful of Easter candy, utterly mystified about the strange happenings on Beechnut Street.

I looked toward the blue Victorian again, hoping that Matt had come home in the last few minutes, but his driveway was still empty. I recalled that he had another house in the country, and the *Tribune* office closed on weekends. If I wanted to talk to someone, I had to find another victim.

ANNORA MAY SAT ON my porch, slowly turning the pages of the scrapbook she'd put together so long ago, while I refilled our glasses with lemonade. The sun had burned away the morning mist, and the world was new and wholesome again. In the midst of a pleasant visit, I found it hard to believe that a mysterious light and a vanishing girl or statue had disturbed my morning.

I definitely needed to socialize more.

A soft smile played on her lips. "Listen to this. Amaranths, radiance, magnificence… These poems don't rhyme or scan. They're mush-and-gush, but once I thought they were so good."

"How old were you when you wrote them?" I asked.

"Sixteen. I wish I'd kept the scrapbook Minta made for me. She was a fledgling author. Her stories could have been published."

"What did she write about?"

"Love, dogs, robots, space travel…whatever captured her interest."

"You both must have known Libby Dorset," I said.

"Yes, but she liked to be called Elizabeth in those days." She glanced at the fountain and looked down at the plate of sugar cookies she'd brought. "The way Libby died was ghastly. They say most accidents happen at home."

"You didn't mention her the last time you were here." I

handed Annora a glass of lemonade and added a smile, hoping she wouldn't recognize a gentle interrogation.

"That's because I felt terrible that I didn't visit her as soon as I came back to town. When I finally got around to it, I learned that she was dead."

"No one could know what was going to happen," I said.

"I guess I'll have to remember Libby the way she was when I last saw her." She dabbed at her eyes and turned to a black page crammed with color prints. "Here's Main Street. The Royal Theater and Sanders. They're both torn down now. Minta and I used to go to the show and then stop at Sanders for sodas."

"They were before my time," I said, thinking of the new restaurant and little antique shop with its nautical window display. Suddenly I remembered the canoe. It must belong to Annora. Maybe she could tell me something about its history.

"I wonder if you can still find old-fashioned sodas with cream mixed into the syrup," she said.

"I don't know where. Annora, are you ever going to use that old boat?"

"Heavens, no. I don't have a death wish. My Uncle Rick left it there. He used to take a trip up the Au Sable every summer."

"It doesn't look very seaworthy."

"He kept it in tip-top shape, but he passed on years ago. I'll have it hauled away so you can enjoy a nice view of the woods."

I suppressed a sigh of relief to be so easily rid of an eyesore. If the girl in green came back, she could find another seat. "I'd appreciate that. It isn't serving any purpose."

"None at all. I'll take care of it." She turned another page. "Oh, darn! Some of my pictures are missing."

I glanced down at the sheet. It contained three views of Spearmint Lake with obscure figures in the background, and, underneath, two blank rows. The small black corners used to hold the photographs still clung to the page.

"They must have slipped out." She looked under the table, as if expecting to see them scattered on the floor. They weren't there.

"I should have reinforced them with Scotch tape," I said. "Maybe it happened in Matt's office. I'll give him a call."

"Oh, yes, Matt Emmerton used them to write the story." Her eyes took on a new shine. "Does he still live around here?"

"He rents that blue house across the street during the week."

"The one with the flag. I remember now." She closed the book and set it on the table. As she reached for a cookie, she said, "It's too bad he has that horrible limp. Otherwise he'd be quite a catch for some lucky girl."

In a flush of anger, I rushed to Matt's defense. "The way he walks doesn't change the man he is."

"Sure it does. Think of all the things he can't do anymore."

"For instance?"

She held up her right hand. Two diamond rings and long, shimmering nails sparkled in the light. "Well, dance, for one. He can't run, can't ski…"

"You don't know that," I said.

"He can never go back to the war, but that's a fringe."

I broke a cookie in two but left it on the napkin, considering. I couldn't argue with that. And could I say I'd never thought of Matt's limp? When I adjusted my pace so that we walked together on the sidewalk or allowed myself a fleeting thought of Jase Clayborne who was whole in every way? That I'd never considered how it would affect my life if Matt and I were ever to have a relationship, which wasn't likely, but still…

I felt as if one of my own failings had been held up to ridicule by this glossy woman in her pristine white sundress. My own guest, whom I'd been ready to like, a woman without a single visible imperfection.

A slight blush betrayed Annora's discomfort. "I'm sorry, Cressa. That must have sounded terrible. Sometimes I speak without thinking. Like now. Poor Matt got wounded serving his country. He deserves our gratitude."

I felt my anger at Annora subside a little. She appeared to be sorry; and who doesn't occasionally make an insensitive comment? "Matt Emmerton is a good man," I said. "That's all that matters."

"Any one of us could be in his place one day. I know."

She picked up an oversize beige bag embroidered with sequined flowers and butterflies splashed across both sides. "Thanks for letting me view the scrapbook, Cressa. It wasn't as wonderful as I remembered, but then what is?"

"A time capsule doesn't need to be fancy."

"No, of course not. What will you do with it?"

"Maybe give it to someone in Minta's family."

"I'm sure her parents are dead. Her younger sister may be alive. I don't know where she's living."

In the long pause that followed, I suspected that Annora was waiting for me to offer the scrapbook to her, but I was reluctant to part with it. I wasn't sure why.

Later, after she had gone, I flipped through the book again, wondering if somehow the missing pictures had landed in another section. Toward the back, I found a sliver of jagged notebook paper clinging to a page by a strip of tape.

Someone had torn out one of the poems. And when had that happened? While it was in Matt's possession? Would he have been so careless? I remembered that I'd left Annora alone on the porch for about ten minutes to make the lemonade. But before leaping to accusations, could I positively swear that there had been a whole sheet of paper here when I'd first examined the scrapbook?

Unfortunately, no. And, at the time, the pages could have been stuck together.

But I had an uneasy feeling that I was the one who had been careless. The scrapbook was slowly losing its contents. Maybe that was coincidental, but maybe not. For the present, I'd better stash it out of sight before something else disappeared.

ELEVEN

SOMEWHERE IN THE NIGHT a dog was barking. The annoying high-pitched yelps dragged me out of a fitful sleep. They were near and frantic, almost in the room with me or on the balcony. But how could any animal be so close? I was on the second floor, high above the ground.

Then I remembered. I'd left the French doors open in the hope that an occasional breeze would cool the room. Instead, a stream of muted sounds had flowed freely in: a car door slamming in the distance, fleeting snatches of radio music and soft laughter in the street. Now noise from an agitated canine, most likely in the woods.

I lay still, letting the fragments of the dream dissolve. They centered around a fork in the road and two signposts shrouded in fog. I didn't know which way to turn, but it didn't matter, as the choice wasn't mine. Some malignant force followed me, propelling me forward into the unknown.

That was a nightmare, best forgotten.

I fluffed my pillows, lay back, and listened. The blades of the ceiling fan turned gallantly, but the hot air beneath them refused to move. In my sleep, I'd twisted the edge of the sheet into a bunch. My hand ached from clenching it so tightly, and a dull pain throbbed above my left eye.

A restless night and rude awakening boded ill for the coming day. I rearranged the covers and tried to go back to sleep, but the barking continued.

Come see what I want. Now! Now! I won't stop until you do.

Only an arrogant, inconsiderate jerk would allow his dog to disturb the neighbors. Maybe he was the same person who had slammed the car door earlier. Or the dog might be mourning for his soldier master. At any rate, this canine was making enough noise to wake the entire block.

And the dead?

I reached across the nightstand and turned on the lamp. It was only three. I couldn't possibly get up now. By noon I'd be ready to fall into bed again. Nor could I relax with this ungodly racket filling every inch of my bedroom.

I swung out of bed and into my slippers and made my way across the hardwood floor. In the brief time it took me to reach the balcony, the barking ceased.

Out here it was sultry, but there was a hint of a breeze. I stood at the railing, gazing at the sky. The moon was a luminous sliver surrounded by stars. The farthermost boundary of my property swam in thick darkness that hid the canoe and the skeleton dog's grave from my view.

That grave… A strange thought slipped into my mind. Could the panicked barking be coming from beneath the ground?

No. Of course not. Never. Maple Creek had plenty of living dogs. I didn't have to create a canine phantom.

Nonetheless, the idea took hold and, like the stagnant air in my bedroom, refused to move. Feeling the prickle of apprehension again, I stepped back inside and locked the doors. That was a little better, but the image of a barking skeleton lurked in my mind, one more detriment to slumber.

When first exposed to the lights, those bones had an eerie glow, an unnatural shine… I'd saved them from an ignoble fate and buried them in a new resting place. Why should they haunt me?

That isn't happening.

At present, in the real world, it was so quiet that I could hear my own breathing. Someone must have brought the barker inside. Now that I thought about it, every newly unearthed bone would look strange when first disinterred. Once again, logic saved me.

Suspecting that I wouldn't be able to fall asleep, I sat up in bed with a notebook and pen and began to plan the day's activities. The next minute, or so it seemed, I awoke in a pool of warm sunshine. The pain above my eye had progressed to a full-fledged headache. Outside, the barking had resumed, as loud and insistent as before, now laced with a note of despair.

The first item I'd written on the page was "Deal with the dog."

I CARRIED MY COFFEE OUT to the balcony and sank into the chair, feeling as if I hadn't slept at all. At seven-thirty, the morning was already hot and steamy, and a strong vile odor rode on the air. It overpowered the fragrance of lilies that usually accompanied my outdoor breakfasts.

A toxic substance seeping up from the ground or a malfunctioning sewer or…something burning?

My peripheral vision caught a drift of smoke, coming from… *My house?* The cup slid out of my hand and crashed to the floor, spewing hot liquid on my leg. I looked up. No, Libby's house! The old white Victorian was on fire! Smoke billowed out through the seams of the third floor, steaming the air and spiraling around the gables. It looked as if the structure were ready to burst.

From a distance, I listened to my mind give a series of orders. Call the Fire Department; leave the cup; step around the mess. Move!

I hurried downstairs and fumbled in my handbag for my cell phone. Kady should know about the fire, but I didn't have her number. And the Fire Department's number was…? With shaking hands, I dialed 911 and gave my message to a calm dispatcher.

There. Now wait.

If the firefighters arrived in time…if the blaze was confined to the top story…if it didn't spread to my house…this didn't have to be a disaster.

I slipped the phone in my pocket in case another emergency arose. Response time for fire fighting crews was ten minutes. I'd read that in the *Tribune*. Sixty seconds times ten, with no wind to carry the flames to my home. It should be all right if they'd just hurry. Thank God no one was inside the Victorian. Nothing

would be damaged except the walls, the ceilings, the floors…
Libby's antiques. The crystal lamp, her cherished spinet, the
vintage oil paintings…

An anguished howl broke through my feverish catalogue of
endangered possessions.

I looked through my bay window directly into the dining
room next door. A black dog with tan markings above his eyes
stared back at me. His paws were on the sill, his nose pressed
against the glass. Across the several yards that separated us, I
could sense his panic.

Her panic. The dog looked like Pepper.

Here was the barker. Trapped inside the house, Pepper had
sent out a plea for help last night, but I'd ignored it.

I hurried outside, wading through the overgrown area between
the two houses. The smoke was thicker now, impossible to
escape while I moved toward it.

I'm always racing next door. Ever since Libby died.

At the dining-room window, I peered inside. Apparently the
fire hadn't spread to the ground floor yet, but the dog was gone.
Surely not upstairs. Where then? Another door. There were three
of them.

Excited yips led me to the back. Pepper had fled to the kitch-
enette where she pawed furiously at another window, raking the
surface with her nails and whining loudly.

"It's okay, girl!" I shouted.

On an impulse, I tapped on the glass. It was old and rimmed
with condensation, most likely, breakable. The window was
close to the side door. Within arm's reach, I'd guess.

"Fire! The house is on fire!" Patti rushed up to me, holding
the folds of her flimsy white bathrobe together. Her makeup had
a slapped-on look, and a blue roller dangled from hair. "Cressa,
what are you doing?"

"There's a dog inside. I'm going to get her out."

"How?"

"I don't know yet. I need something heavy."

"Look on the porch. The outer door doesn't lock."

I did. The porch had been swept clean.

I dashed back to the fountain where Patti stood looking up at the smoke. The satyr cast me a mocking smile, watching and beckoning. If only I could break off one of his arms. That could smash through glass in an instant.

"It looks like just smoke for now," Patti said. "You'd better wait for the firemen. I called 911."

"So did I."

But I didn't hear a siren yet. I was on the scene; they weren't.

What was strong enough to break a window? Quickly, I scanned the yard looking for a makeshift implement. An overlooked garden tool? A brick? The stones on the skeleton dog's grave!

Then I noticed the aluminum lawn chairs from the reception. I could use one of these—or take the sensible, sane course and wait for the firefighters to arrive.

Behind the glass, Pepper screamed like a terrified child in a world turned hostile. Her terrified eyes burned into my heart, along with the smoke.

"Just a minute, pooch," I said. "Stand out of the way, Patti."

I lifted a chair and sent it driving into the window. It landed with a crash on the floor inside. Jagged fragments flew back at me. Dodging their lethal edges, I reached through the opening, above the glass that still clung to the frame, and groped along the inner wall for the doorknob. My calculations were a fraction off. What seemed an arm's length from outside was beyond my grasp. But not by much.

"Can you get it?" Patti asked.

"Almost…" I raised myself up on my toes and reached inside again, grasping air several times. Finally, my hand closed on the knob. I turned it and gave the door an outward shove.

With a joyous yelp, Pepper leaped through the porch to freedom, knocking me off balance. I fell to the ground, taking the dog with me and lay there for a moment, stunned. Her fur smelled of smoke and felt warmer than it should.

"Some gratitude," Patti said. "Are you hurt?"

"Just a little shaken," I said.

I took Patti's hand and stood up, waiting for my heartbeat and breathing to synchronize. "That was easier than I thought."

Pepper whined and thumped the side of the house with her tail. "How did you get inside that house, you silly mutt?" I asked.

"You cut your leg, Cressa," Patti said.

Suddenly aware of a sharp pain, I looked down, expecting to find blood. The skin around my knee had the angry red color of a rash, but there was no laceration.

"I spilled hot coffee on myself," I said.

"That looks like a third degree burn. Let's get away from here."

We moved to the sidewalk, just as Mr. Harrison appeared. "It looks worse from down here. I called the Fire Department."

"So did we," Patti said. "I hope the chief won't be mad because you broke a window, Cressa. He doesn't like civilian heroics."

"It doesn't matter if he is. Saving Pepper was more important." I petted the dog and was rewarded by a wagging tail. "Besides, they're taking too long."

Patti said, "I think somebody's been living here all along, using Libby's things."

"Like a squatter?"

"Sort of. This place would be paradise to someone who doesn't have a home. Just imagine…sleeping in a clean bed, boiling water on the stove. I'd say eating Libby's food, but Kady pretty much got rid of everything edible. Then last night this person got careless and started a fire."

I'd had a similar thought when I'd seen a figure moving through the dining room, even though the police and Kady had summarily dismissed my eyewitness account. Still the theory had problems.

"That's possible, but I don't see how anyone can get in or out without breaking a window like I just did. The dog probably wandered in with Kady, and she didn't notice her."

"Someone might be inside right now burning to death."

"I'll go look," Mr. Harrison said. "Do one of you ladies have a towel I could wrap around my face?"

Patti glanced at the open door. "There should be one in the kitchen, or a tablecloth. Libby always…" A distant siren drowned out the rest of her sentence.

At last. It seemed impossible that only ten minutes had passed since I noticed the first wisps of smoke from the balcony.

"They made good time," Patti said.

I let my hand rest on Pepper's head. "There's no need for you to risk your life, Mr. Harrison. The firemen will take care of everything."

BY THE TIME the fire engine pulled up in front of the white Victorian, a small crowd had congregated across the street, well out of the way. As we joined them, Mr. Harrison announced that he was going to a later mass today. "Just in case it gets windy again," he said with a glance toward his own home.

"There's always something going on at the Dorset place," a voice behind me remarked.

"Talk about déjà vu. Isn't it empty now?" another asked.

"It's supposed to be." That was Gwendolyn wearing a blue-checked apron over her tailored suit.

Patti had vanished into her house and emerged a few minutes later in a red sundress with her hair brushed. The roller was gone. She came back in time to hear Gwendolyn's question, but she had one of her own. "Did I miss anything?"

"Not much. I think they're finishing up," I said.

The firemen had worked swiftly and efficiently, storming the white Victorian with impressive equipment and determination, doing whatever they did behind the walls. Now the smoke had dissipated, but its smell lingered, heavy and unpleasant on the air. From the sidewalk, I could see the crystal lamp in the window clearly. Maybe the damage wasn't so extensive after all.

"We have a first-rate Fire Department in Maple Creek, but I hope I never have to call on them again," I said.

Gwendolyn waylaid the chief, a grim, austere giant of a man. "How did the fire start, Bruce?"

"I can't say. Luckily someone noticed smoke and called or there might have been more damage."

"That was Cressa," Patti said. "She saved a dog, too."

"How did a dog get inside an empty house?" he demanded.

"We don't know." She looked at me.

"Maybe when the new owner was here," I said.

As Bruce moved out of hearing range, Gwendolyn said, "I went to school with him. You think he'd be more forthcoming."

"Could the dog have started the fire?" Patti asked.

"I can't imagine how."

"By knocking over a small appliance? A hair drier?"

Gwendolyn scoffed. "How unlikely is that! He'd have to turn it on first. You need hands to do that."

"Not necessarily," Patti said. "I read about a case…"

I stopped listening to their good-natured bickering and looked toward my house, longing for a quiet sanctuary, needing to regroup. My head still ached and now my hip hurt from the backward fall. Absently I rubbed my leg. I was a mess.

"Shouldn't you have that burn looked at?" Patti asked.

"I'll put some ointment on and wait," I said.

Then I'd take two aspirin, wash the smell of smoke away, change clothes and once again start a day over. Since it was Sunday, I'd fix a special dinner and read over my plans for the coming week. The firemen would likely notify Kady and in time I'd learn more about the extent of the damage and perhaps its cause.

My fantastic new life, I thought. *When is it going to get better?*

As the fire truck pulled away, Gwendolyn said, "I guess the excitement is over. Just in time for church."

I said goodbye to my neighbors and the dog and crossed the street again. The trampled lilies between the houses were a mass of broken stems and crushed flowers, a sacrifice to save a burning structure. I gathered a few survivors that had escaped the firemen's boots, and held them up to my face. They smelled of smoke, but the sweet fragrance I loved was still there, buried deep inside the petals.

Carrying the bruised flowers, I walked across my lawn to the walkway. Pepper trotted alongside me, wagging her tail tentatively. When we reached the front porch, she sat down and looked from the door to me and back again, her eyes alert and bright with hope.

Oh, no!

"Go home, girl," I said, opening the door.

She sat still, her head tilted to one side, watching my hand.

"If I didn't rescue you, the firemen would have," I said. "That's their job."

She whimpered and offered me her paw to shake.

"You must have a home," I said. "Somebody's going to miss you."

But that wasn't true. She wasn't wearing a collar. No one had bought her a tag. Pepper had lean ribs and expressive eyes. All dogs know exactly how to look when they want something and Pepper's desire couldn't have been plainer.

I spared a fleeting thought for the lovely Gracie with her gorgeous blue mottled coat. Pepper wasn't the dog I would have chosen, if the choice were mine. Obviously it wasn't, and Gracie already had a home.

"Okay," I said. "You might as well come in for something to eat and a drink of water. But we're going in through the back."

She didn't look very clean. Her white forelegs were crusted with dirt, and her fur was matted. I'd use the porch as a grooming station and confine her to the kitchen until I decided what to do with her. I opened the porch door, and she slipped past me like a dark ghost.

What a strange ending to a tumultuous morning.

Before following Pepper inside, I paused to look at the white Victorian. Still and solemn, the old house was determined to keep its secrets. But surely this time, for this crisis, there must be a clue. Fires don't set themselves. Had a squatter appropriated Kady's house for himself, assuming that it was abandoned? Or was something more sinister going on?

Choose the second option, the satyr seemed to say. Something sinister.

TWELVE

THE DAY AFTER THE FIRE at Libby's house, the temperature soared to ninety degrees. In the extravagant heat bath, the perennials at the back of my yard burst into bloom. They were graceful spires with deep pink petals, similar to phlox.

I poured through my botany book trying to identify them without success. They might be an invasive species or a weed, but in the end all that mattered to me was their beauty. The plants were almost tall enough to hide the red canoe. Which reminded me. Annora had promised to have it hauled away. She must have forgotten, or clean-up occupied a low place on her priority list.

Ah well… It was too hot to fuss about a single flaw in the landscape. I moved the sprinkler to a bed of white impatiens near the house and hurried back to the porch where Pepper lay panting in front of the floor fan. She looked up and wagged her tail.

"Poor girl," I said. "You're not a summer animal, are you?"

Her answer was a soft, plaintive whine.

I was becoming a pathetic caricature of my former self, tending flowerbeds and commiserating with a dog. Ever since coming home to Maple Creek, my almost perfect life had settled into a slow motion pattern, and I wasn't happy with the new order.

It's bound to change, I thought. *Only yesterday you took on a fire.*

"Cressa! Are you busy?"

That was Matt's voice. I pushed a strand of hair away from my face and wiped the mud from my hands with a paper towel. "I'm back here on the porch."

He came around the side of the house slowly, limping as always, looking exceptionally handsome with a darker tan and a light blue shirt that emphasized the color of his eyes. Pepper scrambled to her feet and trotted to the door as I opened it. I let her out and let Matt in.

I felt his gaze resting on me and sensed his approval. "Are you doing some gardening?" he asked.

"Just watering."

"The lawn can use a long drink. It's ninety-three by my temperature gauge." He surveyed the wicker furniture and my lacy knit top. "That's an unusual shade of green," he said. "What do you call it?"

"Teal."

"It looks good with your red hair."

"Why thank you, sir!" I reached for the wayward strand again, but it was where it belonged. I was as tidy and attractive as I was going to be.

"This may be the coolest spot in Maple Creek," he said.

"It's my secret oasis."

"I came to take you out for an ice cream cone, if you're interested." He glanced at his watch. "In exactly ten minutes, we'll hear music."

"There's nothing I'd like better." I moved a magazine off the rocker, and he sat down. "You're pretty sure about the time."

"Give or take a minute. I hear that you saved Pepper from certain death and the Dorset house from the flames."

"Who told you that?"

"Patti, just now. I had a reporter on the story, but he didn't mention your part in it."

"I was one of three people who called 911, and yes, I rescued the dog. I'm going to have to pay Kady Dorset for a broken window. It's temporarily boarded up."

Through the screen, I checked on Pepper's activities. She was racing around the yard, keeping within the invisible boundary lines.

"Do you know if Pepper has a home somewhere?" I asked.

"It looks to me like she does." A teasing sparkle appeared in his eyes. "With you."

"I asked because you seemed to know her before," I said.

"Not really. She's been hanging around the neighborhood for a few months. One of the kids told me her name. Maybe the kid named her."

"I made her a nice, soft bed in the kitchen, but she likes to roam through the house."

He laughed. "Like a typical dog."

"Look what she's doing now," I said.

We watched her advance on the sprinkler as if it were a mortal enemy, only to spring back, barking furiously, when the water hit her face.

"Do you have any inside information about how the fire started?" I asked.

"The most probable cause is a candle left burning on the third floor. It was one of those tall tapers in a china holder."

"And this happened in a supposedly unoccupied house? The mystery deepens."

"Patti thinks someone has been living there."

"She could be right."

"The squatter won't be likely to come back now that the police are on to him," I said.

"Not if he's clever. My guess is that he doesn't think beyond the present."

I looked at the section of the white Victorian that I could see from the porch—the curtain-veiled windows behind the railing and the gingerbread trim dripping from the arches. The house was as silent and secretive as it had been since Libby's death except for the day when Kady had emptied the refrigerator and cupboards. Only the sound of water suggested habitation.

The fountain continued to puzzle me. Why did Kady keep it running when she was living elsewhere? Because of that old "appease the satyr" tradition?

Matt leaned back in the rocker, taking in that other view that always enchanted me: white impatiens shining like fallen stars, pink perennials and dark, lean trees throwing their shadows on the skeleton dog's grave.

"You're lucky to live next to Annora's woods," Matt said. "I'm surrounded by families with little kids. I look out on sandboxes and about a hundred plastic toys."

I nodded. "I hope a developer never gets his hands on those acres."

"I don't think Annora has any plans to sell her land."

If she kept the acreage intact, then those maples and oaks, like Libby's house, would keep their secrets. I recalled one of them now: a mysterious young woman, her features blurred by distance and mist.

"I saw a girl in the woods the other day," I said.

"Doing what?"

"Sitting on top of that old canoe. She vanished before I could find out what she was doing there."

"Maybe you saw a ghost," Matt said.

My heart skipped a beat. I felt as if Matt had accused me of some indiscretion, as if he knew my own secrets—which was impossible. In retrospect, I should have chosen a different verb. Any word except "vanish."

"She was real enough," I said. "She wore a green dress, which I thought was a little unusual…"

"For a girl today, I agree," he said.

And her hair didn't move in the breeze. I kept this detail to myself lest Matt think I was delusional. Surely he hadn't been serious about that ghost comment.

"It was all very strange, but I only saw her on one occasion. Then again…"

There was the light-in-motion person who had moved too quickly for me to see clearly.

"She might have been around before," I said. "Some of Libby's piano students have been visiting the place where she died."

"People used to come by occasionally even before that. The fountain is a neighborhood institution. Can you describe this girl in the woods?"

"Not too well. I saw her from the balcony and through the mist, but she was slender with long brown or black hair. The oddest thing about her was her dress. It had a vintage look. Oh, and she never moved. For a moment I thought she was a garden statue."

"I haven't seen anyone like that," Matt said. "She sounds like a rare young lady who enjoys solitude." A sudden sparkle brightened his eyes and made them seem more green than blue. "Or, like I said before, a ghost." As quickly as the sparkle had appeared, it vanished. "What's wrong, Cressa?"

"That's a word I don't use lightly."

He leaned over and touched my arm with a warm strong hand. "You may have to rethink that position, honey. You're living on Beechnut Street now. The longtime residents claim that it's haunted."

"You're joking," I said.

But I recalled the weird goings on in the white Victorian and the strange aura that hung over the house and yard; sentimental old songs drifting out from the unoccupied rooms; a woman's form moving slowly behind a window.

A candle lit by a spirit hand?

My mind searched for the best rational explanation—a homeless person with a portable CD player finding temporary shelter in an abandoned house. That could explain everything, but I had a chilling suspicion that the answer lay elsewhere.

"I'm dead serious." His voice lingered on the word "dead." There was the green twinkle in his eyes again.

"You're obviously teasing me," I said. "Diverting our attention from the *killing* heat."

"Not at all."

"Tell me, then. How can an entire street be haunted?"

"Just our part of it is," he said. "The Smith house on the corner was the scene of a murder in the nineteen twenties. Now it has a resident ghost, or half a ghost, I should say. I'll tell you about it later. Closer to home, there have been lights in the woods, music that comes and goes with the wind, sobbing and bells…we ran a feature on the haunts of Maple Creek last Halloween. I know what I'm talking about."

"Those are all ghost story staples," I said. "How about barking in the night?"

"That, too. And let's not forget the living satyr statue next door. You moved into a hotbed of psychic activity, Cressa."

At this crucial moment, the first notes of "Nelly Bly" rang out in the distance, coaxing us back to the sweltering afternoon and an impromptu ice cream invitation. Matt consulted his watch again. "Eight and a half minutes! Let's go beat the neighborhood tykes to the truck." He rose and held out his hand.

"I want to hear more about these so-called supernatural manifestations," I said, letting him draw me up out of the chair.

"Sure thing, when we come back, but I thought you were afraid of ghosts."

I didn't say that. Did I?

"I don't believe in them, but if by some very, very slim chance you're right…if the girl in the green dress is a spirit, I want to be forewarned."

"Then you wouldn't be frightened or upset to find a phantom visitor at your back door?" he asked.

I hesitated, wondering how to say exactly what I meant. "Neither. Maybe a little unsettled. I would never disrespect a ghost, if such an entity existed, but I don't intend to meet one on Beechnut Street or anywhere else."

"You may not have a choice," he said.

ROCKY ROAD ICE CREAM has a way of overriding spirit talk, but as we passed the Smith place on the way back to my house, Matt brought up the dual subjects of our street and its supernatural history again. If he hadn't, I would have. He appeared to be serious about local ghost lore, but I wondered why I'd never heard these tales before—especially in conversations with Patti who loved to talk.

Half a ghost and an enchanted forest indeed. And I might not have a choice? The always-objective facts-only editor of the *Tribune* had a Romantic streak. That was Romantic, as in the Romantic Age, not hearts and flowers romantic, although he held my hand until we reached my house.

His touch felt slightly intrusive, but at the same time nice. More than a little presumptuous, but overall pleasant.

Make up your mind, I scolded myself. *It's a gesture, not a declaration.*

Back on the porch, we sat close together in companionable silence, finishing our cones, while Pepper fixed her wistful eyes on us. I brought a pitcher of ice water from the kitchen because Matt declined anything stronger, and gradually we began to talk about the other world. That is, Matt talked and I listened. Each new story convinced me anew that he was amusing himself at my expense.

The tragedy at the Smith house was his apparent favorite. On the last night of 1925, Venetia Smith, a sweet, self-effacing matron, donned a glittery ball gown and hacked her unsuspecting husband to pieces with a butcher knife. Then she went to a New Year's Eve party. All evening, she laughed and danced, welcoming 1926 with champagne. The police found her husband's body a week later.

"My goodness! What did he do to deserve such an end?" I asked.

"According to rumor, he had a girlfriend on the side."

"So it was revenge? A punishment?"

"Madness," Matt said. "Venetia claimed that a robber had committed the crime, but all evidence pointed to her. Before the end of January, she lost her hold on reality and ended her days in a mental ward. The house remained vacant throughout the next decade—except for the Half-Ghost observed flitting through the rooms."

"The resident spirit you mentioned?"

"Venetia. Over the years, twenty-three people swore they saw a black-haired woman in a white blouse with a huge brooch clasped at her breast. That's documented. There was no body beneath the waist."

"What was the significance of the missing parts?" I asked.

"The best answer is that they were there, only hidden by a thick red vapor that moved when she did."

"Very dramatic," I said. "But wouldn't you think the husband would make a better half-ghost, since she hacked him to pieces?"

"I guess so. But this spirit is definitely a female."

"It must have made for an exciting Halloween edition," I said.

"Sales tripled that day," he said with a wink. "In the forties, the house was a bed-and-breakfast. An elderly guest encountered the Half-Ghost on the stairs one night and fell over dead of heart failure."

"Has anyone seen Venetia lately?" I asked.

"On Halloween night, five years ago."

"You know I don't believe a word of this, Matt."

"You should. We live on a street of strange happenings. Look at your own house. Remember Minta Bransford's disappearance."

I shifted on the seat, rearranging the sunflower patterned throw that was slowly slipping to the floor. "I don't know about half-ghosts, but everything else you mentioned can be explained rationally."

"For example?"

"The bells are wind chimes. People carry flashlights in the dark and listen to radios and CDs in all kinds of places. Sometimes they cry. Dogs bark day and night. I've heard mysterious music myself."

"In the woods?" he asked.

"No, coming from Libby's house, after she died. For a while I kept hearing Stephen Foster songs. But not lately," I added quickly. "She played them so often that I figure they imprinted themselves on my mind."

His smile had an odd new element to it. Understanding? Empathy? Maybe he'd heard ghostly music, too, and therein lay his newly-revealed fascination with the supernatural.

"It's like a tune that runs through your head," he said. "A television jingle."

"Sort of."

"There's nothing strange about that."

"It happens all the time. Is the Smith place still a bed-and-breakfast?"

"No, a couple with young children lives there. They're renovating the spookiness right out of it."

At that moment, Pepper scratched at the door. I let her in and she flopped down at Matt's feet, giving him her special canine-in-need look.

"What does she want?" he asked.

"More dinner."

"It's getting late." He looked at his watch. "Cressa…" he said. He paused, his hand on Pepper's head.

I waited, thinking he'd recalled another ghost yarn.

"Would you like to have dinner with me some night soon? There's a new restaurant I'd like to check out for the paper, and I don't like to eat alone."

"That would be nice. Yes."

"How about this Saturday? Around seven?"

"That's perfect."

In spite of his quick smile, he appeared a trifle uncomfortable, almost as if he'd expected a rejection. Because of his limp? I didn't think so. We'd been together before, in a casual way, and even shared a meal at the Blue Lion once. But this encounter would be different. Planned. A date.

No man issuing an invitation can ever be one hundred percent certain that it'll be accepted. If he was uneasy, that was most likely the reason. I'd accepted rather quickly, which should reassure him.

Casting about for a comment to put him at ease, I said, "Do you suppose Minta ever took her collie out in the woods?"

"I'm sure she did. Have you ever explored them?"

"Only the fringes. I'm not fond of mosquitoes or snakes. Or poison ivy."

He was quiet for so long that I suspected my answer had somehow disappointed him. Finally he said, "Except for the long hair, the girl you described could be Minta. In spirit form."

That thought had occurred to me, of course, but I'd been trying to ignore it. I hadn't seen the girl on the canoe properly, and I didn't remember what Minta looked like in the *Tribune* photograph. Then, how many Maple Creek girls were slender with long dark hair? Dozens.

I reined in my thoughts. They were crossing over into dangerous territory.

"Are you trolling for another sensational *Tribune* story?" I asked.

"Always."

"This has to be some other girl."

"It probably is," he said.

"That reminds me. I invited Annora over to look through the scrapbook, and we found several pictures missing. Then I found a page with something torn out. Probably a poem."

A frown darkened his eyes. "You're not implying that I lost the items, are you?"

"No."

"Because I'm always careful with sources."

"Maybe they slipped out when you had the book on your desk."

"I don't think so, but I'll look, and I'll find that picture of Minta for you. Just to satisfy my curiosity. I'm becoming interested in your girl in green."

"Remember that I didn't see her clearly," I said. "Minta might have a daughter who resembles her. Who knows? Maybe they've both been living in Maple Creek all this time."

He stood up and pulled me close, brushing his lips across my cheek. "Don't try so hard, Cressa," he said. "Some things can't be explained."

THIRTEEN

TWO HOURS LATER, I faced another sweltering night with no breeze to stir the oppressive air. The sun held on to its position in the sky as long as possible, burning the water out of the grass and plants. The leaves on the trees were still, as if they were too exhausted to move.

At nine o'clock I took a mystery novel out to the balcony and managed to read four pages before Matt's phantoms insinuated themselves into my concentration: Venetia, the Half-Ghost, and her murdered mate danced through my head to a discordant melody made up of mysterious sounds. If I wasn't careful, I'd soon hear a Stephen Foster song wafting over from the white Victorian.

Matt. My Saturday night dinner date. He was an enigma, a man I had hoped to see again, preferably in a social setting. Whenever we were together, I felt that I'd known him at some previous time in my life, that he was familiar and comfortable. Yet, in a sense, I didn't know him at all.

Was he hiding something?

I couldn't imagine what, except perhaps his true relationship with Annora May. Matt had spoken of her as if they were well acquainted. I didn't receive the same impression from Annora, who had made that unkind comment about his limp and asked me which house he lived in. But she knew that he'd been injured in battle.

Maybe Annora was the one with the secret. Why did his address matter to her unless she harbored a private interest in him? They couldn't be romantically involved. Annora was too old for him, although she looked youthful and was very attractive. But to some people, age disparity was irrelevant, and Matt could well be older than I thought.

Instead of idle speculation, I should formulate two discrete questions, one for Matt and one for Annora. But, most likely, I was creating a mystery where none existed. Matt had a friendly nature, and Annora was open and gracious. She'd given me no reason to doubt her sincerity. Still, I was going to have to remind her of her promise to remove the canoe.

The fire-engine shade and peeling paint spoiled the graceful sweep of pink perennials. Annora's discard was pure junk. From a different perspective, though, its very unattractiveness served as a striking backdrop for the flowers. Perspective was the keyword—perhaps about everything.

No matter. I wanted the eyesore out of sight.

I looked down at the book in my lap, intending to finish a chapter, but the sky had already begun to darken. Without warning, an unwelcome old memory surfaced.

Once, on another night in Maple Creek, I'd stepped out of the world as I knew it to walk with a ghost. The incident had haunted me for years. Every now and then I dusted it off and allowed myself to remember, always hoping that this time I'd understand.

My life might have ended that night. By the grace of God, it didn't. So why shouldn't I, of all people, believe in the spirit world? I knew the answer to that.

I closed my eyes, and it came rushing back: the blizzard, reports of a massive traffic tie up on the freeway, my evening class at the University cancelled, the impulsive decision to take a shortcut home to Maple Creek on a narrow little-traveled country road…

Drive slowly, be prepared to stop at a moment's notice, keep your eye on the beams of light.

My late father's mantra played over and over in my mind. But steering shouldn't be this hard. The snow seemed to grip the wheels, pulling me down.

Afterward, I couldn't remember when the car left the road and plowed into a deeply drifted field. Suddenly it stopped, as if an invisible barrier had materialized in its path. I stepped down hard on the accelerator. The engine whirred, the wheels spun. I realized what I'd done.

The road was about a hundred yards away, barely visible in the beams cast by my headlights. About a mile back, I'd passed a farmhouse. I made another impulsive decision to walk back to the road. Leaving the emergency lights flashing, I set out. A hundred yards into blowing snow turned into a thousand.

Pain scissored through my fingers. A cold wetness made its way through my boots. The car lights grew dimmer, and the road appeared to be in motion, slipping farther away from me with every labored step I took. I couldn't do this.

"Stop there, Cressa!" My father's voice boomed out into silence. "You're going around in circles."

Through swirls of blowing snow, I saw him. He wore the same brown corduroy jacket we'd donated to the Salvation Army after his death and his favorite hunter's cap that I'd kept for a remembrance.

"Turn right," he said, and I felt his hand against my back guiding me. "This way."

"Dad…? You died. You can't be here."

"I am."

I turned and walked until I felt myself sinking down into deep snow.

"Keep moving," he said. "You can do it. Just a little farther."

At that moment, something compelled me to look down. Ahead of me lay a large pond at the end of an abrupt five-foot drop. Shards of ice glittered on the surface, sharp and deadly. Between their cutting edges, the dark water threatened. Three more steps and I would have walked into it. If that happened, I could never have made my way out.

My heart turned cold with fear. I stumbled backward and found myself alone in the snow swept field. My father was gone, and thank heavens for that. He'd told me to go the wrong way—straight toward the pond. That didn't make any sense. He'd loved me, always protected me.

The rest of the story was anti-climactic. I mustered the last *bit of strength and reached the road. By luck, two men from my class had chosen the same shortcut. They moved my car out of the snow bank and followed me home.*

All's well that ends well, except...

My father's spirit tried to kill me.

I couldn't deal with a beloved parent who had somehow transformed into a demonic force bent on my destruction. Not then, not ever. It was easier to reject all things supernatural and believe that I'd had a hallucination brought on by the snow and cold and panic.

And so I did, and in time concocted a logical reason, rooted in guilt, for the apparition's strange behavior. I'd kept a vigil by my father's bedside during his final days, but when he drew his last breath, I was in another room asleep. That was an unsatisfactory explanation in every way, but I held on to it.

Guilt combined with being stranded in a killer blizzard added up to a dreamlike experience that had never happened. I forced myself to believe that explanation. Still, how could I ever know for certain what was true?

With a sigh I closed my book and leaned back against the plump cushion, made my mind a blank screen, and consigned the chilling images to the darkness. I didn't want to think about that time, especially now with Matt's ghost tales playing in my mind.

The last streaks of daylight had already disappeared. From the white Victorian, there was no sound at all, and that was good. Behind the house, the water in the fountain splashed down into the basin. Usually the sound reminded me of Libby's death. Tonight it was soothing, conjuring visions of all things cool and healing. How odd!

No, not really. I couldn't see the satyr in the dark. That changed the ambience.

Forget him. Focus on something beautiful instead.

I looked straight up, above the motionless leaves, at a pitch black expanse sprinkled with glitter. *The lights in the sky are stars.* So numerous that I could never count them. Too far to touch. Each one different, as individual snowflakes are different.

One of them shone especially for me. Quickly I found it, a tiny burst of brilliance winking at me from the top of Libby's maple tree.

Star light, star bright… Like a child, I uttered a child's rhyme for an adult desire. For a successful evening with Matt, because that was important to me. For time to build a deeper friendship with him, if we proved to be compatible. For a chance to be truly happy in Maple Creek again.

That was an immense wish to hang on a brief dinner date. Still, it might come true. Sometimes the stars worked their magic. Now, on this hopeful note, I'd better end the day.

I closed and locked the French doors, even though it was several degrees warmer than it had been last night. Pepper lay asleep on her side, directly under the ceiling fan. She didn't move as I crossed the room, but when I came back from the shower, clad in my lightest nightgown and ready to climb into bed, she was gone.

The last sound I heard before drifting off to sleep was a dog howling in the distance.

"THIS IS WILD PHLOX," Patti said. "An invader. I don't want it in my yard." She yanked a tall plant out of her pansy bed and tossed it on a heap of weeds. Its delicate rose-pink petals still held dewdrops, still glittered in the morning sunlight.

"Oh…" I retrieved the hapless flower and examined the root system, which was intact. "Don't throw it away. I'll transplant it."

"Why don't you let me give you some real phlox a little later in the season? They have a pretty blue color and a compact shape."

"I like these."

"The first hard rain will knock them down, and you'll have a mess to clean up," she said.

"That's okay." I held the petals up to my face. They had no fragrance, only deep, rich color and beauty. "Your trash is my treasure."

Across the street, Pepper leaped out of her porch nap to chase a squirrel into a tree. I shouted at her to Stay! To my amazement, she obeyed me, freezing in the middle of the lawn.

"Did you hear a dog howling last night?" I asked. "In the woods, I think."

"My bedroom is at the back of the house, and I had the AC on," she said. "Once Aleta comes home, nothing much disturbs me."

"It was so mournful. Really spooky."

"Probably you heard one of the strays baying at the moon."

"Or a neighbor's dog wanting to come inside."

"That could be. There's the Hilton hound and the husky at the corner. They both live outside in their houses. The people three doors down have a new retriever pup. Dogs are taking over the street. You can't call a cop if all you have is a noise."

"I'd never do that," I said.

Patti turned her head at the low hum of a motor. "Speak of the devil! A visitor!"

A squad car cruised slowly down Beechnut Street, coming to a stop at the white Victorian. Lieutenant Gray got out, waved to us, and strode around to the back of the house. Pepper dashed after him.

"I wonder what's happened now," Patti said.

"I'll go ask him."

Carrying the rescued flower and dripping dirt in my wake, I crossed the street just as the lieutenant emerged from the backyard. His expression was grave, and his stance a trifle intimidating. In one gloved hand he held a scarf splashed with bright rainbow colors. It might have been cut from the same material as Libby's recital dress.

Pepper ran around his long legs, yipping frantically, which was probably not her best idea. I grabbed her collar, wishing I'd brought the leash outside.

"She isn't bothering anything," he said, giving her a gruff smile.

I freed her, and she lay down at my feet, proving him correct. "Is there a problem?" I asked.

"I'm just checking out the Dorset place this morning." He

gestured toward the white Victorian. It looked vulnerable in the sun's glare and grateful for a policeman's attention. "We've had a rash of robberies lately and reports of a woman looking in windows over on Walnut."

"And you think there's a connection?"

"There could be. Have you seen any signs of suspicious activity around here in the last few days?"

"Only the fire and a few kids hanging around." I set the plant down in the shade and considered what I might have said.

Only a figure who moves as fast as light and a girl who resembles a garden statue.

My low key answer was the wiser choice.

"Were they older boys?" he asked.

"No, girls. We—that is, some of the neighbors—think someone has been camping out in the house."

"Yes, because of the way the fire started. That makes sense, but I didn't find any obvious way in."

He held the scarf up so that I could see it more clearly, let it unfurl from his grip. "Did you lose this, Ms. Hannett?"

"It's not mine. Where did you find it?"

"Back by the porch, lying on the ground."

"It wasn't there yesterday, and I don't think one of the firemen dropped it."

A ghost of a grin softened his expression. "That's a good guess."

"Doesn't it remind you of Libby Dorset's dress?" I asked.

"The color and pattern are similar."

"That's one more mystery."

"Maybe. Or maybe it's just a red scarf."

But he was handling it with great care, treating it with importance.

Missing balloons, a shadow tenant and a lovely lost accessory that might have belonged to Libby Dorset—the strangeness kept growing. Perhaps the elements were all related, all part of the larger mystery.

"The curious woman might have dropped it while she was scoping out the house," I said.

He ran his hand along the material and glanced at the label. "Unlikely. This was expensive."

"It was part of her last haul?"

As he looked from me to the Victorian, his mouth arranged itself into a full smile. Then, as quickly, it faded.

"An unoccupied house is a burglary waiting to happen," he said. "Especially when it's loaded with valuable antiques." He scanned the area, his gaze sweeping the silent acres beyond the canoe. "You have one of the best views in town, Ms. Hannett, but this isn't the safest location."

"Because of the woods?"

"Exactly. Anyone can hide behind those trees waiting to pounce and make a quick getaway afterward."

He had a point, but I refused to worry about an eventuality that might never happen. At any rate, what could I do about it?

"None of those robberies took place on Beechnut Street—or did they?" I asked.

"Not yet," he said. "You still want to be careful. From here I can see that your back door is wide open, and you were all the way across the street. Our thief has been targeting homeowners when they're working in their yard. He takes money left lying around, watches and other small items. They don't know he's been there until it's too late. One woman had her engagement ring stolen."

"I was only talking to my neighbor," I said.

"How long do you think it would take someone to stroll right into your house while you're working in your flowerbed and make off with your jewelry?"

"If you're talking about a pro, ten or fifteen minutes?"

"Right. You should get in a habit of locking your door if you're going to be outside for any length of time," he said.

In spite of this official warning, I suspected that I wouldn't remember to do that, but I *did* have an unfortunate tendency to leave valuables and money strewn around. At this moment, my purse was open on the buffet, and my cherished star pendant lay on the dresser upstairs, easy to grab. I couldn't bear to lose that.

"I'll try to be more aware, but I have a watchdog now," I said.

"She'll sound the alarm all right, but that's no substitute for commonsense precautions. Look around every now and then. Give us a call if you see anything out of the ordinary."

"I usually sit on my balcony until dark," I said. "If anyone comes around to this side of the Victorian, I'll see them."

"I remember."

Even though I knew what his answer would be, I asked, "Did you ever find the woman who stole the cakes at Libby Dorset's reception or the person in the cloak?"

"They never turned up—not in those guises anyway."

"Now we have a fire setter, a woman peering in windows and a robber."

"They're all part of the town's population, inside and outside the law," he said. "Mostly out."

"And they could all be the same person."

He tipped his cap, and the grin returned. "Keep those doors bolted, and you should be all right, Ms. Hannett."

GOOD STRONG LOCKS could protect me from the Maple Creek burglar but not from everything that threatened me.

I frowned as I clasped the star pendant around my neck.

What had inspired that thought? Nothing threatened me. I might be surrounded by strange happenings, but I had no reason to believe that anyone was out to get me.

These were new feelings, and they had appeared out of nowhere, just now, as I dressed for my dinner date with Matt.

Three days had passed since Lieutenant Gray's melodramatic warning, three ordinary blocks of time during which nothing significant happened. Deciding to be prepared for trouble, I replayed his advice and added cautions of my own.

I hung my purse on a hook in the front closet and found a new place to keep my necklace when I wasn't wearing it—in a tin containing stamps at the back of my desk drawer. Before going outside, I locked the door and slipped a key in my pocket, and if anyone came near the white Victorian, I was unaware of it. Having done all that I could, I put the matter out of my mind.

Now, this thought, this feeling, had materialized, demanding to be noticed, and it involved more than theft.

Someone or something intends to destroy you. Beware!

After Libby's death, for a short time I'd wondered if her killer might try to silence me as a possible witness, but that transient fear had evaporated a long time ago, around the time of the coroner's report.

Still… Without apparent cause, this afternoon I felt jittery. I imagined myself glancing over my shoulder, searching for the source of an innocuous household sound or, toward the end of the day, peering into the shadows, looking for one that moved. Like a timorous heroine in an old Gothic novel, I saw myself climbing up to the castle tower, three steps ahead of the Horror.

That was an amusing comparison, but it wasn't Cressa Hannett, space engineer of the new millennium.

I didn't have premonitions and didn't fret about tomorrow's calamities. Only the satyr had unnerved me, and I had nothing to fear from him.

From *it,* Cressa. From *it.*

I frowned again, realizing that I might not know myself well at all.

Pepper padded through the upstairs hall. Her nails clicked on the hardwood floor, an aggravating nail-on-blackboard sound. But I knew what it was. She scrunched the rag rug beside my bed into a cottony ball and curled up for an afternoon nap. My alarm system was temporarily disabled.

If I were a burglar I'd avoid any house where a dog lived. It might be a good idea to take Pepper with me wherever I went, to leave her toys on the grass. To post a "Beware of Dog" sign outside? No—that was overkill.

Before leaving Maple Creek for all those new worlds I intended to conquer, I'd never once considered the possibility of home invasion, burglary or worse. Trust a doomsday policeman to drain the spontaneity and freedom out of life.

And count on an enterprising newspaper editor to restore it.

I checked the neckline of my black dress, decided it was a little too low, and made the pendant an inch longer. Whether Matt liked dark red hair or not was another mystery, but I was going to proceed as if he did. He'd be certain to admire my black dress. What man wouldn't?

It was time to quit fussing with my appearance and go downstairs to wait for him. Hours of diversion and pleasure lay spread out in front of me.

So, summon a party mood. Smile. Add another spritz of Spring Spice, and you're ready.

But I couldn't shake the sense of impending threat.

FOURTEEN

THE MARBLE LAKE INN was an old white Victorian, built in the same style as Libby Dorset's house, with gables and turrets and a more generous helping of gingerbread trim.

It nestled in a surround of maple trees, and rosebushes in bloom lined the walkway. The lake was nearby, within walking distance. From our table in the Terrace Room, we had a view of still blue water and pristine shoreline.

The country décor dripped with gingham and lace. Old-fashioned bouquets in creamy pitchers adorned the tables, and the day's specials leaned heavily toward comfort foods. As soon as I'd stepped through the door, I felt instantly at home.

All I needed was an evening in a different environment with good company. Matt Emmerton provided both. In truth, he was excellent company and exceedingly handsome, as well. With his first warm smile, I began to relax. The sense of threat seemed far away. It had stayed behind on Beechnut Street.

"This place is wonderful, Matt," I said. "I've never been in such a pretty restaurant before."

"So far I'm favorably impressed myself." He closed the menu. His herringbone suit gave his eyes a green cast and emphasized their light golden flecks. "What would you like for dinner?"

"Everything looks good, but since I have to choose…" I scanned the day's specials one last time. "Pineapple Glazed Ham and buttermilk biscuits."

"I'm going to have fried chicken."

"Does the owner know you're from the *Tribune?*" I asked.

"I hope not. We want the kind of service and food they give ordinary diners."

"And no bribes for a good review," I added.

The cake-shaped dessert menu described six tempting confections, each one accompanied by a color illustration. I skipped over the elaborate ice cream creations and cobblers to Michigan Old-Time Strawberry Shortcake. This choice was easier, but were strawberries in season already?

The month of June was moving at warp speed. Balmy spring breezes and delicate blossoms had given way to summer before its official beginning. That was a typical Michigan weather pattern. Fair days sped by; winter lasted forever.

"For years, this place was an antique shop in need of renovation," Matt said. "It opened as a restaurant last month."

The Terrace Room was rapidly filling up, and all but a few of the tables were occupied. The wait staff moved so unobtrusively that it was easy to believe we'd wandered into a private country residence, an illusion that contributed to the ambiance.

Matt placed our orders and filled two flutes with the special red wine he'd chosen. Our evening was speeding by, too. I hadn't expected a simple dinner date in a country inn to be so enjoyable. Nor had I envisioned such an attentive companion.

"I have a surprise for you," Matt said.

"Something nice?"

"I think so. It's information. First, I did a little searching and came up with a better picture of Minta Bransford. I'll show it to you after dinner."

"So if I see the girl in the green dress again, I'll have a basis for comparison?"

"That's the idea."

"I hope I don't," I said.

"You may not, but if you do…" He let the thought trail away.

"Then I hope she'll be a neighbor's daughter wearing blue."

Apparently Matt wanted to believe the mysterious visitor had come from another world. Then he could add her appearance to his ghost collection and write a story for the paper. But was this his only reason for pursing the Bransford disappearance?

"I'm supposed to be living in a quiet part of town, but it seems like Grand Central Station sometimes," I said.

"I haven't noticed any change."

"It might be my location—only a few yards from the place where a tragedy occurred."

"The notoriety will pass," he said. "It always does, eventually."

Unless something else were to happen, and I didn't want to think about that.

"What first drew me to my house was its resemblance to my family home and the woods," I said.

"Did you want to recreate your past?" he asked with a knowing smile.

"Not intentionally, but I guess I did just that. I took my parents' furniture out of storage and bought a few new pieces. So the rooms are pretty much the same as the ones I lived in growing up."

"I wish I could duplicate my old homestead in West Virginia," Matt said. "You and I are a pair of romantics."

"All I know is what I like, and it isn't contemporary furniture. Did you find out anything else about Minta?"

"One of her cousins still lives in the area, over in Spearmint Lake. I have the address."

"She might like to see the scrapbook, and maybe she can tell me something no one else knows."

"Looking for secret knowledge may be a long shot," he said.

"You never know. One tiny detail that nobody noticed at the time may change everything."

"We make a great sleuthing team," Matt said. "I'll do the research, and you work in the field."

"That would be fun."

"Unfortunately, my recent information isn't going to take us anywhere," he added. "Libby's stalker has been in a mental institution for three months. She couldn't have had a hand in Libby's death."

"What if she was out on a pass?"

"According to her doctors, she wasn't."

"We can cross Jacqueline off the list, then. Darn. She was a natural suspect."

I picked up the dessert menu again and looked at the sundae pictures from a different angle. Jacqueline wasn't the gypsy; she couldn't have been the cloaked figure. Who was, then? The mystery surrounding Libby's drowning was as puzzling as the Bransford case.

"Do you still think Libby was murdered?" Matt asked.

"Deep down, yes, and by a clever killer. The fire and everything else—they're connected somehow."

He leaned forward, elbows on the table, and fixed me with a green-eyed stare that Lieutenant Gray would have envied. "What do you mean 'everything else'?"

Not expecting this challenge, I took time to think through my response. Music in an unoccupied house, a shadowy woman lighting a candle that started a fire, the people who came and went on the fringes of the property, the howling dog?

That last one especially. Pepper had padded back into the bedroom last night, moments before the howling resumed. I'd turned my bedside lamp on, just to be sure. There was nothing unusual about that, and each of these elements might well have a simple explanation rooted in reality. But I couldn't let them go.

I said, "Libby's death seemed to start a chain reaction of bizarre occurrences." I listed each untoward happening for Matt and for myself, to make certain they were clear in my mind. "It's hard to explain, but when I put them together, something feels wrong. I sense that I'm in danger and don't know why."

My words sounded melodramatic, paranoid even, and paranoia didn't become me. Nor did vague feelings. At least, they never had until I came back to Maple Creek and moved into the small white house on Beechnut Street.

Matt fell silent. He drank his wine, frowned across the room, and appeared to be considering what I'd said. While I waited for him to answer, I delved into the bread basket, distracting myself with rolls. I wanted someone to agree with me, to hand me a neatly wrapped package of answers across the dinner table.

Then Matt said, "You explain it very well, Cressa. I think the police closed the case too soon."

Ah, validation. What could be sweeter?

Michigan Old-Time Strawberry Shortcake. The whipped cream was real, and the Michigan strawberries were small and sweet, not the tasteless jumbo variety sold year around in grocery stores. Matt's blueberry cobbler was delicious, too. He had broken off a piece for me to sample.

"You have to give the Inn a good review, Matt," I said. "This is the best dessert I've ever had."

"I will. Five golden stars. Everything was exceptional."

It was almost ten now, and the lake view had retreated into darkness. The window in front of our table threw back my own reflection: a red-haired woman in a black dress wearing a diamond pendant. She looked radiant and energized, as if the evening were starting rather than drawing to a close.

"It's still early," Matt said. "What would you like to do now?"

"I'll leave that up to you. I'm game for anything. Any activity, that is."

"How about a moonlit drive along the lake?"

"Marble Lake?"

"I was thinking Lake St. Clair."

"That sounds lovely, but isn't it a little out of the way?"

"It'll be an adventure. Then we can head back to Maple Creek. You can invite me in for a nightcap… Or we can go to my house. You said you wanted to see the inside. We'll look at Minta's picture and plan our next move."

Our next move?

Oh, in our mystery solving project. Matt's smile was genuine, without guile. He had no ulterior motives, even though a casual eavesdropper might think otherwise.

And I?

I was accustomed to reading men's subtleties and generally astute. Matt offered unencumbered friendship—no more. The thought that he was lonely crossed my mind. That led to my curiosity about Annora. How could I slip her name into the conversation and at the same time clarify my position on ghostly phenomena?

I said, "If the girl in the green dress likes to trespass in the woods, Annora should know about it. If she gets hurt, Annora could be held responsible."

"You can't control who walks across your property, and Annora has several acres of undeveloped land. That's a real temptation for just about anybody, especially kids. I agree with you though. Whoever—or whatever—this girl is, Annora should know."

Here was my opening. "You mentioned that Annora's real home is somewhere else, that she's just here visiting."

"She has an apartment in New York and travels for her job."

"Which is?"

"She works for an airline."

"So you know her well?"

"We're old friends. She used to go out with my cousin. He died in the Gulf War."

"Oh, I'm sorry."

"Annora doesn't come to town very often. When she does, we catch up."

The waiter handed Matt the bill. As he signed it, adding a generous tip and lavish praise for the fried chicken and cobbler, I mulled over his words. Apparently Annora was the one who had skirted around the truth. Now why?

"All ready?" he asked.

"I'll mention the girl the next time I see Annora," I said.

He laid his arm on my shoulder. "That's a good idea, Cressa. She'll appreciate knowing."

MATT SET Minta Bransford's picture on my kitchen table. The light from the Tiffany ceiling fixture seemed to infuse the image with life—to add a rosy glow to the young woman's features. She wore a short dark skirt and a white blouse with a deep V neckline. The gold chains around her neck made her look older.

"This was taken by Oaklane Photographers a month before Minta vanished," Matt said. "They're no longer in business."

"Her hair is longer and curlier. It's more reddish than it was in the other picture."

"That could be in the developing."

"Or maybe it's a tint. The news story described Minta Bransford's hair as dark brown."

"Would girls that young color their hair?" he asked.

"Sure. All females like to experiment with their appearance."

The hour was late, past one-thirty by the stove clock. The coffeepot was empty, and Pepper had long since stretched herself out in the doorway and gone to sleep. All of my brilliant stars had burned out. Now Matt was the energized one.

We had made every possible observation about Minta Bransford. We'd leafed through the scrapbook again, collecting stray details of life in Maple Creek, as documented by Annora: A birthday picnic in Elizabeth's yard, heart cutouts from the Sweethearts Dance at the high school, autographs by Garnet, Patti, Janelle, Mari…scraps of a young girl's life.

Now there was nothing left to be said or perused. Minta seemed more real to me than ever before, almost a presence sharing our space. She had once sat in this small kitchen eating breakfast or an after-school snack. She had moved through the rooms with the speed of a springtime breeze, perhaps sensing that she had too much to do and time was running out.

Then she walked off the face of the planet. Her story ended. Without solid evidence, I refused to believe that, for some reason, she had come back.

I picked up the sheet of notepaper containing the address of Minta's cousin. Tomorrow or the next day, or sometime, I'd be in a mood to contact her. Tonight I was too tired. I tried to stop my yawn and failed, but Matt didn't appear to notice.

"We can start our P.I. business and set up shop in your house or mine. Emmerton and Hannett." The merry sparkle in his eyes told me that he was joking. "We already have our first two cases."

"I'm not that dedicated to detective work," I said. "For me, the disappearance is an intriguing diversion. As for Libby's killer, I'd leave that to the police, but they don't think he exists."

"Looking into the Bransford mystery should be harmless, but if we're right about Libby, you'd better be careful. Don't forget that cloaked figure you saw the night she drowned."

"Lieutenant Gray doesn't believe in that, either," I said.

"Did you ever think of having a security system installed in your house?" he asked.

"Wouldn't that be overkill?"

"Better overkill than over killed."

He laughed at his own joke. He laughed alone, as I wasn't amused by the macabre little word play. By the fireplace, Pepper barked in her sleep. For the present, I'd rely on her to alert me to danger and hope that she would be awake if it made a surprise appearance.

"Do you ever hear a dog howling in the night?" I asked.

"I can't say that I have. I'm a sound sleeper." He laid his coffee cup on the table and stood. "We should call it a night, Cressa, but let's do this again soon. Next time, you choose the place."

"I'd like that, and thank you for the evening."

"Thank *you*." He drew me into his arms for a goodnight kiss that was quick and gentle and nice, like Matt himself. I walked him to the door and kept my hand on the knob watching him limp across the street and over to the blue Victorian.

Well, Cressa, what do you really think about Matt?

The evening had been nice, that was true. Matt's kiss was nice. It was nice to get dressed up and go out.

Nice was an anemic word. It bestowed the kiss of death on a relationship. The only stars I had were the diamonds in my pendant and the real ones up in the sky.

With a sigh, I closed the door and double-checked the lock. What accounted for this uncharacteristic mood swing? A few hours ago, I'd been practically euphoric in the midst of gingham, garden flowers, and country ham.

Something troubled me; something nagged at me to recognize it.

I tried to analyze my changing feelings. My hopes had been too high. The night's long, low-key end could never match its beginning, and most likely, we'd hexed this first date with all our talk of Minta and murder. We should have discussed happy subjects and kept the atmosphere light.

That was it. Maybe. At the moment I couldn't think of

anything else. Still, I suspected that if I wanted the entire super nova experience I'd have to look beyond Matt Emmerton.

We were still friends, though, and nothing needed to be sorted out tonight. I checked on Pepper who didn't move, turned out the lights, and went upstairs, still trying to isolate the off element that eluded me.

FIFTEEN

THE NEXT MORNING Lieutenant Gray parked a vintage blue Cadillac convertible in a pool of sunshine across the street from my house. He strode down the walkway with a slight swagger, like the quintessential romance novel hero moving into a scene. His jeans and blue shirt suggested that this wasn't an official visit.

What then?

I dropped a large dandelion into my weed pail and set the trowel down. "That's an impressive car, Lieutenant! How old is it?"

"Almost a half century. It's my new baby." His scanned the white Victorian quickly. "Is everything quiet on Beechnut Street these days?"

"As far as I know." I rose and pulled off my gardening gloves, wishing I wasn't wearing torn denim shorts. "At night a dog keeps howling, but no one's peering through windows or breaking them." I drew a key out of my shirt pocket. "And my house is all locked up and safe."

He glanced down at the newly cultivated lily bed. "Did you find any more balloons?"

"No, only bits of clay pots and bones."

"Bones?"

"Marrow bones. The kind you give to dogs."

Pepper had already snatched one and carried it off to some secret place. Now she grasped her Frisbee between her teeth and ran up to the newcomer in her world, tail wagging, dark eyes communicating her desire. He threw it for her, high into the air and across the yard. It landed in the middle of the skeleton dog's grave. She dashed after it but froze several feet from the first row of stones. Whining loudly, she cast imploring looks in his direction.

"What's the matter with your pup?" he asked.

"She doesn't understand the rules of the game. Go fetch your Frisbee, girl," I called.

Instead she lay down on the grass, facing the bright yellow disk and occasionally glancing back at us.

"Somehow Pepper learned to stay inside the property line," I said. "It's like I have an invisible fence, but there's nothing there."

Only the grave. I'd never seen Pepper walk across the grave. She made an elaborate show of ignoring it.

"You won't have to worry about her running away," he said. "Now, Ms. Hannett—Cressa—I came by to see if you'd like to join me for a movie and a bite to eat this weekend. I have some downtime and need someone to share it with."

I couldn't have been more astonished. But hadn't a few sparks ignited at our first meeting, on the morning I'd discovered Libby's body? They were soon extinguished, drowned in crime scene formality, stern warnings and occasional condescension. Still, I'd never thought of the lieutenant as a serious romantic prospect.

Apparently he'd been thinking of me, but he could hardly act on his interest while on duty. That would be breaking the Police Department's code of conduct. I doubted that Lieutenant Gray ever broke anything. In any event, it was clear that this man would never be lonely for female companionship. He was far too handsome.

A gorgeous hunk, Gwendolyn had called him. I, of course, always looked beyond a man's attractive features.

"Unless you're dating someone else," he added. "If that's the case…"

"Not at the moment," I said quickly. "A movie sounds like fun. I haven't seen one lately, except on DVD."

"We can remedy that."

His cornflower blue eyes had a light similar Matt's, but they were darker and brighter, strikingly vivid in his tanned face. Matt. I glanced across the street at his house. He hadn't said anything definite about seeing me again. Anyway, more than one escort was like money in a savings account.

"When?" I asked. "Saturday or Sunday?"

"Saturday night. Six o'clock. It's a date, then?"

"A date." An impish streak compelled me to add, "Will we go in that snazzy car?"

"We sure will. Rain or shine." He winked. "She'll be all washed and polished for the occasion."

"Then so will I, Lieutenant."

"Call me Dalton."

"Okay, Dalton. Till Saturday."

He nodded and walked back to his car, driving away in police cruiser mode. At Elmsleigh he turned, and the convertible disappeared from sight. A blue-eyed knight on a powder blue horse. The lieutenant had come and gone so rapidly that the encounter scarcely seemed real. It had a romance novel flavor—brief, brilliant and irresistible like the man himself.

Suddenly I had a social life again. The lilies had never smelled so sweet.

Pepper trotted back to my side and nudged my hand, looking toward her toy.

"You silly creature," I said. "You're supposed to retrieve it."

Nevertheless, I walked to the back of the yard with Pepper bounding along behind me. Here, the pink phlox stood tall and proud in the manner of rosy sentinels guarding a dark forest.

All except for the plant I'd rescued from Patti's throwaway heap. Although I'd given it water and food, the stem drooped close to the ground with the top half leaning on the skeleton dog's grave. The leaves were beginning to shrivel, and the pink flowers were limp and faded.

Almost as if the color were draining out of them. Almost as if they were bleeding.

I shuddered at the gruesome notion. This particular transplant would most likely die, but, as long as the roots were alive, a baby phlox would soon emerge from the ground, new and fresh. At least, that was what happened with the wild ferns I constantly moved around.

Stepping between the stones, I picked up Pepper's Frisbee and held it for a moment, surveying the Maywood acres, as always listening for tell-tale sounds of wildlife or danger. All appeared peaceful. The woodland scene fairly cried out to be preserved on film or canvas.

But there was a discordant note. An old mulberry tree had begun to drop dark red berries on the ground, even staining the stones I'd placed on the grave. Some of them were mashed into a blood-colored pulp. By shoes? Or paws? By something from the woods.

I didn't know whether the tree was on my side of the property line or Annora's, but she wouldn't be likely to object if I trimmed the overhanging branches.

Still the berries would continue to fall from those I couldn't reach.

At that moment I felt a sharp sting on my knee and looked down at a rapidly reddening spot. And another on my arm... I slapped at a mosquito. Too late. I had a second bite. Dozens of tiny insects buzzed through the air. This wooded wonderland might make a pretty picture, but it was no place to linger in a skimpy gardening outfit.

No wonder Pepper avoided it. She remained several yards behind me barking her excitement but not moving forward.

At this close range, the canoe was even more of an eyesore. Shards of red wood chips littered the ground, mingling with berry splatters. Wild ivy had wrapped itself around the sides and rusty chains made a show of anchoring it to a rotting stump.

Had anyone ever attempted to steal the boat when it was new and freshly painted and tied to a living tree? Did anyone besides me even realize it was here?

I made a mental note to remind Annora to please, please have it taken away. Then, if Kady would only dismantle the satyr fountain and the pests would disappear, my yard would be perfect.

Nothing can ever be perfect, I reminded myself.

Okay, then, my yard would be more hospitable. I turned and inadvertently stepped in berries. Nature was showing her disagreeable side today. I threw the Frisbee back toward the house with more force than usual. Pepper dashed off, leaping up to catch it in mid-air. I followed her, newly aware of the high humidity and annoying bites. At the porch, I looked back at the woods.

From this vantage point, they were more appealing, even with the offending canoe in the forefront. I couldn't see the berries, and the bugs had stayed behind in the shady, damp places. As I watched, a robin hopped down from a low branch and nibbled eagerly at the fallen fruit.

"The next time, bring all your friends," I said, as I turned to the lily bed. I was almost finished with this task; then I could move on to a more enjoyable one, preferably on the porch or balcony.

I could never keep up with the weeds, and a hundred birds couldn't make the berries disappear. Several hard rains would do it, but next year they'd be back again, so there was no point in fussing over a natural cycle.

In this town, in this yard alone, there were more important things to deal with, none of which could be swept away with a garden broom.

LATER THAT AFTERNOON Gwendolyn appeared at my door with a pad of yellow lined paper, a pen and a bright smile. Obviously she wanted something.

"Did anyone tell you about our July Fourth block party?" she asked.

"Not yet." The top sheet was covered with writing, leaving little space for additions.

"We always have a big outdoor bash on the street for the Fourth of July. It's an all-day affair. After dark, we shoot off firecrackers or go down to the park where there's an official display."

That seemed like an unusual tradition for a sedate street of Victorian houses whose owners tended to stay inside. But seeing this as a chance to be a part of the community, I easily caught her enthusiasm.

"We hang flags and everyone contributes something to the menu," she added.

"It sounds like fun. What do you need?"

She handed me the list. "One of your homemade specialties and bread. Hamburger or hot dog buns. Dinner rolls. Whole loaves, sliced. It's your choice."

I glanced at the long list of offerings. "A specialty?"

"A covered dish, like baked beans. I'm making my famous potato salad. We need…" She ran her finger down the page. "More desserts."

"How about a blueberry pie?" I said. "That's all-American. And I'll bring the hot dog rolls."

"Wonderful. Make it four pies and seven dozen rolls."

"My goodness!"

"We're expecting around a hundred people, some of them kids, and you know how they eat. Barbecue Central is the Ghost House."

"The what?"

"The old Venetia Smith place on the corner. Lance Baldwin mans the grill. He can take a plain all-beef frank and turn it into a gourmet meal."

I signed my name and added my contribution, noting that Matt was bringing paper cups and Caesar salad. How many bowls, I wondered? Or how many packages of salad-in-a-bag?

Would Gwendolyn know if I ordered the pies from a bakery? Probably. She'd mentioned a homemade specialty, and I could make a good crust—a great one, with a little practice.

"We have two bachelors in the neighborhood," Gwendolyn said. "Here's a heaven-sent opportunity for you to impress them with your culinary skills."

I smiled at the thought of two Lieutenant Gray clones falling on their faces in the grass. "I never try to impress men. They come of their own accord, or they don't."

She gave an exaggerated sigh. "Oh, to be young, beautiful— and thin. Make the most of it, Cressa, dear. Some of us have to work hard for every crumb of attention."

I felt a wave of warmth wash over my face and hastily

changed the subject. "It'll be quite a sight to see Beechnut all decked out for a party and people on the street."

"We need a little cheer. It's been dead around here ever since Libby Dorset took her plunge. Well, I'm off. Looks like you have some company."

As Annora May turned onto the walkway, Gwendolyn swept past her with a civil nod. Here was another woman she might envy, one who truly was beautiful, if not particularly young and thin. In her long white sundress and gleaming gold locket, Annora looked like a bride. To enhance the illusion, she carried a bouquet but no purse.

"Hello, Annora," I said.

She came up the stairs, stepping gingerly in her high-heeled white sandals, and handed the flowers to me. They were fresh and fragile, still glistening with dew. "These are for you, Cressa, a little thank you for sharing the scrapbook with me," she said.

"I love columbines. They're like little orchids."

"I have a field full of them."

"Do you have time to work in a garden if you're in town on vacation?" I asked, remembering my endless weeding sessions.

"Oh, I'm not a gardener. Flowers come up every year on their own. My mother planted the original batch of columbines in different colors years ago, but only the pale yellow ones survived."

"That's my favorite color." I took hold of Pepper's collar with my free hand. "Come in. We can sit on the porch where it's cooler."

"Just for a minute," she said. "I wonder if we could have lunch tomorrow. Around noon?"

"I'd like that," I said.

"I'll pick you up, then. We can go to the Blue Lion or some other nice place."

I led the way to the kitchen where I stopped to fill a vase with water. It was a cream-colored urn, a perfect container for the delicate columbines. On the porch, Annora settled herself in the rocker while I arranged the flowers.

"Is Elizabeth Dorset's place going on the market anytime soon?" she asked.

"Her niece is supposed to move in. I'm not sure when."

"These old houses don't like to be unoccupied," Annora said. "They get unhappy and restless without their people."

That certainly described the white Victorian. But what a strange observation.

"Three of Kady's college friends are going to join her," I said. "They should bring it to life again."

"That'll be different," she murmured. "And is Kady going to keep Libby's old furniture?"

"I have no idea."

"I thought she might have an estate sale."

"She might. I don't know her very well."

Annora was practically a stranger, too, but she'd just handed me an opportunity to learn more about her. Still, I didn't want to turn a pleasant visit into an interrogation. My plan was to proceed slowly and begin with an innocuous inquiry.

"Does anyone stay in your house while you're—living elsewhere?" I asked.

"My cousin stops by from time to time, and I have a good neighbor." She leaned forward in the chair. "The woods look different from your porch. They're so much darker and wilder."

"They're lovely," I said. "Are you still going to have the canoe hauled away?"

She flushed faintly. "I'm looking for someone to move it. We may end up chopping it for firewood."

"The other day I saw a girl sitting on top of it. She could have fallen off."

"Oh, no!" Annora's voice took on a sharp edge. "What girl?"

"I can't say, but I thought you'd want to know."

"I do. Thanks for being observant," she said. "I have 'No Trespassing' signs posted."

"That doesn't mean much to inquisitive kids."

"No, and those woods have a magical pull." Her eyes grew soft and her voice took on a dreamy tone. "We used to play there when we were kids. My father built us a tree house with a ladder right in the middle of the acreage, just a simple structure, but to an eight-year old it was like a castle."

"I wonder if it's still there."

"Probably, and in the same condition as the canoe. I wouldn't trust that ladder now." She ran her hand down lace inserts on her dress. "On my first day in Maple Creek, I followed the sound of water all the way to the fountain, but I couldn't go any farther because there was a picket fence around Elizabeth's house in those days. Then I met Elizabeth and Minta, and eventually we all grew up."

"And you were too old to go tramping in the wilderness?"

"Too old and sophisticated. We used the sidewalks, like everybody else, although if you're coming from my house to yours, it's shorter to cut through the woods."

"That must be what this girl was doing," I said. "Taking a shortcut and looking at the fountain."

"The fountain has the same strong pull, but I'd hate to have a kid tumble off that old tub. Yes, it has to go, and I'll hire someone to clean up the area."

"I may trim the mulberry tree on my side," I said. "It's a major mess maker."

"If you feel like picking the berries, you could use them in baking. That's what my mom used to do."

For the Fourth of July bash. I'd never thought of that. Why not bake mulberry pies instead of blueberry? But as soon as the idea formed, I rejected it. I wasn't sure why, and Annora was talking about her house, so I didn't pursue the matter.

"I'm attached to it but I wouldn't want to live in Maple Creek again."

"Why not?" I asked.

"The place is too small. It's my property but not my home. When I visit, I reconnect with old friends, sometimes meet new ones, and fly away. You can't go home again."

"I've done it."

"But don't you find that nothing is the same? The past is gone. The dead don't come back. You walk down the same streets, but everything is different. It's all very sad."

"That's true, but I'm not trying to relive my childhood and this is a perfect town. It's picturesque and close enough to almost any place I want to go."

"You should work for the Chamber of Commerce," she said. "Well, I'd better be going." She got up and fluffed Pepper's fur. "I'll see you tomorrow at noon?"

I nodded. "Would you mind if I explored the woods someday? I'd like to take pictures of the tree house and see what else is there."

She hesitated. "Be my guest, but watch your step. Over the years, a lot of branches and trees came down, and there may be snakes."

"Are you talking about garden snakes?"

"Those, too. But my uncle killed a Massasauga rattler there once. They're lethal. I believe that was my last walk in the woods."

"Maybe I'll skip it," I said.

"Oh, don't do that. I didn't mean to frighten you."

"You didn't. I can't allow myself to fear life."

She laughed softly. "Why not, Cressa? There's so much to be afraid of."

I looked at her, wondering what the laughter had to do with her pessimistic remark. Perhaps I was dense today.

"When you go, take a large branch," she said. "Take your dog and keep your eyes on the ground. You should be safe enough, and as you leave the woods, you'll see my garden. Help yourself to whatever flowers you like. There's something blooming all through the summer, and there's no one left to enjoy them."

"I may do that."

She opened the screen door and we walked together around to the front, stopping to admire my lilies. But she seemed more interested in the white Victorian, with its silent, curtained windows and air of desolation.

"Three young schoolgirls," she said. "When they move in, it'll be almost like old times."

SIXTEEN

ANNORA'S OBSERVATION about unoccupied houses being restless and unhappy stayed with me throughout the evening. It tottered on the edge of my consciousness as I cooked a light supper. It sprang up at intervals, stealing my attention from the mystery I tried to read. The idea might be ridiculous, but its hold on my imagination was powerful.

The house hungers for footsteps in the silent halls and voices in the rooms. It won't let the music die or the shadows melt away. It needs light and life. When kept in darkness, the boards cry out, and neighbors gossip about ghosts.

Surely Annora didn't believe this. Houses were insentient structures built of brick or stone or wood. They didn't feel. You could love your home, but it would never grow attached to you.

So why couldn't I stop thinking about Annora's odd theory? Obviously she had spoken figuratively.

At ten-thirty, I let Pepper outside for the last time before bed and moved up to the balcony. For some reason, I was wired tonight. Three pleasant prospects promised to enliven the coming days, and nothing stressful loomed on the horizon except for a new round of interviews. Still I couldn't relax.

The night was heaven-perfect with a generous sprinkling of stars in the sky and a warm wind that sent a delicious new fragrance into the air. I found Venus and my wishing star, a fiery white pinpoint that seemed closer to the earth than the others. *But always beyond my reach.*

Pepper growled. An indistinct sound that I couldn't identify drifted up from the ground.

Gripping the railing, I looked downward, afraid I'd see a

cloaked and hooded figure shamble out of the darkness, as I had on the night of Libby's death, but nothing moved. The scene was a still life, colored in shades of black. I listened for footsteps but heard only shrilling crickets and splashing water.

Then a ripple of feminine laughter, soft and seductive, slipped into the night and disappeared in a sudden silence. For a moment, it seemed as if an invisible hand had turned off every sound in the world except for the beating of my heart. I laid my hand on Pepper's head, took a deep breath, and waited. An instant later, the fountain came alive again, and the crickets resumed their incessant chirping.

The laughter had come from my yard or Libby's. No one appeared to be in the immediate vicinity, but a strange energy charged the night. Sharp needles of apprehension raced up and down my bare arms. Something was there.

Only a few hours ago, I'd said, "I can't allow myself to fear life."

"Why not?" Annora had asked. "There's so much to be afraid of."

Maybe I should take her words seriously.

I glanced at the white Victorian, searching for a light in the third story window, a shadow walking across a room, or flames leaping skyward. An old house, dark and silent, stared back at me. Whoever had laughed in the night didn't move within its walls.

The disturbance was outside. Someone taking a late walk, the Walnut street robber trolling for his next victim, or a homeless woman in search of a makeshift bed. Or perhaps a young girl keeping a romantic tryst with her boyfriend in a quiet, quasi-private part of town.

That must be it. Now they'd moved on, perhaps to a parked car. The electrical charge in the air was my imagination, and the sensation in my arms had passed. Pepper lay quietly at my feet, resting her head on her paw. Tomorrow I'd examine the grounds for evidence of an intruder and maybe inform Dalton. The non-incident was officially over.

But a vestige of uneasiness stayed with me, as Annora's words had. Something was wrong with this night. Failing to pinpoint the problem, I'd seized a likely explanation of teenaged lovers. But what was really going on? An entire drama might be playing out around my house to a clueless spectator.

I told myself that yet another Beechnut Street mystery was unlikely. Settling back in the chair, I fluffed the pillow, looked up at the sky that always offered comfort, however cold and faraway, and remembered to make my wish.

The lights in the sky are stars— We think they do not see…

Archibald Macleish's chilling poem always set my nerves on edge. Why remember it tonight when soothing stanzas from Sara Teasdale's "Stars" were more appropriate for the occasion?

You know why. Someone, somewhere, is always watching. There are no secrets, and there is no escape.

MORNING DAWNED with rumbles of thunder, low clouds and the sense of threat that never seemed far away. Wind gusts had flung the neighborhood chimes into a frenzy of ringing. They sounded like alarm bells, all clang and no melody.

After a night of broken sleep, I felt edgy and tired. A cranberry muffin and tea should set my day on the proper course. Then I'd check the yard.

I took out a Milk-Bone biscuit for Pepper and dodged her paws while pouring boiling water in the teapot. Trying to ignore the beginning of a headache, I carried my breakfast tray out to the back porch and stepped into a blast of hot, muggy air.

I wasn't alone. The girl in green stood in the back of my yard where the wild phlox grew. She was tearing the petals off a flower and tossing them on the ground. Long strands of dark hair blew across her face, and her dress flapped around her knees. I knew I'd see her again but was unprepared for the shock that jolted through me.

Stay calm, I ordered myself. *Does she look like the girl in the pictures?*

Not really. Rather, I didn't think so. Her blowing hair obscured her features. Her fingers tore at the plant, and blossoms sailed through the air, mixing with the fall of mulberries brought down by the wind. I couldn't possibly mistake her for a garden statue today, and she didn't look particularly ghostly.

Relief flooded over me, then anger. This young vandal wasn't worth the hours of speculation and discussion, not worth a single minute of apprehension.

I slammed the tray down on the table. Tea spilled onto the tablecloth, and the muffin rolled to the floor. Opening the screen door, I cried, "Stop that!" and advanced on her, hoping that I or the presence of a barking dog would intimidate her.

Pepper dashed toward her but came to a stop midway across the yard. She flopped down on the grass, the way she had when her Frisbee landed on the grave. I stopped with her and glared at the girl, not believing that anyone could be so bold and defiant.

She continued to ignore me, yanking the petals from the plant and throwing them around as if they were confetti. They lay at her feet, a spreading pink pond, along with several mutilated stalks. My flowers!

"Who are you?" I demanded.

She pulled another petal from the plant.

"You're destroying my garden! That's breaking the law."

She stooped down, retrieved a handful of petals, and crushed them. I thought I saw a stream of bright red gushing from her hand, staining her dress, but…no, it was fresh and unmarred, a flowing sweep of light green. The phlox were pink, as they'd always been. It was the mulberries that were red.

"That's enough!" I made my voice so sharp and cutting that I hardly recognized it. "Stop what you're doing right away!"

She must have heard that because she hurled the shredded stem to the ground, turned and ran into the woods. Her hair blew back behind her like a dark wing.

Thunder rolled over my head, and the wind chimes clanged their warning. The rain was minutes away, but the girl had a head start. I took off after her, vaguely aware that Pepper ran alongside me.

Almost immediately the woods grew thicker. Long, low branches scraped against my arms, and tangled vines reached up to trip me. Downed branches lay where they'd fallen. Like snakes. *The Massasauga rattler.*

I came to a stop in a slippery quagmire of rotted leaves and stepped quickly to one side. This was a bad idea. "Pepper, wait!" I called. "Come."

She bounded back and pranced around my feet while I stared ahead at the nightmarish obstacle course ahead of me. There was no path stamped out by previous footprints, and it was too quiet. No one could navigate this wild tract soundlessly. Had the girl already crossed through the woods and disappeared into a house on the other side?

In the end, the eerie silence convinced me to turn around. Someone in Maple Creek must know her. Making discrete inquiries in the neighborhood would be more productive than chasing her through an unfamiliar stretch of woodland.

Calling Pepper to heel, I started back home, keeping an eye on the ground.

Now that I'd seen the girl in green at close range, I'd never wonder if she was Minta's ghost again. She was just a troublemaker who took pleasure in destroying beautiful things. In fact, she could be last night's visitor, laughing softly as she planned her vandalism. I intended to find out where she lived and what had prompted her bizarre behavior.

As I came out of the woods, the first raindrops fell. Pepper dashed ahead of me to the house and pawed at the porch steps, whining for her biscuit.

"Hold on, girl," I called.

At the property line, I stood in the rain, looking down at the fallen blossoms. Most of them had come to rest on the skeleton dog's grave. They lay there with the mulberries like a strange pink snowfall, while the phlox that had escaped the massacre swayed in the wind.

Explain this, Cressa.

I could, eventually, but first I needed a little time to figure it out.

I WANTED TO TALK TO Matt about the new developments, but Annora was the one who sat opposite me in a booth at the Blue Lion. Sleek, cool, and all in white, she rambled on about her

August trip to London. She had ordered a quiche and English Breakfast tea, explaining that she hadn't slept well last night.

"So this is brunch," she said.

I had a cup of chicken soup, an enormous salad and a tiny banana muffin that I'd eaten in two bites. I also had a headache caused by too little sleep, too much aggravation, and the storm that had left steamy, oppressive air in its wake. Two aspirin hadn't dented it, but I hoped a meal at the Blue Lion would.

Annora cut a small piece of quiche with her fork, and I leaped into the conversational lull. "That girl came back."

I gave Annora a brief summary of the incident, including the laughter I'd heard the night before, but I didn't mention Matt's idea that the girl might be the spirit of Minta Bransford. That was his story to tell. If he and Annora were friends, as he claimed, let her hear it from him.

"She's either evil or demented," I said. "Maybe both. It was raining too hard this morning to check the grounds."

"What are you looking for?"

"Anything. Tracks, a discarded candy wrapper, more damage…" Something that shouldn't be there, like the red scarf, evidence I could present to Dalton.

"I'll bet she came through the woods again," Annora said. "If she's damaging your flowerbeds, you should report her to the police."

"First I'm going to try to find out who she is. Do you know if there's a disturbed child living in the neighborhood?"

"Not offhand, but remember, Maple Creek isn't my permanent home."

"She has to live somewhere," I said.

Annora laid her fork neatly on the plate beside the last small square of quiche. "There's a woman on my street who sits on her front porch every day. She might know her."

"And I'll ask my neighbors. Do you suppose she's homeless?"

"Didn't you say she was well dressed?"

"She appeared to be."

"Then no."

"That dress could have come from a Salvation Army bin," I said.

But she looked well-groomed and well-fed, as if she belonged somewhere. I pushed a slice of cucumber around my plate. A basket filled with rolls and decent sized muffins beckoned to me. I broke one of the muffins in two and ate it slowly, envisioning myself on Beechnut Street, posing my questions to people I knew only by sight, if at all. With a headache. All I wanted to do was go home and take a nap. I felt my hand stray to my temples. I needed another dose of aspirin and more carbohydrates. Also, I felt that I had to start my investigation today before something worse happened.

Matt would be able to help me, and once I learned the girl's name, I could bypass the police and ask her parent or guardian to keep her away from my house and Annora's woods.

There was a good chance that wouldn't work. Teens were notorious for going where they pleased.

Then maybe I'd better call Dalton.

"You could take out a restraining order," Annora said.

"Against a kid?"

"If you feel threatened. Sure."

Legally, the incident would be classified as property damage, but it felt like harassment. The wild phlox were my flowers, growing on my property, and I loved them. Besides, she might come back another day and destroy the new ornamental birdbath I'd bought for the yard. Or hurt Pepper, if she was truly disturbed.

I let that thought die. In a few short days I'd come to care deeply for Pepper. She was my family now, and I wouldn't let anyone harm her. I was beginning to think that the girl had a vendetta against me. But that was so unlikely. We'd never even met.

"Are you all right?" Annora asked.

"It's just a little headache," I said.

"That's natural after all you've been through." Her smile was warm and solicitous. "We could have postponed lunch."

That's what I need, I thought. *Someone to care.*

"No," I said quickly. "I wanted something that I didn't have to cook, and I love the Blue Lion."

"It's my favorite restaurant, too. Do you know the legend of the yellow lion?"

"Find the lion that isn't blue. He'll make your deepest wish come true."

She laughed. "Your little verse reminds me of the poems I wrote for Minta's scrapbook. By the way, did you ever come across those missing pictures?"

"No, and Matt doesn't know anything about them, either."

"That's funny." She picked up her fork again and pushed the uneaten portion of quiche to one side. "That girl—the nameless one…she really upset you."

I nodded. "I'm worried about what she'll do next."

"I don't think I've ever seen a teenaged girl in a dress unless she's going to a dance. Sometimes not even then."

"It's unusual."

"So we've established that she's different and weird. Maybe there was a full moon last night."

"There wasn't," I said, remembering bright stars and a luminous quarter of light wreathed in haze. "Anyway, I don't believe that the moon's shape affects behavior."

"Then I don't know, but if it's any comfort to you, we're supposed to have rain for the next two days. That'll keep her inside."

"We can only hope," I said, and took another muffin out of the basket. Knowing that Annora was concerned made me feel better about the morning's episode. If only she wasn't leaving Maple Creek so soon. We'd just become friends. I hadn't realized how much I'd missed having a female companion.

There'll be others, I told myself, *and Annora will be back.*

Although Annora claimed that her primary residence was New York, I suspected that she still had a deep connection to her Maple Creek home. It was evident in the way she spoke of it.

Just before we left the restaurant, she said, "My house perks up when I come home. The rest of the time it's in mourning."

SEVENTEEN

THE RAIN RETURNED IN the afternoon and pounded the ground into a sodden mess. I waited on the back porch for the storm to pass, anxious to begin my search for the girl in the green dress. Once again I tried to read, but the mysteries in Maple Creek held more interest for me than the convoluted plot unfolding between the pages.

Occasionally I glanced at the woods, knowing that the girl in green wouldn't be outside in this dangerous weather and wondering how I'd react if she suddenly materialized in a flash of lightning.

At the back of the yard, the wild phlox that had survived her touch whipped around madly in the wind. They wouldn't last long in this onslaught, but the climbing rosebush near the door was heavy with red blooms. I breathed in their fragrance and imagined the girl marching brazenly up to my house and ripping them from the canes.

She'll scratch herself on those razor-sharp thorns and bleed...or maybe she doesn't have blood.

What inspired that gruesome thought? I reminded myself that the girl was a living antagonist. Not a garden statue and not a spirit. As for the roses, I'd cut them myself, beating her at her sick game. But I shouldn't have to do that, shouldn't even think of doing that. It was a form of surrender.

"We have to stop her, Pepper," I said.

Finally at five the rain tapered off, leaving waves of muggy air behind. Sunshine broke through the clouds, and the temperature rose. My sleeveless blouse felt as if it were glued to my chest, but the last two aspirin had taken the edge off my headache.

I closed my book in mid-chapter and tossed it on the side table. Pepper sprang up and dashed inside, never doubting that she would be invited to accompany me on an exciting jaunt.

Well, why not? I put on her leash, slipped a small notebook and pen into my pocket and stepped outside, making sure to take my key and lock the door. With Pepper bouncing along happily at my side and stray raindrops falling from the moisture-laden leaves, I felt buoyant and optimistic.

The sidewalks glistened, and the gracious old Victorians on Beechnut Street had a fresh glow in the sunlight. Libby's house looked almost happy, as if all of the sorrows and shadows had been washed away. These were good signs.

Now where should I start? I looked to the right, then to the left, considering. No one had ventured outside yet, but several cars were parked in their driveways. Matt's convertible wasn't one of them. I wished I could talk to him right now, but he rarely came home this early. I'd have to catch up with him later. With luck, by then I might have some new information.

So I'd begin my quest with Mr. Harrison, that gallant elderly gentleman who had been willing to go into a burning house. Although he lived next door, I hadn't seen him since the fire.

I rang his bell and waited, while Pepper sniffed at the small flag in his geranium planter. He came to the door wearing a crisp striped shirt with a maroon tie. His smile was slow but courteous. I had interrupted something. Dinner, perhaps, or he was on his way out.

"Why, Miss Hannett—and New Dog," he said.

"This is Pepper."

"She looks a lot better than she used to." He stepped to one side. "Won't you come in? Both of you?"

"Thanks, but not today. I'm looking for someone." As I told him about the girl who had ripped my flowers to shreds, an angry scowl creased his forehead. "The same thing's been happening in my garden! My strawberries get eaten before I can pick them. All this time I thought it was the birds and wild rabbits."

"It might be. All creatures love berries."

"But birds don't stamp down plants. Some of my vegetables

have been yanked out by the roots and left there to die. Young people today have no respect for nature." He brought his tirade to a halt and gave me a strange, questioning look. "On second thought, that doesn't sound like something a sixteen-year-old girl would do."

"That's one reason it's so disturbing," I said.

"Are you sure of your facts, Ms. Hannett?" His voice was kind and a trifle condescending.

"Positive."

"I wish I could help you, but I can't think of anyone who fits that description." He glanced across the street where Patti had emerged from her house to pick up fallen branches. "There used to be more young people around here when Libby gave her piano lessons. They were a different breed, refined and polite. You won't find a young musician trashing flowers or rampaging through a private garden."

"Making music and destroying property don't go together," I said.

He held out his palm for Pepper to sniff. She wagged her tail politely. "You could sic your dog on her if she shows up again."

"That would get me in trouble with the law," I said. "Besides, Pepper isn't aggressive."

This morning, she had remained in the middle of the yard, a good distance away from the girl. That was unusual behavior for a dog who loved to make new friends.

"I'll keep an eagle eye out for our delinquent," Mr. Harrison said. "I can't afford to have my vegetables destroyed. They get me through the summer." He rested his hand on the doorknob. "She won't be wearing that same dress though, will she?"

"Probably not. Watch for a slender, long-haired brunette. She may come out of the woods."

I thanked him and led Pepper back to the sidewalk, trying to get beyond my disappointment. Although Mr. Harrison's garden had suffered damage, I suspected that he doubted my story. It did sound unlikely. While the girl's age and the green dress were important, in the interest of credibility, I'd better omit them in my next encounter.

I made my way down Beechnut, knocking on doors and ringing bells. No one I talked to knew anybody capable of such wanton destruction. Besides, with the exception of Ginger who drove the ice cream truck, Patti's daughter, Aleta, and Linda, the local girls were in elementary school or college.

But there might be a new family in the neighborhood. Or a visiting niece or granddaughter. Somebody besides me must have seen the girl. She couldn't move through town wrapped in a cloak of invisibility.

By now I'd heard nine variations of the same response. The sun was hot, and the thick, humid air seemed to push me backward. Pepper kept stopping to nibble at grass or investigate the wonders that lined our route, and my initial enthusiasm had plummeted with the day's comfort level.

Don't give up, I told myself. *The girl is out there somewhere. And I can't keep calling her "the girl." She has to have a name.*

At Cherrylane, I turned and walked more slowly to Willow Court. I'd visit a few more houses, then head home. Maybe I was questioning the wrong people. Didn't most kids know one another, perhaps even go to the same school? This evening I'd seek out Aleta.

I gave Pepper's lead an encouraging tug and we moved on.

Willow Court was a quiet, densely shaded street of storybook bungalows and brick ranches. Annora lived in a pale lavender cottage topped with a graceful trio of gables. Dark purple shutters and window boxes created a charming contrast for the siding, and a fancy white railing wrapped around the front porch.

This was one of the prettiest houses I'd ever seen, even more picturesque than Matt's blue Victorian. I'd envisioned Annora in a gloomy estate painted earth tones and surrounded by forest. The reality surprised me.

I looked for her perennial garden, but caught only a glimpse of tall bright flowers in the back. Several yards from the ribbon driveway, the woods began. A "No Trespassing" sign issued its stern warning from the trunk of a weeping willow, while a narrow dirt path wound through dark trees, only to vanish in shadows. An adventure-loving child wouldn't be able to resist it.

But I wasn't dealing with a child.

I walked on and came to another house, this one plain and white with a simple square shape. Built sideways on the lot, it faced away from the woods. The front yard was crammed with an overwhelming collection of statuary: small animals, fairies, and a stone mushroom the size of a lawn chair.

A silver-haired woman sat on the porch, swinging listlessly in a creaking glider, with a golden retriever at her feet. The dog began to growl. In answer, Pepper gave a playful yip, and the woman looked our way. Her blue shirtwaist dress and pearl necklace gave her the neat but dated look of a homemaker from a 1950s television show.

"Good afternoon," she said. "Callie, be quiet!"

I smiled and shushed Pepper who was determined to greet the other dog. "Could you spare a few minutes to talk to me?" I asked.

She pointed to a sign on the door. "I'm sorry but there's no soliciting here."

"I'm not selling anything. This is a private matter, an investigation."

"Come up then and have a seat, but please keep your dog restrained. Callie is temperamental."

The retriever wagged her tail as we mounted the six steps to the porch. She had a jewel-studded collar around her neck and gray hairs in her muzzle. The woman motioned me to a wicker love seat opposite the glider and closed her magazine. It was *Mary May,* a glossy fashion-and-dating tome slanted toward women in their twenties and thirties. Readers like me.

I told Pepper to sit and looped her leash twice around my wrist. "My name is Cressa Hannett," I said, with a smile. "From the other side of the woods."

"Pleased to meet you. I'm Edith Kruger. Do you live in one of those beautiful Victorians?"

"No, mine is the smallest house on the block, but I like it."

"That must be the Bransford place," she said. "You were Libby Dorset's neighbor, then. That poor lady. What a tragedy that was!"

"Libby was a wonderful friend," I said. "Did you know the Bransford family?"

"Not until all the brouhaha about the disappearance, but I used to see Minta walking her collie every now and then. They made such a charming picture. Then they were gone. Just like that." She snapped her fingers, and both dogs came to attention.

Leaning forward on the glider, she added, "Aren't you the one who found Minta Bransford's scrapbook in the attic?"

"You're partly right. It was in the basement."

"Imagine that! I read about it in the *Tribune*. Are you investigating the old case? Because if you are, there are a lot of dead ends in that story."

"Not exactly," I said. "Naturally I'm curious about it, but I'm looking for someone else who should be easier to find."

"Is another child missing?" she asked quickly.

"Just the opposite."

Once again, I told my tale and, on an impulse, added the girl's probable age and the fact that she wore a dress. "I feel threatened, even though I don't know how she could hurt me," I said.

"Oh, my goodness!" Mrs. Kruger's reached out to touch Callie's head. "What color was the dress? And the style? Do you remember?"

"Light green, a soft spring shade. It had a high waist and square neckline with crochet or lace trim." I hadn't realized until this moment that I remembered those details. "Oh, and it was sleeveless. When she ran from me, I noticed a long back tie."

Imperceptibly Mrs. Kruger's friendly demeanor seemed to fade. Was that fear that flared in her eyes or hostility? Before I could decide, it disappeared.

She stared at me, pale and silent, clutching the magazine. Her unease transferred itself to me, and I felt the apprehension rushing back. All the thick, humid air in Maple Creek seemed to have settled on this one porch, holding me in a tight grip.

Mrs. Kruger said, "Don't you realize that you've just described Minta Bransford?"

"But that's impossible. Minta is dead. If she were still alive, she'd be old—much older than this girl."

"When you've lived as long as I have, my dear, you'll find out that nothing is impossible."

"What are you saying?" I asked.

"Minta Bransford was wearing that dress when she vanished. It was in all the papers. The same color, the lace trim, those long back ties. She made it in school and modeled it in a school fashion show."

"That has to be a coincidence," I said. "Or some kid who knows the story is pretending to be Minta."

"That could be. For a prank or a costume party?" She waved the magazine back and forth in front of her face. "The dress could have been stored in a basement all these years or in a resale shop. If it was offered for sale, another girl—this vandal of yours— might have bought it."

I tried to recall the articles I'd read from the *Tribune* archives. Had there been a picture of Minta's dress? Was it even mentioned? It must have been.

"What do you think happened to Minta Bransford?" I asked.

"That she's been dead and buried all these years. That she was killed shortly after she went missing."

"Then we're back to a Minta impersonator. The real Minta couldn't be wandering around today in her home-sewn dress."

Mrs. Kruger turned her head to look at the trees that cast their long shadows on the lawn. "It isn't likely. Only possible."

I was about to ask her what she meant when she said, "Annora Maywood keeps her acreage intact because she likes the atmosphere, she says, even though she's rarely here to enjoy it. A developer could clear the land and build ten nice houses on it, but Annora won't sell. I'm glad...I enjoy my view." Her eyes grew sharp. "You said this girl came out of the woods..."

"I assume so. I know she left that way. Do kids play there?"

"They used to. Not anymore. It's too overgrown and wild. After Minta disappeared, the police searched every inch of every acre. They never found a single clue." Mrs. Kruger set her magazine down again in her lap. "I don't know what you saw, Cressa, unless it was whatever remains of that unfortunate girl."

Her words hung in the air like drops of moisture about to dissolve. I had to respond quickly.

"A ghost, you mean?"

"Minta's spirit. Her soul."

I let my hand drop down to Pepper's head. Contact with a warm, living animal kept me grounded in reality.

"If you believe in ghosts," I said. "The idea of a Minta impersonator makes more sense to me."

"Now that I think about it, whoever ruined your flowers couldn't have been Minta in any form. Her friends described her as sweet and gentle, and I could see how much she loved that pretty collie of hers. I don't believe that people's personalities change when they die." She shivered. "But that dress…the very thought of it chills my blood."

"It doesn't sound so unique," I said. "I have a green dress myself."

A sleek A-line silk in hunter's green with no lace trim and no back ties, ordered from a catalog. Nothing at all like the ghost dress.

Thunder rumbled in the east. Callie trembled and whimpered, resting her chin on Edith's knee. While we'd been talking, the sky had turned dark. Usually I loved storms, but at the moment I felt like shivering, too.

"They said the rain would come back," Edith said.

"We'd better be on our way, then." I tore a sheet from my notebook and wrote my cell phone number on it. "If you see anyone who looks like the girl I described would you please let me know?"

She nodded and tucked it into her magazine, and I tugged on Pepper's leash again, just as a lightning bolt slashed across the heavy clouds.

"I guess you don't want to go back through the woods," she said.

"You're right. I'll take the long way on the sidewalk."

"Come for another visit soon, Cressa. This can be a lonely street sometimes."

"I may do that," I said. "Goodbye."

Now that I was going home, I found that I could move with ease, down the six steps to the walkway, past the stone fairies and animals. Here the air seemed lighter. I could hardly wait to be safe in my own house with time to mull over what Edith Kruger had said.

Ghost talk came easily to the people in the neighborhood, but I wasn't ready to believe that the spirit of the lost Minta had come back to earth to torment me. The girl in the flowerbed was made of flesh and blood. I'd been almost close enough to touch her but not fast enough to catch her.

I would have liked to share Edith Kruger's belief that nothing was impossible, but a normal person didn't see ghosts. Dead people stayed dead.

Of one fact I was certain. No matter who or what the girl in green was, I didn't like her.

EIGHTEEN

I TURNED ON Beechnut Street and coaxed Pepper into a run. My house was half a block away, but the storm was closer.

Lightning crackled across the clouds. A large black bird screamed as it flew for cover, and somewhere behind me, a dog howled. Combined with Edith Kruger's revelations, this display of Gothic atmosphere inspired unsettling thoughts.

If you see a ghost, it means that you're going to die soon.

That was my grandmother's favorite saying, always accompanied by the tale of her cousin, Anne, who had seen the form of her dead mother walking down a snow-covered country lane. Anne died two weeks later of pneumonia. Grandma had countless other shivery stories, most of them dealing with death's harbingers.

As a child, I'd believed them. Now that I was an adult, I wanted desperately to think this was superstitious nonsense, part of her Old World idea of amusing the younger generation. Still, my irrational side whispered, *What if it's true?*

It isn't. Eight years ago you saw your father, and you're still here, dodging raindrops and racing down the street with Pepper. So this new manifestation, if it is genuine, can't be a forewarning of your death.

If I had to die in the near future, I didn't want to know about it ahead of time.

Another lightning bolt sizzled in the sky. We ran faster. Seven more houses now. Six. Matt's car was still parked in the driveway, and his downstairs lights were on, tempting me to make a stop at the blue Victorian. *Later,* I thought. *After he's had a chance to unwind and eat dinner. After the storm.*

Thunder crashed overhead, and water splashed down in the satyr fountain. Just four more yards. I cut across Mr. Harrison's lawn and stood at last on my own porch, fumbling for my key, going through the doorway a few steps ahead of the downpour. In the vestibule I waited for my heart rate and breathing to slow down.

Safe home and only a little wet.

While Pepper shook herself, I turned on the television. A severe thunderstorm warning crawled across the bottom of the screen, but there were no tornado watches, at least for the present. Reassured, I hurried out to the back porch. No one was in the yard. Nothing disturbed the peace except for the rain, once again pounding the earth into an endless mud puddle.

Ghosts didn't have to take shelter from a storm. If there were ghosts.

Remember—nothing is impossible.

Twenty years ago, Minta Bransford had lived in this house. Her family owned the yard and the flowers that grew on it. Maybe she didn't realize they were different plants, no longer her property to enjoy or destroy at will. She might not know she was dead.

One question in particular puzzled me. Whoever the girl was, delinquent or revenant, why tear plants apart? What was the point? I had no idea how to answer it.

BEEF STEW and a cup of hot tea brought me back to the rational plain. Before entertaining the phantom theory, I should talk to Aleta and Ginger, and I wanted Matt's perspective and his company.

Once again, the storm had moved on. Although only a few hours of daylight remained, the sky was bright again. I turned off the television and glanced through my front window. Matt's car was still parked in the driveway.

At seven-thirty, I left Pepper asleep by the stove and walked over to the blue Victorian. One of the hanging baskets had fallen, spilling red petals on the porch. I righted it and rang the bell, waiting for what seemed like an inordinate amount of time.

Finally Matt came to the door. "Hi, Cressa," he said. "Where's your partner?"

"She's napping. If you're not busy, I'd like to discuss something with you."

"That sounds intriguing."

"Something ghostly," I added.

"Even better."

The light in his blue-green eyes lifted my spirits. I hadn't realized how much I'd been looking forward to seeing Matt this evening, even though I had to initiate the encounter.

"Come have coffee and dessert with me," he said. "I just finished dinner."

He led the way through the house to a small but neat kitchen where a bubbling coffeemaker filled the room with an irresistible aroma. An empty container from the Rib Shack lay on top of the counter.

As he pulled out a blue chair, I noticed that the walls were painted a soft robin's egg shade, and the dishes had a striking cobalt-on-white pattern. Practically everything in the room was blue to coordinate with the color of his house.

He opened an Awrey's cake box. "It's chocolate marshmallow."

"That's perfect," I said.

While he cut two pieces of cake, I told him about the girl's vandalism, my futile search for somebody who knew her and the green dress. "Do you recall what Minta Bransford was wearing when she disappeared?" I asked.

"Not offhand, but I can look it up in the archives."

"I don't know what to think anymore, but nothing about this strange affair is good."

"We need to find her," he said. "Soon."

He filled two mugs with coffee and sat down. I relaxed. As worrisome as the matter had become, as potentially dangerous, I didn't have to deal with it on my own. Obviously Matt was motivated by a desire to sell papers, but I'd accept any help he was willing to offer.

He said, "How about if I contact Minta's cousin and we pay

her a visit? Say some afternoon next week, whatever works out
for everybody?"

"Let's do it. If nothing else, she might remember the dress."

"I'll have my secretary make copies of the stories," he said.
"We'll start a Bransford File. Don't worry. Between the two of
us, we'll crack this case. If you see this mysterious girl again,
take a picture. What we need is hard evidence."

"I'll leave my camera out on the porch."

"And here's some advice. You probably shouldn't keep asking
people about her."

"Why not?"

"That's how rumors start. Some women on the block love
to gossip."

"Only women?"

"Mostly women," he said. "Mostly two of them. I'm speaking
from personal experience. Tomorrow, you may find a more
colorful version of your story winging its way back to you."

I'd never considered that, but he had a point. Both Patti and
Gwendolyn had broadcast the suicide version of Libby's death.
The Ghost in the Garden wouldn't make as strong an impact as
a tale of self-destruction, but the meager facts I'd revealed could
easily be bandied about. And my name with them.

Also, the phlox plants bloomed in the shade of the satyr
fountain. A creative gossipmonger could weave a flamboyant
yarn out of the shreds I'd so freely dispensed today. *Ghost Girl
Murders Libby Dorset. Get all the sensational details here!*

Unfortunately, I couldn't go back and undo any damage I
might have caused.

"I'll just ask Aleta then hold my peace," I said. "But I *will* call
Lieutenant Dalton."

"That's a smart move, and we can check out the neighbors
during the block party. Someone of interest may show up. The
cake is good, isn't it?" he added.

"Delicious. Awrey's is the best."

"Next to homemade. Libby's baking was famous all over
town. I'm going to miss her banana bread." He picked up a
knife. "Have another piece? More coffee?"

I declined the cake but accepted a coffee refill, and we sat together in companionable silence, while the mysteries and apprehensions slipped away. I was about to ask him if he would show me through his house when he laid his hand over mine. "I'd like to take you out to dinner on Saturday. We could go back to the Inn or try a new place."

"Yes—I'd love that… Oh, no."

My date with Dalton! Thank heavens I'd remembered it in time or I'd be in the unenviable position of having promised the same evening to two men.

"I can't, Matt. Not then."

"I see."

The happy expression on Matt's face shifted perceptibly, and he withdrew his hand. Had the brightness left his eyes or was it the effect of the old-fashioned light fixture above us?

Quickly I said, "I already have an engagement on Saturday night. Could we do it another time? After the Fourth, maybe?"

"Sure. Why not?"

He didn't suggest another evening, and I had a sinking feeling that I'd unwittingly stolen his enthusiasm and trampled on it. But, in the next instant, his smile was as warm as ever. "I'll call you about tracking down Minta's cousin as soon as I know something definite," he said.

This sounded like a prelude to an ending, and, in truth, I had no reason to linger in Matt's house and no reason to feel guilty. Dalton had issued his invitation first. What else could I have done?

Nothing. This kind of situation happened all the time between single people. But our easy, fragile connection had begun to fray around the edges, and I didn't know how to repair it. I finished my cake and carried the empty plate to the sink.

"I'll take care of that," Matt said quietly.

At that moment the ice cream truck's music floated through the air, light, merry notes that somehow made a poignant melody.

"There's Ginger now," I said. "If I hurry, I can catch her."

I hoped that Matt would offer to accompany me, but he chose to ignore our fledgling tradition. And why not? In his view, we weren't going anywhere.

You could change that, I told myself. *Easily. But not today, and only if you're truly interested.*

Suddenly I wasn't certain about anything. I reached for my key. "Thanks for the cake and coffee and your input, Matt. I *do* value it."

"Anytime," he said and rose to escort me to the door.

GINGER HANDED ME an ice cream cone that I didn't really want. As I'd anticipated, she had no relevant information. "Most of my customers are little kids," she said.

"But I thought, maybe, in your school…"

She shook her head emphatically. "Nobody I know wears their hair long."

That left Aleta, as Ginger thought Linda was on vacation with her family. When a few raps on Patti's door went unanswered, I decided to end this frustrating endeavor and wait for the next occurrence. I had no doubt there would be one.

At home, I wandered through the backyard, surveying the storm damage. Although the wild ferns and phlox were beaten down by the force of the rain, no stems were broken. Small branches littered the grass, and toward the back, the ground was bright with pink petals and mulberries. A fallen nest lay near the skeleton dog's grave. That was all. I was lucky.

Everything smelled of rich wet soil and unseen flowers blooming in the woods. Mr. Harrison's vegetable garden looked fresh and neat, and the fountain splashed unendingly in Libby's forsaken garden. Tomorrow I'd rake the debris, and the ferns would begin to straighten themselves out in the sunshine.

Pepper barked. I whirled around, startled by the sudden noise. She lay in the middle of the yard, her ears at attention, her eyes fixed on the dark trees beyond the grave. I told her to Come! Instead of obeying, she pulled a twig toward her mouth with her paw and began to chew it.

Something in the woods kept her at bay, possibly that red canoe. Every day I expected to see space where it had been, but this never happened. I had a feeling that Annora didn't plan to have it hauled away. One morning she'd go back to New York and that unsightly relic would continue to annoy me every time I looked at it.

Why not go ahead and have a privacy fence installed? It would be safer. I'd still have a view from the balcony, and high pickets wouldn't easily be scaled by a girl in a dress. Unless she could walk through it.

Not liking the turn of my thoughts, I headed back to the house. Pepper abandoned her makeshift chew toy and raced across the grass in a successful attempt to beat me to the porch.

Inside, without any distraction, my lingering guilt over Matt resurfaced. I told myself to stop brooding about the incident. It was over. I hadn't meant to hurt his feelings, and if our bond could be so easily dented, it hadn't been substantial to begin with.

With a sigh, I tabled the Matt issue. Puzzles and riddles were easier to understand than men, and my own private mystery kept tugging at me. Still, there wasn't much more I could do about it at the moment, except work with my only clue.

I took the scrapbook out of my desk drawer and carried it to the dining-room table, into the light. Now that a little time had elapsed and I knew more about Minta and Annora, perhaps I'd find something relevant in its pages. Something like a scrap of green fabric.

I came across a length of ivory lace framing a lock of reddish-gold hair, but as it was unaccompanied by a label or notation, there was no way to determine its origin. Turning pages slowly, I skimmed romantic verses, greetings on Valentine cards, and invitations to long-past schoolgirl events. I lingered over autographs and sentimental messages: Always remember me... Remember this... Don't forget...

What had happened to the girls who wrote those lines? Did they ever think of Minta Bransford?

My gaze fell on one name: Patti. The garish blue-green ink was smeared, but the letters were carefully formed and slanted, and a tiny heart dotted the letter *i*. Could this be Patti Graham?

Not likely. Hadn't Patti once said that she was new on Beechnut Street? I frowned, searching for the memory. Those were her words, but this didn't necessarily mean she was new in town. Patricia and its variants were fairly common names; Patti spelled with an *i* was a little unusual.

This matter could be resolved by asking Patti if she had lived in Maple Creek in 1975 and if she'd ever known Minta Bransford.

I turned another page. The top half held two photographs of the beach at Marble Lake with indistinguishable figures in the background. The bottom half was blank, reminding me of the items that had inexplicably vanished.

Annora had asked about them. Matt claimed not to know how they'd disappeared, and I couldn't be certain they hadn't simply slipped out unnoticed. I flipped through the scrapbook counting empty spaces. If Annora had filled every available inch of the book, as she claimed, approximately four pages of material were missing.

Why did I feel that what wasn't there was important?

After leafing through the scrapbook again, I returned it to the desk. Suppose… An idea appeared suddenly, creeping out of nowhere, another question in a long line of tantalizing "what if's."

What if Minta wanted her scrapbook back?

That's right, Cressa. Scare yourself. Lay the groundwork for a series of nightmares.

That made no sense. Minta had never even opened the package.

But she knows the scrapbook exists. You couldn't possibly keep it a secret. Not when the very walls have eyes. Dark green eyes flecked with topaz and misted with tears.

Dear God! That was enough! And at what point had I accepted the idea that I was dealing with the supernatural?

Before going upstairs to bed, I moved the scrapbook to the bottom drawer of the buffet and, as an afterthought, stacked my linen tablecloths on top of it. I was overreacting and felt more than a little foolish. However, taking extra care was a sensible precaution until I knew more about the mystery girl who haunted my backyard.

NINETEEN

ALL ALONG MAIN STREET, flags waved languidly in the breeze. The quaint nineteenth century storefronts basked in the sunshine, and red, white and blue flowers sparkled in window boxes. With the Fourth of July two days away, the festive atmosphere was contagious.

Feeling happy and festive myself, I parked in front of a purple Victorian that housed Sky and McKay Title and walked a half block to the Bakery on Main. There I lingered in front of the store's display window admiring an elegant flag cake set among an assortment of doughnuts, Danish and croissants. I had come to pick up my order for the block party, but I knew I'd also be going home with pastries for myself.

As I pushed open the door, someone came up behind me. The rough edge of a purse brushed against my arm, and a wave of hot breath hit my neck. I stepped to one side and turned to see who had ventured into my space. In a low, raspy voice, a woman said, "Excuse me."

I recognized her. She was the uninvited guest at Libby Dorset's reception who had stolen a plateful of strawberry tortes; the person Gwendolyn called the gypsy.

There wasn't a bit of color about her this morning. She wore an ill-fitting brown dress with long sleeves that covered her wrists. Her dark eyes glittered above high, weathered cheekbones, and grayish hair hung down in limp strands.

It wasn't a purse that had touched my arm but a grimy shopping bag. She hugged it close to her breast. "Miss? Could you spare some change for a cup of coffee?"

Although I'd never been approached by a vagrant before, I'd

heard the usual warnings: *Open your purse and they'll grab it and take off before you can cry, "Stop, thief!" Or they'll pull out a gun.*

But how could I ignore this request? "I may have."

Just be careful, I told myself.

The sidewalk was deserted, but there were a few people in the bakery. The clerk behind the counter, a woman eying the assortment of day-old pies, and a blond man with a little towheaded boy. The man was at least six feet tall and muscular. It should be perfectly safe.

The woman fidgeted in the entrance, holding the door open. I stepped inside and set my purse on one of the cafe tables, keeping my left hand firmly around the handle. Delicious smells drifted through the air: fresh-baked bread; spices and sugar; rich hot chocolate and coffee.

The bakery was as homey and inviting as a grandma's parlor—if you had money in your pocket.

The young clerk held her chilly stare in place while I rummaged through my coin purse. The man paid for his order and hurried through the door with the boy, both of them munching cinnamon twists. The other customer never looked away from the pies.

I found three quarters and hesitated. What if I were the one who couldn't afford a cup of coffee? Bypassing the jumble of coins, I pulled a five dollar bill out of my wallet. "Here you are."

The glitter in the woman's eyes intensified, and a grin stretched out her thin lips. "I thank you." She slipped the money in the shopping bag.

"Haven't I seen you somewhere?" I asked.

"Maybe. I get around. Thanks again, Miss." She backtracked out to the sidewalk, almost colliding with an elderly man who was passing by. I wondered where she was going to buy her coffee. Or if it was something else she really wanted?

That was her business now.

The clerk's frown turned into a sunny smile. "May I help you, ma'am?"

"Is the order for Cressa Hannett ready?" I asked.

"I'm sure it is." She ducked behind the counter and moments later brought out an enormous white box with my name and the contents printed on top. "Seven dozen hot dog rolls! You must be having a party."

"It's a block party for the Fourth," I said. "Do you know that woman?"

"Just her name. Ruby. She's always hanging around outside. The owner doesn't want her in the store. He won't have her bothering the customers."

I hadn't felt bothered, only startled. But if I encountered her again...

Once you give them a handout, they'll keep pestering you for more.

"Does she ever buy anything?" I asked.

"No, she just asks people for coffee money. There's a law against begging, but the cops don't enforce it."

"I wonder why."

I'd never seen a police cruiser on Main Street. Presumably the officers of the MCPD patrolled the neighborhoods and country roads. That left the small downtown area a pandering-free zone. Matt once said that Maple Creek was hospitable to the homeless population. Obviously not everyone in town felt that way. This young woman, for example, whose *I (heart) Life* sweatshirt jarred with her dismissive attitude.

"They have to catch them in the act first," she said. "Will there be anything else for you today, Ms. Hannett?"

"Yes..." I took another bill, a twenty, out of my wallet, and surveyed the day's offerings, grateful that I could afford anything I wished. "Six cinnamon rolls and six jelly doughnuts, please."

Was there any truth in that old stereotype of policemen gobbling doughnuts from morning to night? If Dalton invited himself in after our date, I'd have something to offer him. He might prefer beer though. All right. Beer and doughnuts.

I left the store, balancing boxes awkwardly, and retraced my steps back to the car. Once I was outside in the fresh air and sunlight, the desire to do something different today, to go some-where, overwhelmed me.

All of the obvious choices were appealing. I could spend the afternoon at the beach, take a short road trip, or head south on I-75 to one of the down state malls. Any place would do, as long as it was far from fountains and ghosts and people who moved like wraiths through the streets, searching for the comforts of home.

IN THE END I DECIDED to go for a ride in the country. I left the baked goods on the kitchen counter, picked up Pepper and drove slowly out of town, savoring a heady sense of freedom. The air blew in through the window, and with every mile I put between myself and Maple Creek, my spirit grew lighter.

The house on Beechnut Street was my home, but it was also steeped in mystery, and vague threats lurked in its shadows. The murder, the disturbances at the white Victorian, the scrapbook and now the girl in green all haunted me.

How could so many strange things have happened in such a short time?

I needed to separate myself from them, if only for a while. Then perhaps I could view the strange events from a new perspective.

Enjoy the sights, I told myself. *Look forward to an exciting evening with one of the most sought-after men in Maple Creek. Let everything else fade to black.*

So I focused on the scenery and allowed the enchanting Michigan countryside to work its magic. Lakes and woods and villages untouched by time reminded me of how much I loved my home state. At a vegetable stand, I bought six quarts of blueberries and a country bouquet. Then I drove another seventy miles and only turned back when I noticed that the time of my next outing was fast approaching. Home was two hours away.

That evening, as I dressed for my date with Dalton, I recalled past Saturdays in Texas, those lost golden days and star-spangled nights. They were always filled with entertainment and laughter. At least that was how I remembered them.

I can have that again, I thought.

My turquoise dress managed to be both classy and sexy. For

sparkle, I added my diamond star pendant and emerald earrings. Now, I'd shine in any theater or restaurant Dalton chose. I vowed to bring all the color back to my life and make this night spectacular.

Later I began to think that might not be possible.

It was half past six. I stood at the bay window, watching Patti struggle with her lawn sprinkler and wondering if Dalton was going to stand me up. I was certain of the day and time but not of the man.

Would he dare treat me that way? The date was his idea, after all. Certainly if he was going to be delayed, he would have called. "Six o'clock," he'd said. It was now almost seven.

By the time I spied his blue convertible cruising up Beechnut Street, I'd mentally revised my evening plans. Now there was no need to regroup. I breathed a sign of relief and glanced one last time in the hall mirror.

He parked in the driveway and sauntered across the grass to my house. From her yard, Patti stared at him. I stared, too. In his dark blue suit and tie, Lieutenant Gray was indeed a gorgeous hunk, incredibly handsome and no doubt well aware of it. How could he not be?

I opened the door and told Pepper to Sit. She sank to the floor with a little yip of protest. Dalton stepped inside and ruffled her fur. "Sorry I'm late, Cressa," he said. "I had to take care of some police business."

"I'm glad you could make it," I said.

Noting that Patti still stared in our direction, I closed the door.

"You look fantastic," he said, his gaze fastened on my pendant.

"Thanks. That's my intent." I gave him a bright smile and reached for my evening bag.

"We missed the first hour of the movie, so we'll have dinner first," he said. "Are you ready?"

Quickly, I consulted my mental checklist. Pepper had fresh water, the lamp in the window was on, my keys were in my purse. "Whenever you are."

"Let's go, then." He took my arm, and we walked to the convertible. Patti was still in her yard, rearranging the pots on the porch steps. I waved to her, and she called, "Have a good time!"

"Mrs. Graham takes the Neighborhood Watch seriously," I said.

He opened the door. "That's a good thing."

I settled myself in the passenger's seat, sinking into the marshmallow soft upholstery, breathing in the new car smell of a vehicle that was older than I was. Dalton started the engine, turned on the radio, and a sixties folk song came on, plunging us into the ambience of another decade.

"The Kingston Trio?" I asked. "How appropriate!"

"I have an old radio," he said. "Naturally it's going to play old music."

"Or you have a modern CD player in it?"

"Let me have some secrets, Cressa."

"Whatever it is, I'd love to have a car like this," I said.

"You could, but you'll spend a fortune on it. I did all the restoration myself. Even the painting."

He backed out into the street, and Patti waved again. Thank heavens she couldn't follow us.

Like an exotic bird from another age, the Cadillac skimmed down to Main Street, past the ice cream truck, past a group of gawking young people. Here Dalton made a left turn into nonexistent traffic. The Blue Lion, the park, the bakery and the Carousel Theater—one by one, the familiar landmarks sped by until we were driving on a dark country road moving away from Maple Creek at a high speed.

To where? I decided to let myself be surprised.

"Has everything been quiet on Beechnut Street?" Dalton asked.

"More or less."

"Does that mean something happened?"

"There was an incident. I meant to report it but got sidetracked."

"Tell me," he said.

Once again, I described the girl in the green dress and her

senseless vandalism, this time adding Mr. Harrison's disappearing strawberries and trampled plants.

"That kind of nonsense usually happens around Halloween," he said. "We get complaints about overturned flowerpots and squashed pumpkins then. Lately we're dealing with break-ins."

"She didn't come near the house," I said.

"Just so I'm clear, these were wildflowers in the woods?"

"They were *my* flowers in *my* yard."

"I see." His fell silent. I glanced at him, but his attention was fixed on the road. An expressway sign loomed in the darkness. I-75 and an arrow. In the long pause that followed, I suspected he thought that I'd imagined the girl or exaggerated the damage.

Finally he said, "If she does it again, give us a call," and he swung onto the entrance ramp.

"I'll do that."

I'd hoped that Dalton would be a little more helpful. Maybe sympathetic. But what exactly did I want him to do? He was off duty, and if I wanted to make this night spectacular, I couldn't keep dredging up that wretched girl.

I let her fade to black, too, and suddenly felt as light and free as I should at the beginning of an evening with a new man. This was the way I'd felt earlier today driving out of Maple Creek looking for something different. Exhilarated, hopeful, and just a little uncertain.

NOTHING EVER TURNED OUT the way I imagined it. Sometimes this proved to be good.

The burgers Dalton mentioned became Porterhouse steaks in a lakeside restaurant. The place had a live band, a dance floor and its own glitter. Topiaries strung with miniature lights wrapped around the room, and jumbo-size silver stars and planets decorated the walls.

By the end of the first course, I knew that Lieutenant Dalton Gray was a dedicated police officer who had joined the Force after a stint in the Air Force. He had a passion for flying and fishing the Michigan lakes. Acquiring a plane was his next project.

As a man, he was dictatorial and a trifle arrogant. These weren't my favorite character traits, but he was also amusing. I felt comfortable with him and, as a bonus, hadn't had to divulge much of my own background. He didn't ask.

"Maple Creek is my town," he said. "It has everything I like and some of the most intriguing people in Michigan." He tipped his wine glass toward me. "Some of the prettiest women in the state."

I rewarded the compliment with another bright smile.

"And some of the oddest," I said. "Yesterday I met a woman who believes in ghosts. She suggested that this girl who's tearing my flowers might be a spirit."

I took a quick sip of wine, surprised at what I'd said. I never intended to allow Minta into our evening. She'd slipped into my conversation as quietly as she'd entered my yard. Since she was here, I might as well solicit Dalton's opinion on the supernatural.

"She meant Minta Bransford, the girl who disappeared in 1975," I added. "No one ever found Minta's body. Therefore, she's a ghost."

His hearty laugh told me what I wanted to know. "Maple Creek is also a superstitious town. I've never been able to figure out why. There's a ghost around every corner, if you believe half of what you hear."

"And you don't?"

"No, I believe what I see."

"Then you don't think one of the town phantoms gave Libby Dorset that fatal shove into her fountain," I said.

"You're joking, aren't you?"

"Just theorizing—since the neighborhood is overrun with ghosts."

"That kind of talk is for the tourists and the kids, Cressa. Besides, the Dorset place doesn't have any unusual history attached to it. That poor lady did away with herself for a reason known only to her or maybe she had an accident. That's the verdict."

"It's what the killer wants us to think."

His voice sharpened. "Do you have any additional information about the case?"

"Only my instincts. That's all I ever had. They keep telling
me there's more to know."

"When they get more specific, give me a call," he said. "For
now the case is closed." He reached across the table for my hand
and pulled me gently up. "Would you like to dance, Cressa?"

I did, of course, but why hadn't he waited for my answer?

I went into his arms anyway, let him lead me around the
dance floor, while the music wove its spell. The silver stars and
shining planets went whirling around us, blurring the edges of
reality. Fortunately, I knew how to dance on the earth.

Lieutenant Dalton Gray was the requisite tall, dark and
handsome hero of every romance novel. His cornflower blue
eyes promised the happy ending every woman longs to find.

But he wasn't the man for me.

TWENTY

ALTHOUGH DALTON WASN'T the elusive one destined to give me a happily-ever-after ending, our evening had its memorable moments. A touch of glitter followed us wherever we went, even to the small diner that advertised breakfast at any time of the day or night. Dalton devoured a stack of French toast and bacon while I nibbled on a muffin and drank tea. For me, it was too soon to eat again.

When he pulled into my driveway, Beechnut Street was a few hours away from waking up. Mine was the only house with a light in the window, but the stars still shone in a clear black sky, and a sizeable chunk of moon nestled in the treetops.

In the shelter of the front porch, he kissed me thoroughly and followed this passionate display with a promise to call. "Get some sleep now," he said.

That was exactly what I intended to do. "Thanks for everything, Dalton. Good night."

I opened the door and almost stepped on Pepper who had stationed herself in the vestibule. She sprang up and leaped at me, barking a loud welcome home.

"My good watchdog," I said, giving her a quick pat on the head. "Did anything happen while I was gone?"

Apparently not. Only the ticking of the mantel clock broke the silence of the shadowy rooms. It was three-forty. Outside, if I listened carefully, I could hear the hum of the Cadillac's engine starting. How sad that Dalton and I hadn't clicked. Like Jase, and perhaps Matt, he was now part of the past. All of my dates seemed to end up there.

I laid my evening bag on the coffee table and turned off the lamp. Pepper dashed ahead of me up the stairs. I followed more slowly, holding on to the railing. Now that the evening was over, I felt exhausted. Freed from the necessity to be attentive and entertaining, I could take care of myself, and the first item on my agenda was sleep. Late hours were for schoolgirls like Aleta and Ginger.

Remember that when Dalton calls again. If he does.

He probably wouldn't, and that was all right.

Upstairs, I washed the makeup off my face. The last traces of glitter were silvery-green smudges on a white cloth. In the bedroom, I turned on the ceiling fan, slipped on a thin nightgown, and lay down on the bed, waiting for the room to cool off. I hoped I'd be asleep before it did.

Unlike a schoolgirl, my time was my own. My life had no schedule, no rules or restrictions. I could stay in bed all day tomorrow, if I so desired, turning day into night.

Just before drifting off to sleep, I remembered that I couldn't do that. I'd volunteered to bake four pies for the block party.

IN MY DREAM, I moved through a world of vibrant green. I was in a forest that seemed familiar, but nothing was as it had been or should be. My body was smaller and lighter, and the dog that padded along beside me was larger than Pepper. I didn't even know if it was my dog.

Trees towered above me, so high that I couldn't see the sky. I felt like a miniature figure in a storybook illustration, lost in a maze, trapped. The intense green frightened me. Something terrible was going to happen in this place, and I was afraid.

I had to find the way out before it was too late. So I kept moving, past hungry vines that reached out to grab me and roots that coiled around my feet. Then somewhere in the green expanse, I heard a loud splashing sound.

"Follow it," a voice said. "Only the water can save you now."

The splashing sound drew me out of the dream. I lay still in bed, coming slowly to awareness. The smell of rich woodland soil seemed to linger in the air. I could almost taste it.

What had spawned this nightmare? Thinking too much about

the woods behind my house? Most likely, that was the cause. But why did I still feel trapped? I took a deep breath and was relieved to find that it was possible.

The room was full of light. The ceiling fan hummed above my head, Pepper stirred in her sleep and whimpered and somewhere water fell on a concrete surface. The satyr fountain?

Maybe, but how could I hear it in my house? With a start, I saw the open window across the room. In my haste to go to bed, I'd forgotten to close it.

Hot air poured in, and bright sunshine, and…what else? The screen had a gaping tear. While I slept, anything from a bat to a robber could have entered my bedroom.

But I was okay. Even if someone had tried to break in, Pepper lay in the doorway. Most people wouldn't tangle with a dog. Nonetheless, leaving the window open was an invitation to disaster. As Dalton had said, "Don't tempt fate."

I didn't want to think about Dalton now or all those hours of merrymaking. I was still sleepy, and a dull pain throbbed above my eyes. The price of staying out so late was a headache. At the moment, I couldn't say that it was worth it.

A BLAST OF SUNSHINE engulfed me as I opened the front door. It was hot. That sweltering Texas-style heat that saps energy and sears skin had followed me up north to Maple Creek.

The Sunday paper lay beyond my reach, cradled in the scrollwork of an awning post. As I stepped out onto the porch, I spied Gwendolyn coming down the sidewalk with her block party pad in her hand. She turned at my walkway, a gliding pink cloud that grew brighter with each sprightly step. She'd changed her hair color to a glossy dark auburn.

"Good afternoon, Cressa. Good. You're up." Her cheery smile and her dress were too bright for the early hour.

Of course it wasn't early for everybody. Just for someone who'd gone to bed a few hours ago. "Good morning," I said.

"You're just the lady I need to see. Do you have a minute?" She handed me the *Tribune*. A yellow sun symbol grinned above the paper's ominous two-word headline: *Heat Wave*.

"Come in." I motioned her to the Queen Anne chair near the door. "Have a seat."

Pepper sauntered in from the kitchen and headed straight for Gwendolyn who held out her hand and eyed her with trepidation. "Does your dog bite?"

"She hasn't yet, but we haven't known each other very long. Pepper, stay." Pepper froze at my side, wagging her tail slowly. "Now sit," I added, gratified that she obeyed me.

Gwendolyn appeared to relax, but she gripped her pad as if it were a weapon. "I saw a beautiful old Cadillac in your driveway yesterday. That's a pretty impressive set of wheels. Doesn't Lieutenant Gray have a car like that?"

I nodded. "It's his car."

"What a treasure! How did you manage to snag a date with him?"

I hadn't realized that an evening spent in the company of a local police officer would make me famous—or infamous. Then, this was the illustrious Lieutenant Dalton Gray. "I didn't do anything special. He asked. I accepted."

"Are you going out with him now?"

I gave her a demure smile. "I did last night. What did you want to see me about?"

"Oh—that. You can take the hot dog buns over to the Smith place first thing in the morning. Cakes and pies go to the house at the end of the block with the double lot."

"People pick up their hamburgers or hot dogs in one place, then walk all the way to the end of the street for dessert?"

"That's right, and the coolers will be at the Rysling house, two doors down. We'll have homemade lemonade, pop and other drinks."

"That sounds cumbersome."

"It was my idea," she said. "This way, nobody congregates in any one spot. They'll circulate. It'll be safer."

Her tone was casual, but the last sentence caught my attention. "Why should we worry about safety?"

"Because of those robberies happening all around us. People get distracted."

"But if they keep their doors and windows locked…"

"You never know who's going to end up in your backyard. The parade on Main attracts lots of strangers to town. Your boyfriend is going to make a few unscheduled stops at the party."

"My boyfriend?"

"Your lieutenant. Are the pies ready to go?"

"I'm going to bake them today."

"Blueberry, right? Patti's pies are cherry, and I'm bringing homemade vanilla ice cream. We'll give everybody a piece of each with a scoop of ice cream in the middle. That's red, white and blue." The pride in her voice demanded a proper response.

"You *are* clever, Gwendolyn."

"It's just another one of my patriotic ideas." She put a pencil check after my name. "I'll let you get to your baking. Give me a call if you run into trouble."

A SEDATE Sunday silence lay over Beechnut Street. The sun burned on in a cloudless sky, sending powerful rays down through the thick leaf cover, and the air was still. Nothing moved except the water falling in the fountain and the high spray soaking Mr. Harrison's vegetable garden.

It was too hot to turn the oven on. Why not postpone baking until late this afternoon? In the meantime I could take a nap and hope that my second wakening would be better than the first.

I slept for two hours and woke up feeling like I usually did—well-rested and ready for a new day. When I came downstairs again, I saw Patti in her front yard adding blue plants to her red and white flowerbed. Patriotic spirit flourished on Beechnut Street. All I had to offer were my blueberry pies. My pies-to-be, that is.

I strolled across the street, quickly reviewing my questions. Soft piano music drifted out from the Graham house. I recognized "Ah! May The Red Rose Live Alway," Stephen Foster's lament about the death of the beautiful. That was one of Libby's favorites.

Swallowing the lump in my throat, I said, "I came to see what you're planting, Patti. These blue shades are incredible."

"Pansies have the prettiest little faces." She patted a mound of soil around a plant and stood up, holding her hand on her hip. "Speaking of pretty faces, what's it like to go out with Lieutenant Gray?"

"Very nice."

She gave me a sly smile. "That doesn't tell me anything."

"How's this, then? Dalton is generous, charming and a gentleman."

"And he has that classy convertible. What more could you want?"

I smiled. "Not a thing."

"Good luck with him," she said. "You'll need it. He changes girlfriends as often as Gwendolyn changes her hair color."

I didn't want to discuss Dalton with Patti or anybody else. "That must be Aleta playing," I said.

"She's just practicing, but doesn't it sound like angel music?"

"Hearing that song, you'd almost think Libby was still alive."

"You'll have to tell Aleta that. We found her a new teacher in Oxford. Then in the fall she'll be off to college."

"And the music will go away again."

"For a while," Patti said. "Let's move out of the sun, Cressa." She headed to the wide shadow cast by the porch and sat on the top step next to a flat of pansies. I joined her.

"I didn't mean to interrupt you," I said.

"I do everything slowly in the heat, drink lots of water and take frequent breaks. It's supposed to go up to ninety-two today. I think we're there already."

I touched a royal blue petal lightly. It was as soft as velvet, as rare and beautiful as Stephen Foster's song.

"It feels good to rest, and I've only been outside a half hour," Patti said.

"I've been meaning to talk to you about the girl who lived in my house a long time ago. The one who disappeared."

Patti brushed a speck of dirt from a purple pansy face. "Minta Bransford. You found her scrapbook in the basement just last month."

"Did you know her?"

"Ages ago. We were in the same class, but I'd forgotten all about her until you resurrected that old case."

"Did you two ever exchange autographs?" I asked.

She stared across the street at my house. "I may have. We used to have little books for collecting signatures and sayings from our friends. Why would you want to know something like that?"

"I came across a name, Patti, spelled with an *i,* in the scrapbook and wondered if it was you."

"It might be, but I doubt it," she said. "Honestly, I can't remember back that far."

The signature was hers. I felt certain of it by her ambiguous answer and sudden intense scrutiny of her pansy flat. But why did she feel the need to be evasive? All the autograph proved was that she knew Minta, a fact she'd already confirmed.

"I had the impression you'd moved to Maple Creek recently," I said.

"That's partly true. I bought my house last year," she said. "When I was growing up, my family lived on Willow Court."

"That's right around the corner."

"So it is, but I always loved this street. I used to ride my bike up and down and dream of living in one of these beautiful Victorians."

"Then you must have known Minta well," I said.

"During most of our high school years, yes. Toward the end, that changed."

"What happened?"

"With young girls, friendships are always shifting. Minta and I took different classes. She was going to college, I wasn't. She had a fantastic future ahead of her. I had to take business courses and go to work."

"Did you envy her?"

"I guess so, a little, but Minta was always so sweet to me. You couldn't help but like her. Anyway, that was a long time ago. I earned my degree at night school. But if I could have gone to college when I was seventeen, it would have made all the difference."

"Why is that?" I asked.

"I would have been the same age as the rest of the students. Maybe I'd have found a better husband or been able to study archaeology. My other dream was to travel to Egypt."

"It's never too late."

She sighed. "Yes it is. This is Aleta's time. My daughter is going to have everything I didn't. But I'm happy with my house. It needed work when I bought it, and I've been fixing it up a little bit at a time."

Aleta came to the end of her song and began another piece that I didn't immediately recognize. It was classical, by Debussy, maybe, eerie and evocative. Unlike the sweet Stephen Foster melody, it set my nerves on edge.

"Poor Minta," Patti said. "All those wonderful expectations and not a single one came true."

"Life can be arbitrary."

"It can be downright cruel." Patti picked up a pansy plant and held it carefully as if were a delicate bird's egg. Its petals were so deep and luminous that they might have been added on with a magic brush.

A small smile played around her lips. "Minta had her own garden in back of the house. Every summer she used to spend her allowance on seeds and scatter them in the ground. Whatever flowers she planted always came up. They were never more beautiful than that summer when she vanished."

TWENTY-ONE

THE SUN BURNED THROUGH my light cotton blouse as I walked down to the Venetia Smith house, carrying seven dozen hot dog rolls. I'd never seen the sedate street so lively and bright. Everything from landscaping to clothing sported a dash of red, white or blue, and flags flapped restlessly in a substantial breeze.

Once again, I suspected that I didn't quite fit in. My house didn't have a single decoration, and my blouse had pastel stripes. But my hair was red. Not everyone could say that.

A yellow beach ball sailed past my head and landed on a lush square of lawn. Startled, I stepped back, tightening my grip on the bakery box.

"Sorry, Ms. Hannett," Ginger said with a sheepish grin. "The wind made me do it."

Matt limped over to the ball and threw it back to her. "Watch that aim, young lady. You don't want to hurt anybody or rile Mrs. Alistair. She's fussy about her grass."

He turned to me with the warm smile I had thought I wouldn't see again. "Let me help you with that, Cressa."

"Thanks. It's a little awkward." I handed the box over to him. "Would you mind going with me to take my pies to the other end of the block? Together, we can do it in two trips."

"I'm your man," he said, falling into step alongside me. "What kind did you bake?"

"Blueberry."

"What a coincidence! That's my favorite."

I'd forgotten the small flag pin he wore but remembered the lights in his eyes and the curious feeling that we'd been friends in the distant past.

"What's there to do today besides eat?" I asked.

"Tennis, croquet and all sorts of games and contests. Or you can sit under an umbrella and socialize."

"I think I'll sit under an umbrella. It's too hot for anything physical."

"Not for the young or the young at heart. These block parties are a great way to bring people of all ages together. It used to be that you could live near a family for decades and never know their last name."

"Unless there's a tragedy," I said, remembering how we'd first met.

"Some folks don't come out of their houses even then. They're the loners. But there's a good showing today. I haven't seen this many kids in one place since last year."

We walked the rest of the way in silence, passing a rowdy game of hopscotch in the street and a pair of yapping dogs. As we approached the Smith house, Matt said, "It doesn't look haunted today."

That was an understatement. A swing hung from a low maple branch, and toys littered the grass. We followed the "Hot Dogs/Hamburgers—This Way" sign to the backyard where four little girls splashed in a swimming pool. Their clamor would send any self-respecting spirit back to the other world.

The only adult in the yard wore a flag-striped apron and a wide blue band in her hair. She was setting out condiments on a redwood picnic table already crammed with chips and relishes on ice-layered trays.

Matt handed her the box. "Morning, Julie. This is Cressa's contribution."

"They're hot dog buns," I said.

"Thanks so much." She set them next to a stack of bags and similar boxes. "Come back later, Cressa. I'll see that you have the best hot dog in town."

"I'll make one especially for you," Matt said.

"He's helping us on the grill," Julie added.

I had no doubt that Matt fit in and that he always would, wherever he lived.

On the way to the deliver pies, he stopped several times to greet people and exchange news. With me, he made small talk. Neighborhood chit chat. Hot weather observations. The home-owner most likely to win first prize for the most original decorations. We agreed that was Gwendolyn whose tall wood-cut Uncle Sam cast an imposing shadow in her yard.

Something was missing, though. A closeness, almost a spark, that had flickered between us from the beginning appeared to have died out. He had minded my turning down his dinner invitation. Of course…any man would. How could I convince Matt that my rejection wasn't personal, that I'd simply received a prior offer?

Give it time, I told myself. This was a good start.

As we unloaded the last two pies at Dessert Central, I wondered what to do now. I'd never been entirely comfortable at outdoor parties, and although most of my neighbors looked friendly, no one seemed particularly welcoming.

You needed a partner to play tennis, and my only knowledge of croquet came from reading *Alice in Wonderland.* As for games and contests, I'd wait and see what they were like. Anyway, the party was just beginning, and the block was long. I should be able to find at least one activity to interest me.

But it was so hot, already uncomfortable and growing more so with each passing hour. I rolled my sleeves up one more time and undid another button.

"Have fun, Cressa," Matt said, with a light touch on my shoulder, and he left me to flounder.

Where should I go? Under whose umbrella would I find a congenial group of revelers? Or even one person interested in making a new acquaintance?

I looked in vain for Patti and Gwendolyn who always seemed to make unannounced appearances. And where was Mr. Harrison? I was surrounded by strangers, my party contributions handed over, and my next step uncertain.

But this didn't have to be a problem. I'd go back to my house and get Pepper whose plaintive barking could be heard from half a block away. Anyone who owns a dog has perpetual company and a guaranteed ice-breaker. Then I'd move from group to group and keep smiling. After all, anyone who had been ready to explore the stars could manage a holiday celebration in a small Michigan town.

AFTER THE PARADE, the crowd tripled in size. The temperature reached ninety-five degrees, and the noise level soared. As the wind blew heat and dust around, competing for choice spots in the shade became an adult's game.

I wandered up and down the sun-scorched sidewalk, leading Pepper on a leash and enjoying the role of observer. Whenever I passed a gathering of young people, I looked for a girl with long dark hair, knowing that I'd recognize her even in denim shorts and a stars-and-stripes top.

But if she lived on Beechnut Street, she wasn't at the party.

On my third trip past a beige house with fancy gingerbread trim, a gray-haired woman sitting on a bench called out a greeting to me. Her sundress had gingham checks in two shades of pink, and she wore a straw hat trimmed with daisies.

"That poor dog is burning up in the sun," she said. "Come sit down for a spell."

"Thanks, I will," I said, noting that her yard was ninety-five percent shade. I chose a lawn chair facing the bench and told Pepper to lie down.

The woman offered Pepper her hand to sniff. "Would she like a drink?"

"She just had one." I showed her the empty bottle of Alpine Spring water.

"My name is Barbara," she said.

"I'm Cressa."

A bright sparkle appeared in her dark eyes. "Aren't you the woman who saw Minta Bransford's ghost?"

Oh, no. I took a deep breath. "It wasn't me. Where did you hear that?"

"Just around. It didn't surprise me since you're living in Minta's house."

Matt had been right about the downside of my neighborhood

inquiries. Edith Kruger must have twisted the elements of our conversation into a choice piece of fiction. I had to squelch it immediately.

"Something unusual happened the other day, but it has nothing to do with ghosts. A girl did some damage in my garden. She was as real as you are."

"That's funny. Generally, the children around here are well-behaved. You ought to tell her parents."

"I would, if I knew who they were."

She sighed. "So Minta didn't come back?"

"No. It's somebody's idea of a joke."

"Too bad. We could use a little excitement."

"Did you know her?" I asked.

"Not really. She was just one of the girls. There used to be droves of them, walking home from school and hanging out with their boyfriends. Then poof! They all grew up."

All except one.

"Did Minta have a boyfriend?" I asked.

"I suppose so. All the girls did."

"Because I don't recall any mention of one—in the old news articles."

"So you've been reading up on the Bransford Case?"

"After I found the scrapbook," I said. "As you know, I'm living in Minta's house."

Barbara nodded. "Of course, you'd be curious. That makes sense."

At my side, Pepper growled softly. I laid a steadying hand on her head and looked around. Nothing new or unusual had entered the immediate vicinity, nothing that I could see, that is. But Pepper's body was rigid, her head turned back toward our house.

"What's the matter, girl?" I asked.

"There must be too much excitement for her," Barbara said.

"I think I'll take her back home." Pepper sprang up and lunged forward, as if to agree that this was a good idea. "It was nice talking to you, Barbara."

She waved. "Stay cool, you two."

BY LATE AFTERNOON, the novelty of celebrating a summer holiday as a neighborhood began to fade. I'd sampled most of the activities and met a fair number of people. No one else asked me if I was the woman who had seen Minta Bransford's ghost.

Nevertheless, I longed for the street to return to its everyday still-and-silent state. Unfortunately, the party showed no signs of winding down. The day became a dizzying blur of heat, wind and noise.

The last vestiges of my holiday mood evaporated when I spied Matt deep in a private conversation with an elegant white-clad Annora May. They looked like old friends who had met by chance after a long separation. That was what they were to each other, according to Matt.

I still wondered why Annora had given me the impression that she hardly knew Matt. And how could she smile sweetly up at him after making that cruel remark about his limp? Incidentally, why had she come to our party, when she lived on Willow Court?

They didn't notice me.

Julie handed me a grilled hot dog on a paper plate. "Help yourself to the go-withs," Julie said. "Cressa?"

"Oh…" I tore my gaze away from Matt and Annora. Reacting like a jealous girlfriend when I was only a neighbor didn't become me. Still I said, "All these people can't possible live on this block."

"Well, no. Some of them brought guests. Others would go anywhere for free food. Luckily we have enough food to feed an army."

Annora must be here at Matt's invitation. I spared a rueful thought for the special hot dog he had promised me. Well this one looked delicious, far more appetizing than the fat free variety I usually cooked in the microwave.

At the condiment table, I squeezed a wavy line of mustard on it, took a root beer from the cooler, and, with a last surreptitious glance at Matt and Annora, headed back to my house to eat on the porch, once again pondering my next move.

What did I want to do now? Walk down to the opposite corner for dessert? Take Pepper out again? Nothing?

A strange malaise settled over me. Everything I'd looked forward to had fizzled. The date with Dalton. All right, but a dead end. Lunch with Annora. Pleasant, but I didn't want to see her again. Now this party—too loud, too long, too hot. And why couldn't young children play without screaming at one another?

My head began to ache, and my hair felt too heavy, lying on my shoulders like a woolen shawl. Somewhere to my right, several firecrackers exploded in rapid succession. Pepper wouldn't like the noise. I should never have left her alone.

As I neared the white Victorian, the sound of falling water insinuated itself into the general uproar. How glorious it would feel to step over the stony rim into the concrete basin and let the water wash away the dust and heat and, most of all, the depression that had appeared out of nowhere.

If I did that, I could keep my eyes closed and never see the satyr's gloating face above me or his beckoning hand with its talon fingers. There would be only cool, pure water splashing down in never-ending streams. The fountain's lure was practically irresistible.

Abruptly I shook my head and revised the fantasy. What I really wanted was to lay a cold washcloth on my face and get my hair off my neck. Then, maybe, after I ate, I'd feel like rejoining the party.

Taking a shortcut across Libby's lawn, I reached my porch at last. I set the plate and bottle down and fumbled in my pocket for my key. From inside the house, Pepper barked, short high-pitched yelps with a hint of a howl in them.

All around me, the water seemed to roar, louder than the exploding firecrackers or any child screaming in the street. All I wanted now was to get away from it.

TWENTY MINUTES LATER, I gave Pepper the last bite of hot dog and finished my drink slowly, savoring every ice chip. The constant splashing had become soothing background music, and the noise in the street was almost tolerable. No one screamed, no one shouted, and I hadn't heard a firecracker in a while. I felt calmer and more comfortable, even ready for dessert.

In my bedroom, I arranged my hair in a ponytail and changed the striped shirt for a sleeveless blue tank top.

"This is the new you, Cressa," I told myself. "Cool, crisp, confident. On with the dance."

But my head still ached. Aspirin hadn't touched it yet. I needed something stronger.

Pepper streaked past me and ran to the French doors. She raked her nails along the glass, whining frantically, glancing anxiously back at me.

"What now?" I said. "You can't go outside that way."

I walked over to her, and, on an impulse, stepped out on the balcony and looked across the long blocks of sun and shade below.

A dog lay on the skeleton's grave. From here it looked like Pepper, only larger, with a coat the color of autumn leaves. A collie or collie mix, stretched out on its side, it appeared to be sleeping.

Here was the source of Pepper's agitation—a fellow canine who had found a shady respite from the firecrackers on her territory. There was nothing unusual about that, but...

Fear spun an icy web around me as I moved closer to the railing, squinting into the glaring sunshine. On the hottest day of the season, I felt cold. This was no ordinary dog.

Then what is it? And how do you know?

I hurried out of the room and down the stairs, moving faster than I had all day, knowing that I couldn't possibly move fast enough.

I was right. By the time I reached the yard, nothing lay on the grave except the stones I'd placed there, the drooping phlox and fresh new mallow plants about to burst into bloom.

TWENTY-TWO

THE MALLOWS WERE as straight and tall as they'd been yesterday. In the intense heat, their pink bell-shaped petals seemed to unfold even as I stared at them.

But this couldn't be. If a large animal had lain on the grave, at least some the plants would be crushed. I knelt down and ran my hand over the wild grasses that grew between the stones. They felt warm—from the sun. But not a single blade was bent or mashed down.

"What are you looking at, Cressa?" Mr. Harrison sauntered over to join me. He'd been gathering strawberries. Red juice stained his fingers and flag-striped bandana.

"My beautiful mallows," I said.

"You're going to have a real show in a day or two. I wish they were growing in my garden." He tipped two small perfectly formed berries out of his pail. "Taste these little gems, fresh from the vine."

I did. "They're so sweet. Like candy."

"And you don't need any sugar with them. I'll pick more tomorrow, enough for a pie."

"Thanks. I'll bake one and give you half," I said. "Did you see a brown collie in my yard a few minutes ago?"

"No, but there are all kinds of dogs roaming around today."

"It must belong to someone in the neighborhood, then." I looked away from the undisturbed grave. "Didn't you go to the party?"

"For a while, this morning. It's too hot now. How about you?"

"I'm taking a break from the commotion."

"That's a good idea." He paused, then said in a voice newly charged with energy, "If your young man isn't going to escort you to the fireworks, I'll be happy to walk over to the park with you."

"Thank you." I reined in my surprise. Previously, Mr. Harrison had only greeted me in passing. Now an invitation? "I think I'll just watch them from my balcony."

"Whatever you like. Don't stay out in the sun too long." He tipped his straw hat. "Or get yourself some proper head gear."

He went back to his berry picking, and I glanced down at the grave, wishing I could escape the thoughts careening through my mind. The canine skeleton…Minta's collie…the nighttime barking that I'd attributed to a soldier's abandoned pet. Most of all, my own dog's odd behavior.

Pepper had followed me downstairs but not outside. She waited quietly for me on the porch now, her paws resting on the wraparound ledge. She liked to stay at my side whenever she could, except when I strayed into unknown territory.

I pushed my hair behind my ears and headed back to the house. There was no need to gravitate toward supernatural explanations. Still they came. Suppose the spirit of the long dead dog had come out of the grave? What if Minta had sent her into my garden for some unfathomable purpose?

Then something terrible might be on its way. With that doomsday observation, my rational side tried to take over. There was a simple explanation for this apparent manifestation, one I hadn't found yet. For instance, the collie might have been lying in front of the grave rather than on it.

Something else bothered me. When the long-haired girl had shredded the flowers, I'd found them strewn on the ground, evidence of her presence. This dog had come and gone like a shadow. Shouldn't supernatural phenomena be consistent? Also, when the girl first appeared, her hair hadn't moved; the second time, it had blown around her face in the wind.

So what was going on in this place of strange happenings?

Nothing now, as far as I could tell. Except for Mr. Harrison, I was alone. The fountain water sang its never-ending song, the satyr broiled in the sun, and the white Victorian basked in somber silence, its gables casting dark shadows on the grass.

If Libby were still alive, she would have brought out her flag and her banana bread and hung balloons in the trees. The old house would be humming with life, and I would have had a friend to talk to.

I looked up at the kitchen window, and Kady's face appeared behind the glass. She waved to me, and moments later, came out into the yard.

"I didn't know about the block party," she said. "I had to leave my car on Main and walk."

"Are you moving in?"

"Not until late next week. I came over to get ready for my estate sale."

Here was someone else to ask. "Did you happen to notice a collie in my yard, back there toward the woods?"

"Sorry, no. I've been in the basement."

Kady walked over to the fountain and sat on the rocky rim, trailing her hand through the water. I joined her but stayed a good distance from the satyr.

"Don't you just adore this fountain?" she asked.

"Well, it does make the air seem cooler. Are you selling the antiques?"

"Only retired furniture and some small stuff. Aunt Libby was a collector whose collection was out of control. We'd planned to have a yard sale this summer."

"I'd like to buy a small memento," I said. "Maybe something with a musical motif."

"If you like, you can look at everything before I set it out." She splashed water on her arms and neck, oblivious of the drops splashing on her cotton candy top. "You're at home during the day, aren't you?"

"For now."

"Have you ever seen anyone hanging around my house?"

"No one lately."

"Somebody has been using my porch. They left crumbs all over and a sticky spill. I think it's wine."

Kady had moved the furniture inside, leaving no place to sit or lie down, not even a throw rug on the floor. Still, the small enclosed space must be tempting to a person who had no other shelter.

"Maybe a vagrant stopped by to get out of the rain," I said. "Don't you keep it locked?"

"The latch on the screen door doesn't hold. I'm worried that somebody may have gotten inside the house. Every now and then, it seems that a lamp or picture is in a different place."

"Didn't you have new locks installed?"

"Yes, but a determined burglar can find a way in. Maybe it's just my imagination in overdrive." She splashed the fountain water higher up her arms. "Do you think the town elders would give me something to eat?"

"I'm sure they will. Why don't you get a hot dog and walk with me down to the corner for a piece of pie?"

"Just give me a minute to lock up," she said. "You do the same."

GWENDOLYN, SUNBURNED, DROOPING, and all in yellow, presided over a picnic table guarding the last cherry pie. There was no sign of her homemade ice cream.

"You girls are just in time," she said. "I'm going to close up shop any minute and go home to my AC."

"What happened to your red, white and blue desserts?" I asked.

"All we have left is red. The ice cream kept melting before I could scoop it out, and your pies were the first to go. I've been singing their praises to all the men. What's your secret?"

"Just blueberries," I said. "Sugar, cinnamon, and lemon. The cookbook's recipe."

"But what's your special ingredient that makes them so marvelous?"

"I bought the berries at a farm up north," I added.

"Ah! Much better than store-bought." She transferred two pieces of cherry pie to paper plates. "That gypsy is prowling around, loading up on hot dogs like they were going out of style."

"What gypsy?" Kady asked.

"A homeless person named Ruby," I said.

"She turns up wherever there's free food," Gwendolyn added. "Except we all had to pay for this spread."

"There'll probably be some leftovers," I said.

"Not with this hungry crowd." She cut the rest of the pie in small wedges and set each one on a paper plate. "Patti's proud of her baking. She won't be happy to know that people liked yours better."

"Have you seen a brown collie running free?" I asked. "I'm looking for it."

"Nope. Just a few black dogs. I'll wash your plates and drop them off tomorrow, Cressa."

"Anytime is fine." I picked up a plastic fork and broke off a small piece of pie. The filling was a little too sweet, but the crust was good.

"Why are you looking for a collie?" Kady asked, as we walked back home.

"I was so sure I saw one lying in my flowerbed, but then he disappeared."

"Dogs move pretty fast."

"Like light in motion," I said.

THE REST OF THE AFTERNOON passed in a noisy haze. Kady went back to the white Victorian. I sat on the front porch and tried not to think about the dog on the grave. At last, the partygoers began to disperse, and the firecracker blasts moved farther away.

Toward the end of the day, I caught a glimpse of Ruby carrying a plate heaped with food. In her long blue dress and wide straw hat, she blended into the crowd. No one appeared to pay the slightest attention to her as she entered a shaded area between two quiet houses and vanished from sight.

Shortly afterward, a uniformed Dalton made his appearance, hot dog in one hand, pop can in another. Moments later, I watched Gwendolyn swoop down on him like a bird of prey and practically drag him down the street toward her house. No doubt she'd eventually broadcast her reason for abducting the law. I hoped she wasn't setting him on Ruby's trail.

I didn't see Matt or Annora and realized that it didn't matter. Let them keep their secrets. I had my own.

When dark finally came, I relaxed on the balcony with a glass of iced tea and watched the firecrackers explode in the clear sky. Brilliant moonlight swept over the yard, and the stars burned with an unusual intensity. If the mystery dog came slinking out of the night, I'd be able to see him.

And if I didn't, Pepper lay at my feet with her head on her paws. I'd read somewhere that canines could detect the presence of otherworldly beings, whether they walked on two legs or four. Perhaps she had already done so by growling when we stopped to talk to Barbara.

I turned my glass around, clinking the ice cubes, waiting for the fireworks show to end. Even with the noise in the distance, it was easy to think up here.

The time had come to set reason and logic aside. No ordinary stray had curled up in my mallow bed for a mid-day nap. No living girl had torn the petals off my flowers.

Just accept the fact that ghosts can walk the earth. Then move on.

This ongoing game of alternately rejecting and accepting the possibility of supernatural entities had kept me at a standstill. Now, could I move on and trace the strangeness on Beechnut Street back to its beginning?

It had started on the night of Libby's death. Before the recital, I'd focused on lining up job interviews and the porch renovation. Nothing untoward shadowed those early spring days except my frame of mind. My heart was still on the Texas Gulf Coast, and I'd begun to doubt that coming home to Maple Creek had been the best decision for me.

It wasn't. I could have stayed in Texas and found another engineering job and eventually another love interest. Instead, I'd tried to recreate my past and in the process landed in the middle of a mystery with enough strands to choke me.

If I allowed that to happen.
I wouldn't.

Every question had an answer. Every problem could be solved. Drifting could be deadly. I drank the last tea in the glass and felt unaccountably energized.

The firecrackers were still booming when I went inside. The long day was over, but tomorrow, I intended to make a list of every inexplicable event that had occurred since Libby's drowning and investigate each one.

And if this investigation led me into the other world, so be it. I'd been there before.

TWENTY-THREE

IN THE LIGHT AND CLARITY of a new day, I sat at a table in the Blue Lion's outside area creating my mystery list. The satyr statue's power to evoke strong feelings…the cloaked and hooded figure who had shambled through Libby's garden on the night of her death…the missing balloons…

I poured the rest of the tea and broke my croissant in two. The whereabouts of those balloons still baffled me. A few days after Libby's death, one of them had turned up in the fountain. Another lay hidden in my shrubbery. What had happened to the rest? I assumed that the police had stopped looking for them.

I moved on, adding every strange happening that I could remember from piano music in an unoccupied house to the collie on the skeleton's grave. Many of them involved dogs.

Last night I'd been awakened from a restless sleep by a faraway barking that turned into a howl. It seemed to originate in the woods. I turned on the lamp, saw that it was almost midnight, and lay still, listening and wondering. Pepper slept under the window in a wide beam of moonlight, debunking my theory about canine supernatural detectors.

So had I heard a lonely, lost creature broadcasting a lament to the world or a spirit? *The ghost of Minta's collie who lay on her grave without leaving an impression in the mallows?*

As my mind traveled back to my first glimpse of the bones with their eerie green glow, I added the last phrase, "unknown night barker."

Before long, writing filled every line on the page. Setting the items down on paper helped me to see something that should have been clear from the start. They fell neatly into two categories: "Murder" and "Haunting."

Could there be a connection between the two, with the murder as the catalyst? Possibly, but why would Libby's death have brought Minta Bransford back from the grave? That didn't make sense.

But perhaps this did. The skeleton and the scrapbook might have remained hidden for decades if I hadn't commissioned the porch renovation and cleaned the basement. Could these seemingly insignificant acts have set the haunting into motion?

Glancing over the list again, I saw too many odd occurrences attributed to my long-suffering imagination. Suppose something else was going on, a force that threatened my own life or mental well-being?

I took a sip of tea, only to find that it had cooled off. The croissant was gone, and I was still hungry. An order of French toast or pancakes would help me think. In the meantime, what should I do first?

Learn more about Minta Bransford by reading through the old Tribune file again. Then arrange separate encounters with Edith Kruger, Barbara and Patti. Especially Patti. If the scrapbook autograph was hers and she knew more about Minta than she claimed, she might slip and reveal some pertinent information.

Well, I could hope.

None of Minta's contemporaries had said much about her. They'd offered variations on the same theme: *Minta Bransford was a nice girl with a bright future. One summer afternoon she vanished—simply walked off the face of the earth. That's all we know.*

It was as if I'd crashed head on into a decades-long conspiracy of silence. That didn't make sense, either.

"Good morning, Cressa. Mind if I join you?"

Matt leaned over the railing that separated the tables from the sidewalk traffic. The sleeves of his deep blue shirt were rolled up, and his top button was undone, revealing a glimpse of tanned chest. The sunlight gave his flag pin a shine, and, with the bright glints in his blue-green eyes, he looked handsomer than usual.

"Please do." I smiled up at him as I folded the sheet of note paper. By the time he reached the table, I'd slipped it into my purse. "I'm working on my "To Do" list."

"Do you have a busy week lined up?" he asked.

"Just a few job interviews and garden chores."

He sat down, perused the card with the morning's breakfast choices, and set it back in the holder. "It's going to be another hot one."

"Yes, but I love being able to eat outside in the fresh air."

A young woman in a peach and white uniform moved unobtrusively from table to table, pouring coffee. "Belgian waffles this morning, Mr. Emmerton?" she asked.

"Please…with a large orange juice."

"Make that two orders, and more tea when you have a chance," I said. After she left, I added, "Are you taking the day off?"

"I'm going in late. Did you have fun at the block party?"

"Pretty much. I missed the special hot dog you promised me, though."

"That was poor planning." His warm, winsome smile couldn't quite erase the image of Annora May. But I had decided that their relationship didn't matter to me, and this morning Annora was nowhere in sight.

"I owe you one," he said. "That sure was a good blueberry pie you made. A blue ribbon winner in my book."

"Gwendolyn thinks it had a magic ingredient."

"So do I." He winked at me. "On another note, did you hear about the burglaries yesterday?"

I looked at him in surprise. So that was why Gwendolyn had dragged Dalton down the street. But she'd cautioned me about strangers in town and the possibility of robbery during the block party. Hadn't she heeded her own warning?

"The thieves hit five houses on Beechnut this time," Matt said. "They stole small portable items. Gwendolyn White lost an heirloom sugar bowl and her silver teaspoon collection."

"I wonder why she didn't lock her doors."

"She did but forgot to close one window."

"Oh, no…I left mine open, too, on the second story. That's my bedroom."

"You'd better check to see if you're missing anything."

"I think they passed me by. Pepper was inside most of the day, and Kady was working next door. I went back home for a while and didn't see anyone, but…" I trailed off, remembering Pepper's growling and her uncharacteristic restlessness. Had she been alerting me to an intruder in the house instead of reacting to fire-crackers outside?

I touched my diamond pendant, grateful that I always wore it, even to outside activities. Perhaps I was worrying about all the wrong things. I owned several portable heirlooms of my own and couldn't swear that they were still in their proper places. If I didn't want to stay at the Blue Lion, have more breakfast and talk to Matt, I'd be on my way home now to take an inventory.

"Is something troubling you, Cressa?" Matt asked.

Without stopping to think, I said, "Setting the thefts aside for a moment, I saw a brown collie in my backyard yesterday. Then all of a sudden it wasn't there."

"Another stray?"

"I'm not sure what it was."

As I filled in the details, I couldn't help thinking how strange my story sounded, how—ghostly. "What do you think?" I asked.

"Could you have seen something else, like a shadow?"

"Well…with the haze and the deep lot, I might have been a little off on the location, but the dog was there. I'm sure of it."

He said, "I saw a collie with reddish brown fur and white markings running free yesterday."

"You're a kind man, Matt. And here I thought I was halluci-nating."

"We can make sure the bones are still in the ground—if it's going to bother you."

Disturb the skeleton dog's resting place again? I didn't want to do that. Because I didn't want to find out that it was empty?

Of course the bones were still there, wrapped in a sheet, with stones placed on the ground to ward off scavengers, everything just as I'd left it.

"Thanks for the offer," I said. "But you saw a collie, too, and I could be mistaken about where the dog was lying. Let's leave the matter there."

"You're thinking of Minta Bransford's Sunny." He paused, then asked, "Did that girl ever come back?"

"No, but I'm always waiting for something weird to happen. I want my life to go back to the way it used to be."

"Don't we all?" He pulled out his pocket planner. "I'm going to call Minta's cousin today and set up a meeting for us. When are your interviews?"

"Wednesday and Thursday."

"We'll aim for tomorrow or Friday, then."

At that moment, our waitress appeared with waffles, juice, three kinds of syrup and a fresh pot of tea. Matt handed me the pitcher tray. "Blueberry, raspberry, or maple," he said. "This is the right way to start a day."

BACK HOME, I walked slowly through every room, taking a silent inventory. Kady had noticed that occasionally one of her pictures or lamps appeared to have been moved. In my house, everything was where it belonged. Nonetheless, I checked the contents of my jewelry case and the envelope of emergency money hidden in the dresser drawer.

All of my valuable possessions were accounted for, but I couldn't afford to be so careless again. I locked my bedroom window and glanced down at the yard below. There, too, everything was as it should be. The blooming mallows formed a wavy pink line on the grave and along the woods' edge, but no long haired girl reached for them with greedy hands. The only dog outside was Pepper, lying close to the porch.

Taking the Bransford file from the top of my nightstand, I stepped out on the balcony and dropped into the chair. From here I could see Mr. Harrison working in his garden, tossing weeds into a grocery store box. With Kady away again, the white Victorian had reverted to its accustomed somber, still state.

No shadowy visitors or otherworldly goings-on disturbed my little corner of Maple Creek today. Anyone who chanced upon the "Haunted" column in my list would think I was delusional. On a clear, sunny, quiet day like this, I could almost believe that nothing unusual had ever happened to me at 714 Beechnut Street.

I opened the folder and began reading, hoping to find a clue embedded in the yellowing clippings, some slender thread to tie the old disappearance to the girl who had targeted my garden for her flower shredding frenzy. Something I'd missed.

But the articles proved to be a disappointment. Apparently I'd garnered all the relevant information in my first examination of the Bransford papers. The facts repeated the comments of the people who had known Minta.

Unless I could find another written source, I'd have to rely on the recollections of those whom Minta Bransford had left behind.

THE ORDINARY DAY continued, minutes and hours passing by with no untoward occurrences to disrupt their onward flow. None of the women I wanted to see were home. Mr. Harrison gave me two quarts of strawberries and several lavish compliments on my pie-baking skills. A white convertible came to a stop in front of the Graham house. Aleta and Linda got out and stood on the sidewalk, holding tennis rackets and talking to the two young men who remained inside.

All of the girls had boyfriends... Just before her disappearance, Minta might have lingered on Beechnut Street with a young Annora or Patti, gossiping about end-of-school parties or a weekend date, never knowing that her happy plans were never going to materialize.

At four o'clock Matt called to tell me that Minta's cousin, Allyson Camden, had agreed to meet us tomorrow for lunch at the Spearmint Lake Inn. I baked two strawberry pies, gave one to Mr. Harrison, and took Pepper for a walk to the park where I ate a solitary picnic lunch. This was the way small town life should be: serene, sun-drenched and slightly boring.

A sense of well-being settled around me. In all aspects of my life, I was headed in the right direction, and sooner or later, I'd find the answers that had so far eluded me. The ordinary day turned into a quiet night, undisturbed by a dog mourning for her people.

The next morning I opened the buffet drawer and reached

under the tablecloths for the scrapbook. It was gone! The thieves hadn't spared me after all. I ran my fingers through a drift of glitter on a blue lace topper, wishing I'd remembered to close my window. If this had happened during the block party. I'd left my window open more than once and couldn't be sure of the timeline.

Yesterday's robbers had scooped up small articles like sugar bowls, silverware, antique clocks, and jewelry, items that were easy to carry and dispose of. Who would steal a homemade scrapbook filled with schoolgirl writings and mementoes of old dreams?

Several people: Annora, who had hinted that she'd like to have it back? Patti, who might have forgotten that once she'd autographed the book and wanted to destroy the evidence? Matt? Except I couldn't imagine why he'd take it. Or someone else, anybody who had read Matt's story in the *Tribune*. Maybe the same person who had taken the vintage photographs earlier?

I'd almost forgotten about them, hadn't even included them on my list. With this latest development, they took on a new significance. Possibly the scrapbook posed a threat to someone. In any event, now I had another mystery.

Quickly I searched the rest of the buffet, then took one more inventory of my possessions. An hour later, I knew for certain that my only missing object was Minta's scrapbook.

And it wasn't really mine, I thought.

Technically it belonged to Annora, but she had no right to invade my home and rummage through my belongings.

Of course I only suspected that Annora was the thief.

I couldn't accuse her without proof. I couldn't accuse her at all. She'd just deny it.

Disheartened, I went upstairs to dress for lunch with Matt and Allyson. I wouldn't be able to show the scrapbook to Allyson now. More importantly, I might have lost an important clue to the Minta mystery. But these matters paled alongside the real issue. Somebody must be desperate to keep a secret hidden. Once again, I was caught in the middle of a strange affair without knowing why.

TWENTY-FOUR

THE DRIVE TO Spearmint Lake soon took on the air of an excursion, not quite a date but close. It was riding in the convertible, I decided, and the fresh air blowing through my hair, or perhaps this shortcut with its new scenery. Matt navigated the winding road through a light haze while I soaked in the morning's beauty.

Tiger lilies and blue wildflowers sparkled in tall grasses at the wooded verges of the road. As we passed ponds and streams, I watched for a body of water large enough to be considered a lake and wished that Matt would drive a little slower. A day like this wasn't made for the fast track.

"Maybe it's a good thing the scrapbook was stolen," he said.

"Why do you say that?"

"Now we know for certain that something suspicious is going on. Did you notify the police?"

"Yes, but Lieutenant Gray didn't seem impressed. My loss isn't in the same league as family silverware."

"That's a short-sighted view. When we find out who took it and why, we may have a few answers."

Matt was thinking of us as a mystery solving team again. For leisure moments, he preferred cool, polished blondes. This lunch engagement in another town was a combination of pleasure and work. I intended to make good use of every minute we had together.

"Someone besides us is interested in Minta Bransford," I said. "Or, more likely, in the scrapbook's contents. I wish I'd had a chance to look through it again."

"Consider it spilt milk. We may find out something at lunch. Mrs. Camden thinks I'm writing a follow-up story on Minta."

"Are you?"

"As soon as we have more information. I hope her recollections will give me a new way to twist it."

He made a left turn onto a quiet, woodsy trail that rose gently up into a thickening mist. We were traveling through woods fringed with balsam firs that would make good barrier between my yard and the Maywood acres. A natural fence to discourage intruders.

"I hate that somebody was in my home, touching my table-cloths," I said. "I'm going to wash them in hot soapy water tonight."

"Be glad you didn't cross paths with the thief."

"My trusty guard dog was there," I said.

"You don't know what happened. Maybe she bit him or drove him off."

"With my property in his hands."

"Did you mention the theft to Annora?" he asked.

"I don't see her very often." I kept my voice neutral and my suspicions to myself.

"Since she put the scrapbook together, she might be able to point us in the right direction," he said.

Not if she was the one who took it, I thought.

"I'll ask her, but she said she couldn't remember what was on those missing pictures."

"A clue, I'll bet."

"It's too bad that I can't show it to Mrs. Camden," I added.

"We'll have to settle for telling her about it. Look, here's the water."

He pointed to an immense shimmer of pale blue, an enchanted mirror of a lake beneath floating white clouds. Pastel cottages rimmed its eastern edge, and sailboats skimmed the waves. Dark woods framed the farthermost shore, but, to the south, sunbathers on bright blankets crowded the beach, giving a carnival atmosphere to the scene.

Suddenly I longed to run across the sand and dive into the water. To be cool and free. I hadn't gone swimming once this summer, and here we were in July—and here I was in an aqua silk dress with chandelier earrings.

I'll come back another day, I promised myself, *when I don't have an agenda.*

"There's the Inn." Matt slowed down and pulled off the road. "That big white house with the picket fence."

A palatial Victorian, the Spearmint Lake Inn sat in the middle of a sloping green lawn. Old English roses lined the winding walkway, and weeping willows shaded a small black-tarred square. If it weren't for the half dozen cars parked near the entrance, I'd think that we had stopped at a gracious country residence.

"We're right on time." Matt came around to the passenger side and opened the door. "Let's take this show on the road, shall we?"

THE WAITER LED US to a secluded corner table where a petite woman waited for us. Her grayish-brown hair and light summer tan gave her a winsome youthful look. Ropes of pearls lay against the floral bodice of her dress, and three pearl rings adorned her hands.

Pearls for tears, I thought. Mrs. Camden is weighted down in grief.

But her happy face belied that initial impression. She bore a slight resemblance to Minta in the school picture, most apparent in the shape of her eyes.

"Good afternoon, Mrs. Camden." Matt held a chair for me and sat down. "This is my neighbor, Cressa Hannett."

Her bright smile included both of us. "I'm a long-time fan of yours, Mr. Emmerton. We have breakfast together every morning."

Matt grasped her hand. "That's nice to know."

"While I read the *Tribune,* that is. Call me Allyson. I sent you a letter after you wrote those lovely articles about my cousin. You were kind enough to print it."

"We had a tremendous reader response," Matt said. "Lots of people are still captivated by the story."

She glanced at me. "Didn't you bring the scrapbook with you, Ms. Hannett?"

"It's Cressa. No, I'm afraid it's gone."

"We've been having a rash of robberies in Maple Creek," Matt said. "It was stolen from Cressa's house."

"But who would do that?" She looked from me to Matt, her smile fading. "I was so looking forward to seeing it."

"I wish I knew," I said.

After the waiter took our order for soup and club sandwiches, I gave her a description of the pages: a short story that I hadn't read, scenic snapshots, autographs, scraps of fabric and love poems. "Think of a schoolgirl's collage. Maple Creek in the seventies."

"Your robber wanted a made-to-order collection of nostalgia without doing any of the work," Allyson said.

"I'm wondering why he bypassed money and jewelry for scraps of another person's life."

"You have a mystery on your hands, my dear," Allyson said. "Minta didn't know how she'd ever wait all those years to open her scrapbook. As it turned out, she didn't have to."

"We were hoping you could tell us about the days leading up to Minta's disappearance," Matt said. "What she was doing, her frame of mind…"

"That was a busy and exciting time. I was only a junior, but I got swept up in all the graduation fun. Minta and I were like sisters, very close."

"Who were her special friends?" I asked.

"Annora May, Elizabeth Dorset and some of the others who lived on the street. They'd all grown up together and gone to the same school."

"Did Minta have a boyfriend?"

"No one steady, but she had a few dates. All the girls were crazy about a cute cop who'd just joined the Maple Creek Police Department. His name was Dan Byron, and he was so good looking—tall and blond with a rascally twinkle in his eyes. Aunt Marjorie called him a dangerous man."

"That's the best kind," I said.

Matt cast me a quick, inquisitive look that Allyson didn't notice. "Dan Byron was too old for them by about ten years, but Minta thought that age didn't matter. After all, she was a senior."

Allyson moved her water glass forward and turned it around

and around on the table. It was almost a nervous gesture, but not quite. "I ran into Dan a few years back. He's not the town dreamboat anymore. Far from it."

"So he's still alive," I said.

"I assume so." Her smile was wry, her voice teasing. "Some of us are still going strong, no matter what you young people may think. He moved somewhere up north."

I added Officer Dan Byron to a new page on my mental list of people to talk to. To try to contact, I amended. Up north was vague and possibly hundreds of miles away.

"Did Minta have any plans for the summer?" Matt asked.

"Our families were going to take a trip to Mackinac Island. Then when Minta vanished, we didn't go. It took me a long time to realize that she wasn't coming back. Not for good anyway."

"You sound like it was her choice," I said.

"In time, I came to believe it was. That fall, sometime in September, I saw her walking with Sunny in the park. She was on that path that runs under the railroad tracks, close enough to hear me—if she wanted to. I called out to her to wait, but she just kept on walking."

Matt leaned forward. His eyes and his tone were sharp. "Are you sure it was Minta?"

"Oh, yes. She was wearing a green dress with long back ties that she made in Sewing. It was one of a kind. I recognized Sunny, too, and Minta's long hair. There was no mistake."

"What did you do?" he asked.

"Took off after her. In those days, I could run. By the time I reached the street where the park ends, she was gone. Again."

"Could she have stopped at one of the houses near Wyndemere?" I asked.

"I doubt it. We didn't know anyone who lived there. The logical route for her to take was through the school grounds. I rushed home to tell everybody that I'd seen Minta. Aunt Marjorie was the only one who believed me."

"You said the dog was with her?"

"Yes—on a leash. That collie didn't notice me, either, and she knew me from the time she was a pup."

"That's unusual behavior for a dog," I said.

"I thought so. The police brought Sunny home a few days after my uncle reported Minta missing, but she kept running away. I don't remember what finally happened to her. I guess she found Minta at last."

Matt sat silently, apparently mulling over the new information. "So you think that Minta staged her disappearance."

"At first, but not anymore."

"What changed your mind?"

"It happened again. When I saw her in the park the second time, I knew what was going on. She had Sunny with her, and, just like before, they kept walking away from me. She never even turned around. I couldn't run fast enough to catch her, but I *did* try."

"How do you know you weren't mistaken this time?" Matt asked.

"She was wearing the same dress."

Unbidden, my grandmother's story of her cousin's experience with the other world came rushing back to me, along with the fear.

A woman walking down on a snowy lane, ignoring pleas from her kin to come back. My grandmother's voice saying, "If you see a ghost, that means you'll die soon."

"When did this second sighting happen?" I asked.

"Four years ago."

"My—goodness."

"The girl you saw couldn't possibly have been Minta," Matt said.

"Only her imprint or spirit or whatever you want to call it."

"Her ghost," said Matt.

"When you write your story, Mr. Emmerton, you can say that Minta Bransford never left Maple Creek. Maybe you and Cressa can find her."

OVER CLUB SANDWICHES and banana cream pie, Allyson regaled us with memories of Minta: elaborate homework projects, school dances, holiday parties and dozens of lost or wounded creatures, all lovingly tended.

"She always loved animals," Allyson said. "Dogs especially."

A widow whose four grown children lived in different states, Allyson was obviously lonely and loved to talk about the past. I had a feeling that she hadn't done so in a long time. But her most important revelation was the existence of Officer Dan Byron, that devilish blond policeman who had livened up summer of 1975 for the girls on Beechnut Street.

I thought about him on the drive home. Minta's friends had shared their remembrances of her and speculated on her fate, but the early reporters never mentioned an officer of the Maple Creek Police Department.

Perhaps, like Jase Clayborne, he had been a brilliant shooting star in her life, a man to light up the night and quickly burn out. A man who might say, if questioned about Minta Bransford today, "Yeah—I knew her way back when. She had a crush on me. All the girls did. Those were the days!"

Or he simply hadn't wanted to get involved.

Matt slowed down for a curve, and we began an ascent on a road heavily shaded with oak trees. This was a different, darker route with fewer wildflowers and no houses.

"That cute blond cop should be our next project," I said.

"He'll be easy to find. Officer Byron, Maple Creek Police Department, circa 1975. Around twenty-seven years old at the time of Minta Bransford's disappearance. Living somewhere up north."

I smiled as I recalled Allyson's description, picturing white hair, a lined face and a stooping form. "And far from the town dreamboat."

"Over time people grow old and decrepit," Matt said. "Only a ghost stays the same."

Yes. The supernatural aspect of the case. This was the first time we'd mentioned it since Allyson's startling revelation.

"I can understand why Minta would appear to Allyson," I said. "My only connection to her is the house I live in."

"Maybe that's the answer," Matt said.

"What I don't understand is the timing. Allyson saw Minta in the fall of 1975, then again four years ago. Last month she wandered into my yard. Why?"

"There are no set rules," Matt said. "But I don't think ghost time is the same as real world time."

"Still there has to be a reason."

"We'll find it. I promise you, Cressa."

I relaxed, believing for the first time that there might be an awakening from this nightmare, perhaps even a happily-ever-after ending.

"Right now, I'm going to focus on the actual disappearance," I said. "Do you suppose romantic rivalry was at the bottom of the affair?"

"With girls that young?"

"Especially at that age. Don't you remember when you were seventeen?"

He laughed. "That's ancient history."

"Well, I do. Anything was possible. You took chances you'd never take today, and nothing mattered except your emotions. Joys were sharper, sorrows cut deeper and all of your senses were heightened."

I skidded to a stop. Where had these ideas come from? Not my life.

"Your past must have been fun to live through," Matt said. "Are you saying that only the young feel that way?"

"The young and the world's romantics."

"Of which you're one. Good enough." Then he said, "Let's toss around a few ideas. Byron seduced Minta, and she ran away to have her baby in secret. Remember, that was a different age."

"Or her parents sent her away and covered the affair up. But they seemed so genuinely devastated."

"You only know them from quotes in old newspaper clippings," Matt said. "That's not really knowing. I see two scenarios unfolding. One is a deception, the other, foul play."

"I wish that Minta had left something else for us to read, like a diary or letters."

"Since she didn't, it's time for some old-fashioned brainstorming." He glanced at the dashboard clock. "I have to go back to the *Tribune,* but let's get together this evening."

"Good idea," I said. "Don't eat dessert tonight. I have a strawberry pie at home. Baked goods always help me think."

"It's a date. By then I may have a lead on the whereabouts of Officer Ex Dreamboat. He may be a person of interest."

"He may even be the key," I said.

TWENTY-FIVE

BEECHNUT STREET DROWSED in a still, stagnant heat. Nothing stirred except for a squirrel scampering across the sidewalk and Patti who was hovering over her pansies with a watering can. Good. She was finally home and always in a talkative mood when working around flowers.

Matt brought the convertible to a stop in my driveway. "I'm off to track down Officer Byron," he said. "See you this evening with news, I hope."

"Meanwhile, I'll do my own kind of detecting." I waved to Patti. Lowering my voice, I added, "There's another girl from the summer of '75."

"I'm surprised she still lives in the neighborhood."

"Lucky for us she does." Loud frantic whines drifted out into the afternoon silence. I frowned, tracing the source to a dark, furry face in my picture window. "Pepper's been locked up too long."

Gathering my purse and the mints Matt had bought for me, I hurried up the walkway. As soon as I opened the door, Pepper lunged at me, then spun around and streaked through the house to the back.

My heart raced as I followed her. What if the ghost girl was in the backyard right now? Matt had left too soon. I grabbed the camera as I passed the kitchen table and rushed out to the porch, prepared to take a picture of a spirit.

She wasn't there. The canine skeleton's grave with the canoe and woods in the background appeared to be swimming in haze. All was peaceful, all was well, and the only sounds were water splashing in the fountain and the gentle spray arcing back and forth over Mr. Harrison's grass.

I breathed more easily. Pepper had a normal canine emergency—she just needed to go outside.

"Sorry I was so long, baby." I laid my hand on her quivering back, and she wagged her tail.

As soon as I opened the screen door, she dashed across the yard, cutting a zigzagging swath through the tall cornstalks in the Harrison vegetable garden. I watched in dismay as she disappeared into a tangle of trees.

No, this was something else.

"Pepper!" I cried. "Come!"

She didn't reappear.

Quickly I went back into the house and scooped up a handful of Bacon Bites. Pepper could smell her treats from far away and always came running when I had one in my hand.

I wouldn't need the camera now. Kicking off my heels, I slipped into running shoes and hurried back outside. This behavior wasn't normal. Pepper avoided the woods, preferring to lie close to the house or the shady area in the middle of the lawn. What was different today?

Obviously not a ghost, but someone had trespassed on my property, activating her watchdog instincts. Perhaps the burglar on the trail of another old-time treasure or a more lucrative haul?

At the woods' edge, I hesitated, calling Pepper's name again, hoping that she'd come bounding back, exhausted after her brief burst for freedom. When it didn't happen, I knew what had to be done.

I'd always intended to go for another hike across the Maywood acres when I wasn't wearing a flimsy dress. But time to change into jeans would be precious minutes lost. I might not find Pepper.

You might not find her anyway, I thought. *She looked like an animal on a mission.*

"Did your pooch fly the coop?"

Mr. Harrison rose from the berry row where he'd been kneeling. He had a pail filled with blackberries.

"Something must have spooked her," I said. "I hope she didn't mash down your plants."

"No harm done."

"Did you see anyone loitering around?" I asked.

"Not a soul. The dog has been carrying on for about an hour. My guess is that she missed you."

"I'm here now, and she couldn't get away fast enough, so that isn't it. I'm going after her."

He stared at me. "In that pretty dress?"

"I don't have a choice. If I'm not back in a half hour, sound the alarm."

Noting the apprehension in his eyes, I added, "It'll be perfectly safe. Just so you know where I am. Would you watch my house, please?"

With this hasty request, I entered the woods before he could launch a warning-laced lecture.

"No one goes there anymore," he called out. "Be careful, Cressa."

His voice faded, along with the splash of the water. Soon the only sound was a soft buzz. *Bees?* I'd better be on the lookout for a surprise attack. *From snakes or whatever else lived in this wild stretch of twisting trees and treacherous vines.* If a coyote or wild dog appeared, I'd toss it a Bacon Bite and hope for the best.

But aside from insects and possibly my runaway dog, it soon seemed as if I were the only form of life moving through the woods today.

The way was easier to navigate than I remembered. I tried to keep my dress away from sharp-edged branches and walked slowly, looking down with every careful step. Pale blue wildflowers and vines bearing dewberries grew close to the ground. In a small clearing, a wild rosebush spread thin canes drooping with dark red flowers in every direction.

This wasn't such a forbidding place after all, only isolated from the rest of Maple Creek—and secretive.

Ahead I noticed a narrow path of sorts, a winding trail of beaten down grasses and disintegrating leaves from past autumns. Encouraged, I walked a little faster, sidestepping mushrooms and logs covered with green moss.

A detour around a fallen tree and one more turn brought me to large clearing where high bits of bright color blended smoothly with the green leaves. I came to a stop and looked up.

Above my head, an array of deflated balloons in rainbow colors hung from the branches around a weathered old tree house. Libby's balloons!

I'd last seen them fluttering in her yard on the night of the reception. One stayed behind in the drained fountain; one landed in my shrubs; the rest had been taken here to this odd little structure in the woods.

Who would steal party decorations from a crime scene to decorate a tree house? Possibilities churned through my mind in dizzying succession.

A demented child with a fondness for colors. A vagrant, wanting to add a festive touch to a borrowed shelter. Or, of course, Libby's killer, for a reason I couldn't fathom.

All I knew was that I'd found the missing balloons. Maybe I had. Only a forensic expert could tell whether or not they were the ones handled by Aleta and Linda.

They had to be.

I let my breathing slow to a normal rate, trying to harness my thoughts. Gradually I became aware of the pungent bacon smell that permeated the humid air. The treats seemed to be disintegrating in my hand. I set them down on the ground and rubbed crumbs from my hand. That was better.

Turning my attention to the tree house, I noticed small, telling details. Nestled snugly in the embrace of a three-branched oak, it had a small porch and an ancient ladder that appeared to be nailed to the trunk. Through a square window opening, I glimpsed the back of an orange chair. Three small people or one average-size woman could fit comfortably inside the structure.

This could be the place where Annora had played as a child, in which case it should be in ruins by now. Unless someone had reinforced it. The unevenly cut reddish boards suggested that the little house had been recently shored up, possibly with pieces salvaged from castoff patio furniture.

What else hid behind the diminutive front door?

The ladder looked sturdy enough to hold my hundred and twenty pounds. Making a snap decision to sacrifice my dress to stains and snags, if necessary, I stepped on the bottom rung. It seemed stable.

Taking a deep breath, I started to climb the twelve steps to the top, leaned forward, and touched the door. It swung open to reveal another chair and a matching table—children's furniture in lollypop orange, along with a few grown-up amenities.

A red plastic plate, a chipped daisy mug, an unopened package of cookies, a half-burnt pillar candle and a box of matches crowded the table's center. In one corner of the floor, a dark blue blanket had been bunched up in the shape of a pillow.

All the comforts of home-away-from-home, except for a low slanting ceiling.

I stepped inside, listening for a warning creak in the old wood, prepared to grab the closest branch if the floorboards gave way. But they held.

The cookies had a month old sell-by date, and coffee or tea stains coated the inside of the cup. And the color of that blanket looked familiar. As I picked it up, it unfolded into a long sweeping cloak with a full hood. The garment had a vile odor of mothballs and smoke. It jarred with the fresh woodsy fragrance that surrounded me.

A memory of the cloaked and hooded figure formed in my mind.

Shambling, covered in dark blue, stealing out of the dark woods while Libby dozed by the fountain, unhearing and unaware.

The image led me down a frightening path.

The person in the cloak could be Minta who had never left the woods. Or a delusional child—the Minta impersonator. Or someone else who moved in darkness and pursued a murky agenda. A person who had killed once and might kill again.

As usual, something didn't add up.

Wouldn't the police have found this place after Libby's death? I couldn't remember if they'd searched the woods. They must have, if Dalton had taken my story of the cloaked intruder seriously. Even if he hadn't.

In 1975, when Minta disappeared, they'd combed the entire area, all the blocks and yards as far as Wyndemere Park. The tree house would have been here at that time, in better shape, with the orange furniture, without the cookies and matches.

A nearby rustle of leaves ended my speculation. I scanned the treetops anxiously, but the disturber was only a huge black crow perched on a branch watching me. I was, after all, in his territory. Then somewhere, toward the ground, I heard a sound like wind moving through dry grasses—not footsteps but movement.

Snakes...or another person, the tree house dweller. She might object to my entering her lair and touching her possession. Even now she might be waiting below.

Get away from here—now! I ordered myself.

I dropped the blue cloak back in its corner and climbed quickly down the ladder. By now the wind sound was gone; the leaves and the brush were still. Safely on the forest floor, I hesitated, wondering what to do first and which direction to take.

I wanted to report my discoveries to Dalton as soon as possible and mull over their implications with Matt. But I also needed to find Pepper and stay alive. Back the way I'd come or forward?

I must be in the middle of the acreage. Why not continue through Annora's wilderness and come out on Willow Court as planned? Maybe on the way, I'd make another discovery.

So I found the path again beyond another downed tree and moved on.

The rest of my trek proved uneventful except for an onslaught of mosquitoes and tiny insects. Some time later, the trees grew farther apart and streaks of light made their way into the darkness. Finally, I saw the sidewalk wrapped in a golden haze.

A blaze of color greeted me as I emerged from the woods. Towering Hollyhocks marked the border between Annora's backyard and her acreage. They were magnificent plants in red, pink, and yellow bloom, grown to giant size in the benevolent July sunshine. Like the balloons, they gave vibrant summer color to the green vista.

I was certain that the balloons and the cloak were important discoveries. Why did I feel that I wasn't any closer to solving the mystery of Libby's death?

Because I wasn't.

Libby had been pushed into the fountain by a delusional child or a homeless woman who lived in a tree house?

Ludicrous. Ridiculous. Even the ghost theory made more sense. But the balloons did mean something. So did the signs of recent habitation in the tree house and the dark blue cloak. Especially the cloak.

Now I had more questions. For example…

"Help yourself to a bouquet anytime you stop by," Annora had said. "I don't have time to garden. My flowers take care of themselves."

But hollyhocks were annuals. They had to be grown from seeds or young plants. Who had done that this spring, if not Annora?

That bit of horticultural lore didn't have anything to do with the murder or Minta's mystery. It proved that Annora was less than truthful, a fact I'd already suspected.

I took the final steps to Willow Court on the wooded acreage, careful not to tread on Annora's velvety grass. Exhaustion had caught up with me, and I was hot, damp, and itchy—about as uncomfortable as I could ever remember being.

I'd come a long way, made an unusual find, and managed to keep my dress in one piece. But I still hadn't found Pepper and, darn! I'd left her Bacon Bites behind in the woods.

TWENTY-SIX

ALL THE WAY HOME, I walked slowly, calling Pepper's name and asking the few people I encountered if they'd seen a medium-size black dog with white and tan markings. No one had.

She could be miles away by now, perhaps dumped in a stranger's truck, the victim of a dognapper. Still I peered into yards and listened for a familiar bark that I didn't hear. The other dogs on the street were behind fences. That was the best way to protect a pet.

I found Mr. Harrison sitting on his front porch reading the paper. "I was just getting ready to call out the cavalry," he said. "Did you find your pooch?"

"Not yet."

"Don't worry. She'll turn up when she gets hungry. It's been as quiet as a graveyard around here." He handed me a large basket of blackberries. "These are for you. They should make good pies."

The berries were dark and glossy, almost too perfect to be real. "Thanks," I said. "They look wonderful."

I glanced across the street. Patti's car was gone, but she'd left her fancy new sprinkling system on. She couldn't be far away.

"And thanks for keeping an eye on my house," I added.

"Glad to do it. We neighbors have to look out for one another," he said.

That included sharing produce and surveillance. I'd have to do something nice for Mr. Harrison to thank him for his kindness. Make him a blackberry pie or, better still, give him some of my mallows for his garden.

I walked around the house to the back, hoping to find Pepper waiting by the porch, and blinked back a tear at the sight of the empty yard. Enough wishful thinking. I had a dog to find and a quick call to make.

After leaving a message for Dalton, asking him to investigate the contents of the tree house, I drove down the quiet streets of Maple Creek looking for Pepper. From now on, I vowed to be a more responsible dog owner, to keep her on a leash when she wasn't inside, and enroll her in obedience class. If it wasn't too late.

In a few short weeks, Pepper had become an important part of my life. Now, without her, the house would be too quiet. Too empty. Already the change was noticeable.

Admit it, I thought. *It's lonely. You're lonely.*

True but strange. I'd never minded living alone in Texas. Work and Jase had kept me so busy that I'd never thought about it. Everything was different in Maple Creek. On the verge of self pity, I forced my thoughts back to the immediate problem.

Pepper must have had a reason for running away from me. She might have taken off in pursuit of a prowler whom Mr. Harrison hadn't noticed. He tended to lose himself in gardening activities.

But why hadn't she come back and where was she now? I pictured her in a truck again, the distance between us lengthening until it would be so great that I'd never find her.

Still my mind teemed with plans for another drive around town in the morning, an ad in Matt's paper, flyers nailed to trees and a reward. I couldn't lose that scrappy little mutt.

Pepper had been taking care of herself long before she followed me home after the fire. Pets who had to fend for themselves grew resourceful. But she had adopted me, and life at 714 Beechnut Street was good for a canine.

Listen to Mr. Harrison and don't worry. She'll show up in her own time.

With that thought to comfort me, I drove around Wyndemere Park and the school one last time and headed home. It was ten after six. I expected Matt soon, and, at present, I was a crumpled, dusty version of his neatly-assembled lunch partner.

In my bedroom, I took off my earrings and examined the silk dress for damage. Miraculously there was nothing that couldn't be cleaned. But a trace of mothball and smoke odor from the cloak lingered on my hands. I couldn't wait to wash it off.

With a little hot water, lily of the valley cologne, and a change into an orange sundress, I felt fresh and new—ready to entertain my guest and share my latest trauma.

At seven I set the porch table, brought out the coffeepot, and lit my hurricane candle. This cool, serene space was a perfect place to welcome a date, except that Matt wasn't coming to my house for any social or romantic purpose. This was pure business, a brainstorming session conducted by two amateur sleuths. It only looked like something more.

I held my hand over the flame and wondered if the candle communicated another message—if I should blow it out.

No, let it add to the ambiance, I thought, and settled myself in the wicker rocker to wait. For Matt, for Pepper and for the next dire happening.

MATT NOTICED THAT Pepper was gone as soon as he stepped inside the door. "That's too bad about her taking off. If she doesn't come home by tomorrow, I'll help you look for her."

"I hope nothing bad happened."

"Try not to anticipate trouble. Only a short while ago, she was running free."

"But she's been used to living in a house."

He patted my arm. "That's why she'll come home."

"I'll get the pie," I said.

I'd made a fancy lattice crust for it and decorated the top with small strawberries in the shape of an *S*. Matt gazed at the piece on his plate as if it were the most sumptuous confection in all of Maple Creek. It *did* look good.

I cut a sliver for myself and poured our coffee. "Tell me if it's okay. The strawberries came from Mr. Harrison's garden."

"And you added your magic ingredient," he said.

"As always, with a half cup of sugar."

I watched as he tasted it, waiting for his warm smile.

"This is fantastic, Cressa," he said. "It's just sweet enough."

"If only the Michigan strawberry season lasted longer."

"That lead didn't pan out," he said between bites. "Dan Byron declined to be interviewed for the article. He claims he remembers Minta only because of the publicity over her disappearance. He might have exchanged a few words with her. That's all."

"Allyson didn't exactly say they were dating."

"No, only that all the girls were crazy about him. If Minta cared for Dan, it might have been one-sided."

"Unrequited love burns so deeply when you're seventeen," I said, remembering the lost scrapbook with its sentimental poems. "So Officer Byron is a dead end?"

"Maybe—for now."

"Do you think he's lying?"

"He sounded sincere—and emphatic. Like he was protesting too much. I wish I could have talked to him face-to-face, but he's up in Marquette."

"Patti's right across the street, but every time I look for her, she's away from home."

Like our clue, Matt's pie had rapidly diminished. "You're the best baker in Maple Creek, Cressa," he said.

"Pie making is my one domestic talent." I cut him another, larger piece. "Wait until you hear what happened after you brought me home this afternoon."

He listened attentively as I described my discoveries in the Maywood acres. "The police will have to reopen the investigation now, won't they?"

"I'm sure they'll want to look into it," he said. "Maybe we should set Minta aside and concentrate on our current mystery. Based on what you found today, I'm afraid the situation might be getting dangerous."

"It always was. I still think that Libby was murdered, and the cloaked figure and balloons are part of it. I'd rather deal with a killer than a ghost," I added.

"We might have both." He fell silent, his attention fixed on the woods.

Approximately two hours' worth of light remained in the sky, but the shadows always began among the wild trees and crept into my backyard, bringing a vague sense of threat along with the darkness. Usually I felt safer on my balcony than here on the ground level. Today Matt was with me, and the ghosts and killers and whatever else lurked in the Maywood Acres seemed a little farther away.

"I'd like to see the tree house," he said.

"Then we should go now before it gets dark. I don't think the police had time to drape it in crime scene tape yet."

"Let's do it."

I leaned over to blow out the candle. "I'll lock the door and get some illumination first. Just in case."

He waited outside the porch while I found a flashlight and my spare key. By the time I rejoined him, he had armed himself with a large pointed branch.

Once again I prepared to tramp through Annora's wilderness, this time with a stalwart companion and some slight knowledge of the land. We passed the skeleton's grave and the canoe and entered the woods, plowing through silence broken only by intermittent buzzings and chirpings.

"There's the path," I said. "Be on the lookout for snakes. Annora says they're all around."

His low chuckle echoed in the silence. "I don't think Annora knows what lives on her own property, but in this case, she could be right." He brandished his makeshift walking stick. "Never fear. I'm a match for any reptile."

"Let's hope we don't meet any."

"This must be a child's paradise," he said. "Just think of all the games that kids can play in these woods."

"Hide-and-go-seek, Tarzan, Indiana Jones…but I've never seen any children here. Only the girl—Minta—by the canoe. But look! There's a candy bar wrapper."

"A Hershey," Matt said. "Could be blown over by the wind."

As we made our way through the underbrush, I recognized the rosebush that had reverted to a wild state, its red flowers blooming close to the ground. We followed the trail, stepping away from encroaching branches and vines. With Matt's limp, our progress was slow but steady.

"The clearing is just ahead," I said, leading the way around the fallen elm, scanning the treetops. "There's the house and… Oh, no!"

Matt came to a stop, leaning heavily on the stick. "What's wrong?"

"The balloons are gone," I said.

Not a single balloon hung on the branches. All I could see was the old tree house held fast in the oak's embrace and a glimpse of lollypop orange through the window opening. Pepper's Bacon Bites weren't where I'd left them. For some reason, I felt like weeping.

"I'm so tired of all this weirdness," I said. "It's like I've wandered into some crazy alternate reality where nothing ever stays the same."

Matt laid his hand on my shoulder. "More than likely Lieutenant Gray took them away."

"I don't think he's been here," I said. "Where's the yellow tape? I'm going to look inside."

He set the stick down and gripped the ladder with his strong hands. "I guess it's sturdy, but be careful. I'm here to catch you if you fall."

"I won't."

I climbed the ten steps hastily, anxious to check out the interior of the tree house. Pushing open the small door, I saw the chairs and table. Everything else—plate, mug, cookies, candle, matches and the cloak in the corner—had vanished like the balloons.

The sense of being adrift in a mad world returned. I took a step inside, keeping my head low, and reached down to touch the small table.

The imprints of the missing items remained on the dusty surface. If Dalton hadn't gathered them as evidence, their owner had removed them. At any rate, I'd arrived too late, and, if someone was hiding in the underbrush, she would know who had discovered her lair.

The unknown person who moved through dry grasses like the wind might have seen me when I was here earlier.

"Did you find anything, Cressa?" Matt called.

"Just children's play furniture. The rest is all gone. Swept clean."

"Then come down," he said in a new commanding tone. "I want to get you out of here."

That, I decided, was a good idea—while escape was still possible.

AS THE DAYLIGHT FADED, we ate more pie and began a fresh pot of coffee. I'd left a second message for Lieutenant Gray to bring him up to date. Matt and I had reviewed the circumstances surrounding Libby Dorset's drowning and Minta's appearances, along with my sighting of the brown collie asleep on the grave.

At one point, I'd almost told Matt about my previous experience with the supernatural but stopped myself in time. That was a memory I couldn't share with him yet. If ever.

The hurricane candle flickered bravely in the darkness. As soon as we'd come out of the woods, I saw Kady's car in her driveway. Now soft lights glowed on the first floor of the white Victorian, and muted strains of music drifted out into the night air, while the water in the satyr fountain sloshed and gurgled in the background. The evening had a superabundance of atmosphere and a faint hint of menace.

"The person who lives in the tree house might be that vagrant, Ruby," I said.

"The change-for-coffee lady? That's possible. She's been hanging around the neighborhood. For someone without a home, it'd be dry and private. Even better than a back porch in an empty house."

"She stole Libby's cakes and took off into the woods," I said. "What if later, when it started to rain, she put on her cloak and came back? Maybe she saw what happened to Libby. She might even be the one who killed her."

"That's a plausible scenario. Can you suggest a reason?"

"Not offhand. Libby tended to ignore beggars. She said they

made her uncomfortable. It seemed out of character for her. She
was so generous."

"It isn't a crime to set up housekeeping in an old tree house.
Just bizarre."

"But Annora has 'No Trespassing' signs posted on the
property."

"Which nobody pays attention to. Coming back to Minta,
isn't it about time for her to make another appearance?"

"Don't say that. Please."

My backyard and the woods beyond were filled with dark
places where a listener from this world or another could wait in
silence and ultimately pounce. Not that this was likely to happen.
Still I felt as if Mr. Harrison could hear us, and Kady, and perhaps
Ruby and Minta, too.

And the satyr, I thought. *Don't forget him.*

"Do you believe in vibes?" I asked. "Bad ones, good ones,
all kinds."

"I guess so. Why?"

"Because they're all around us tonight. Close and getting
closer."

"*We're* getting closer—to some answers." Matt reached for
my hand and held it in a strong grip. "Whatever happens, we're
in this together, Cressa."

Just for a moment, I felt safe.

TWENTY-SEVEN

SIGHING LIKE THE NIGHT and sobbing like the rain, Wailing for the lost one that comes not again...

The poignant strains of "Jeannie with the Light Brown Hair" drifted through my dream. A collie whose fur had an eerie glow bounded across the backyard, joyfully welcoming me home. Through ribbons of white mist I saw Ruby sitting in Libby's wicker chair, oblivious of the satyr's moving hand.

"We're all mixed together," she said in a sinister, droning voice. "All mixed up. Dogs... People... Old bones... Grief... Then she began to sing: *I dream of Sunny with the dark brown fur...*

The statue's hand hovered over her head, its long curving fingers like talons stained with blood.

A scratching sound insinuated its way into my consciousness. Pushing past the splash of water, it pulled me out of sleep. Recognizing the imperious whine that followed it, I stumbled out of bed and plowed through the thick, hot air to the window.

Pepper stood on the porch steps below, crying and raking her nails across the screen to attract my attention. There was no mist and no vagrant rocking in Libby's chair. In fact, there was no chair. They were all part of one of the weirdest dreams I'd ever had.

I tapped lightly on the window. Pepper looked up and launched a series of high- pitched yelps. The hands on my alarm clock pointed to six, an ungodly hour for a dog to be making even a little noise.

I shook my head, trying to clear it of fuzzy nightmare images. The happy collie, the gypsy in the rocker, the satyr's hand, all of them in motion.

Dogs, people, old bones, grief. It sounded like the beginning of a child's nonsense riddle.

Forget the words, forget the dream, I thought. Pepper was downstairs on the other side of the door, waiting for me to open it.

When I did, she dashed past me without a sideways glance. Woodland debris flew off her coat and landed on the floor. As she pounced on her empty food dish, I ran my hands along her rib cage, quickly pulling them back as they came in contact with the prickly burrs embedded in her fur.

She looked up from her bowl and whined.

"You wretched little beast," I said. "I was so worried. Where were you?"

In the woods, of course. Chasing a wild creature or something more sinister, but now she had found her way home. All was well.

I gave her a double portion of kibble mixed with leftover turkey and watched her gobble it noisily. While she licked the bowl clean, I filled her water pail.

"You should have come back yesterday," I said. "There's food here, your toys, your owner—everything you need."

With a feeble wag of her tail, she stretched out with her head on her bowl and closed her eyes, so unlike the bouncing collie from my dream.

The skeleton I'd buried in my yard. Minta's ghost dog.

But gruesome graveyard thoughts are incompatible with morning sunlight and second chances. The trauma of Pepper's loss was fortunately short-lived. Like the summer's other strange happenings, it came with a built-in mystery. I might never know why Pepper had run away or where she'd spent the night, but it didn't matter.

Later, when she woke up, I'd brush her and cut the burrs out of her coat. From now on, I'd keep her leashed, and, as soon as possible, find a good obedience school.

Now, instead of searching Maple Creek for a lost dog, I could cook a real breakfast of bacon and eggs and concentrate on getting ready for my job interview. With the recent turmoil, I'd almost forgotten about it.

THE BALLOONS WERE BRIGHT rainbow colors, turning slowly in the warm wind. They transported me back to the night of

Libby's reception and its grim aftermath. Was I the only one who remembered?

I watched Aleta tie them to the porch posts of the white Victorian. In another part of the front yard, close to the sidewalk, Linda set a maple dinette table for an imaginary lunch, while Kady arranged lamps on a Victorian dresser.

The two-day estate sale was set to begin at eight, and there was Patti holding a necklace of blue beads up to the sun. Here was my chance to toss a few innocuous questions her way.

Kady looked up from the display. "Good morning, Cressa."

"Do you need any help?" I asked.

"Thanks, but the girls have it covered. Just look around and enjoy yourself."

I did, appraising the nearest offerings with a keen eye. Kady wasn't selling the usual drab household cast-offs. The jewelry looked expensive, and the vases and whimsical figurines sparkled.

"My aunt had several small collections that she'd lost interest in," Kady said. "They're still inside."

"Won't you regret getting rid of these treasures?" I asked.

"Aunt Libby tagged them for sale last year, and I added some old books and papers and other stuff. I can't possibly keep everything. Who has time to do all that dusting?"

I glanced at my watch. With an hour before I had to leave for my interview, I could explore the aisles Kady was creating on the grass. But first I strolled over to Patti who still held the necklace.

"Those colors go well with your eyes, Patti," I said.

She beamed at the compliment. "Libby owned some fantastic real jewelry. This is just costume stuff."

"But vintage pieces are popular nowadays. I don't imagine Kady would sell her aunt's sapphires and emeralds."

"This one is a little heavy. It might be uncomfortable to wear. Still, for five dollars, you can't go wrong."

I picked up a similar necklace in purple. It would be a stunning accessory for the lavender dress I had on, and a slightly vintage look might give me an edge this afternoon. Heaven knows I needed a new good luck charm.

"Ah, the fifties! I wish I'd lived through them." Patti stroked the beads lovingly as if they were priceless gemstones. "What do you think? Should I or shouldn't I?"

"You should. Speaking of the past, I came across another antique back in the Maywood Acres. It's an old tree house in good shape with play furniture still inside. Do you know the one I mean?"

"What were you doing in the woods?" Patti asked.

"Looking for Pepper."

"I should tell you that Annora May is touchy about trespassers. That land is her private property."

"I didn't hurt anything."

"I never saw the tree house," Patti said. "But then I've never wandered around in those woods, either."

"Not even when you were a child?" I asked.

"If I did, I don't remember. Did you find Pepper?"

"She came home this morning."

"Just like a teenager." Patti clasped the necklace around her neck where it made an uneasy match for her grass-stained white top. "Heavy or not, I love these blues. I wish I'd had something so beautiful when I was a girl."

"Going back to those days, do you remember a policeman by the name of Dan Byron?" I asked. "He was on the Force when Minta Bransford disappeared."

A deep flush spread over Patti's face, and anger blazed in her eyes. She tugged on the hapless beads.

"How dare you mention that name to me?"

Her words were sharp and cutting, her voice a screech. I felt as if I were melting in the white-hot force of her fury. From across the yard, Aleta glanced in our direction.

"How dare I—what? What did I say?"

"As if you didn't know!"

"I don't. I just heard the name the other day at lunch and wondered—"

"Sure you did. I thought you were a nice person. Guess I was wrong."

Still wearing the necklace, she stamped back across the street and into her house, slamming the door. As I stared after her, Aleta came up to me, trailing red and yellow balloons on strings. "What's wrong with my mother?" she asked.

Some instinct warned me not to repeat Dan Byron's name to Aleta. "I'm not sure. We were talking about the 1950s."

"That shouldn't upset her." Aleta frowned. "Well, back to work." But as she continued tying the balloons to the long porch railing, she glanced furtively in my direction.

Feeling vaguely guilty, I browsed among the teacups and decorative plates for ten minutes, but Patti didn't reappear.

I should go over to her house and apologize for inadvertently offending her. Maybe, having had time to cool off, she'd tell me why the name of a former Maple Creek police officer had triggered her outburst.

Not now though. The next time I saw her.

If I was going to learn anything significant, I had to tread with care. I still suspected that Patti knew more than she'd been willing to say about the Minta Bransford days. Perhaps Dan Byron had played a part in Minta's disappearance. Certainly he and Patti had been acquainted with each other.

Or maybe she was just one of the schoolgirls who had been crazy about him, someone whom he scarcely remembered. There must be more to Patti's story. No normal woman would react so vehemently to a casual mention of an old crush—unless he'd hurt her in some way. Ah, that might be it.

We're all mixed together, Ruby had said in the dream.

Patti, Minta, Ruby, Dan Byron, Sunny…who else?

I wished I had time to pursue this new angle, but my hour had dwindled to forty minutes.

I found Kady carrying out a gleaming mahogany magazine stand with graceful cutwork sides.

"I'd love to have that!" I said.

"It's twenty-five dollars. Shall I hold it for you?"

"Yes, please, and I'll take this necklace. I'm coming back around three."

"Good. You can have dinner here. The girls are selling hot dogs and brownies."

I paid her and put the necklace on, wondering if I should tell Kady that Patti had absconded with a similar piece. I decided to keep silent. Patti would probably return it when she calmed down or bring Kady the money.

Kady nodded her approval. "You look very vintage, Cressa. Just like a girl from the fifties."

AT MID-MORNING, the clouds began to build. By the time I reached the outskirts of North Mill, the sky was a depressing dark gray, and raindrops splattered the windshield.

"Never begin a new enterprise on a stormy day," my grand-mother used to say. "If you want it to prosper, wait for the sun."

Not even a momentary brightening of the sky could transform North Mill Middle School into an attractive employment prospect. It was an old brick building with dim, silent halls and a somber-faced principal who wanted to hire an English teacher. At present he only had one unassigned science class.

The interview went well, but I couldn't see myself being happy in this dreary place. Still I needed to be working at some job soon, preferably in education. Hoping that I'd receive an offer from one of the livelier schools on my list, I headed back home. A hamburger at a picturesque lakeside restaurant restored my mood, and, three miles outside Maple Creek, the sun came out.

If I were superstitious, I'd look on the change in weather as a clear sign. Farewell, North Mill. My sunshine and happiness lay elsewhere.

I made the last turn of the trip and drove slowly down Beechnut Street, past unfamiliar cars and people loading their purchases into trunks. The white Victorian buzzed with activity. The balloons still moved in the wind, and the delicate music of wind chimes filled the air.

I glanced across the street. Matt was home. Patti wasn't. Mr. Harrison walked by, carrying a garden statue—a gargoyle. I waved to him and wondered if Patti had returned to the sale while I was in North Mill. I had to smooth over our altercation. And was Matt planning to come to the sale? I hoped so.

After taking Pepper for a short walk and giving her a fresh

drink, I joined the shoppers. My first stop was a table covered with sheet music where I discovered a yellowing souvenir songbook with an oval portrait of Stephen Foster on the cover.

I leafed through the pages, finding my favorite selections complete with enchanting illustrations. What better remembrance of Libby could I have?

Taking it with me, I moved on to a garden bench stacked high with paperbacks, composers' biographies and several old series books. The titles intrigued me: *Beverly Gray on a World Cruise; Beverly Gray in the Orient; Beverly Gray at the World's Fair.*

Whoever Beverly Gray was, her life was more exciting than mine. I decided on the World's Fair book and turned to find Gwendolyn standing close behind me, clutching a pretty little parlor lamp that I'd seen in Libby's living room.

"Estate sales are so sad," she said. "Poor Libby's possessions shouldn't be scattered around for strangers to paw through."

"She won't need them now," I said.

"I suppose not." She craned her neck to look at my Beverly Gray book. "I've been trying to find that title for ages! Could I persuade you to part with it?"

"No," I said, softening the refusal with a smile.

"But you won't enjoy such an old-fashioned story. Anyway, it's for kids." She pointed to a thick paperback with a faded cover. "There's *Forever Amber.* More your style. Why don't you take that?"

"I've read it."

"Really?"

She didn't believe me. I didn't care.

"My niece is a serious collector of old time series books," she said. "*Beverly Gray at the World's Fair* will complete her set."

"There'll be other yard sales this summer."

"But what are the odds that someone else has this one?"

"Slim," I said.

In the midst of Libby's charming and unique possessions, it was nonsensical for two women to argue over one obscure book. So why was I doing it? There was no basis for argument. It was mine, or would be when I paid Kady for it. But why not just give it to Gwendolyn and choose another one?

Because I was contrary? Or because the request came from this pushy woman and not someone I truly cared about? Like Matt. Besides, I might indeed enjoy Beverly Gray's adventure. It wasn't Gwendolyn's place to make my reading choices for me.

"I think you should reconsider," Gwendolyn said.

"I won't."

"If you change your mind, don't put the book back with the others. Give it directly to me."

I agreed to do that, knowing it wouldn't happen, and quickly moved over to the next display, but a shred of anger over the confrontation stayed with me. Did estate sales bring out the worst in people, even though they were neighbors?

In some, perhaps. But Gwendolyn White had always been nosy and rude, opinionated and self-serving, and…she wasn't getting her hands on my book.

I stopped next at a large box that had once held a microwave oven. Now it contained fanciful Chagall prints, posters, old calendars and original watercolors signed by Elizabeth Dorset. All were jumbled together for "75 cents. Your Choice."

Libby had been a talented artist, finding her subjects close to home. Apparently she had been especially fond of wildflowers and butterflies. I imagined her standing at her easel capturing spring blossoms, summer sunflowers and melancholy autumn vistas on canvas. She had done several portraits of the fountain in all seasons, and a side view of my house, surrounded by a small white picket fence.

I had to have that one, as well as a picture of the white Victorian decorated for Christmas with wreaths in the windows and a lit fir tree on the front porch. Now what else could I find?

Reaching deep into the box again, I drew out a handmade booklet. My heartbeat quickened. I'd never seen this item before, but it looked and felt familiar. Not long ago I'd held one similar to it.

Yes. Very similar.

The pages were black construction paper, held together with gold curling ribbon. Tiny multi-colored stars spelled out: *Elizabeth's Book of Memories. Compiled by Minta Bransford, 1975.*

Quickly I opened it.

TWENTY-EIGHT

POLAROID SNAPSHOTS OF young people stared back at me under headings like "Remember," "Friends," and "Elizabeth's Party." I lingered over a half dozen exposures taken at the white Victorian with a slice of my house—Minta's house—and the fountain in the background. In the pictures, the satyr seemed different, smaller and not so ominous.

Setting that thought aside as ridiculous, I looked for a familiar face—a teen-aged Patti or Libby, or possibly a male police officer lurking in the background.

But the images weren't very clear, and there was no man.

"Did you find something good in the box, Cressa?"

I knew that voice. Instinctively I snapped the booklet shut and tightened my grip on it, just in case Annora turned out to be another Gwendolyn.

She was close behind me, as Gwendolyn had been, peering over my shoulder. Matt stood beside her. Tanned and fair-haired, wearing a shirt the color of a lake in summer, he appeared more handsome than usual. That man grew more desirable every time I saw him, especially when he was in the company of another woman.

"I'm buying some of Libby Dorset's artwork," I said, stepping away from Annora. "She was quite talented."

"So she was, in many ways."

"Nice day for a sale," Matt said.

"Except for this miserable heat," Annora added. "I've half a mind to jump in the fountain."

Matt winked at me. "I'd like to see that."

"Stick around," she said. "You may get the chance."

It appeared that Matt and Annora had arrived together, but why should I assume the worst? Estate sales were common gathering places for neighbors. They'd probably met in front of Matt's house and stopped to exchange pleasantries. I liked my neatly slanted version of reality, even if it was probably out in left field.

"What do you have there?" Annora asked. "It doesn't look like a drawing."

"Just an old album," I said.

Remembering her interest in Minta's scrapbook and its subsequent disappearance, I shoved the memory book between Stephen Foster and Beverly Gray. Whatever secrets it might contain were mine, and I intended to hold on to them.

"I take it your interview is over," Matt said. "Are you ready to start the search for Pepper?"

"Thanks, Matt, but that won't be necessary. She came home early this morning. Crisis averted."

His warm smile reminded me of how much I appreciated his support. "I told you not to worry."

Annora linked her arm in Matt's. "Then you can stay with me for a while. Let's see what we can find."

"See you later, Cressa," Matt said as he followed Annora to a small Victorian dresser where three vintage lamps glowed in the sunlight.

On an impulse, I turned back to the box and rifled through its contents again. If another important document lay buried among Libby's memorabilia, I didn't want to leave it behind.

I couldn't help thinking that somehow Libby had led me to her papers. Or perhaps the guide was Minta, desperate for someone to solve the mystery of her disappearance so that she could rest in peace.

As Minta assembled the memory book for Libby, she'd have focused on pictures of their friends and end-of-the-year activities, whatever would create memories. Since the material reflected her life at the time, one of the scraps might be a clue. My job was to recognize it.

And I might have another source. An exchange required two

people. Wouldn't Libby have given Minta a scrapbook, too? If so, what happened to it? The idea of another time capsule hidden in my house intrigued me.

But one search at a time. This box contained art-themed keepsakes, nothing I wanted to buy. Only the memory book might be tied to the mystery. Fortunately I had been the one to find it.

As I walked up to Kady to claim the magazine stand and pay for my other purchases, I passed Matt and Annora. They were engaged in a light-hearted argument about the merits of a nostalgic Snow White cookie jar over a plain glass canister. They looked happy, almost like a couple setting up housekeeping—which ranked with my more preposterous notions.

Matt couldn't be so easily fooled by an aging seductress whose golden hair came from a bottle. Could he? After all, I was his mystery solving partner. He'd planned to help me look for Pepper this afternoon. Nevertheless, Annora had some hold on him, a purely physical one, I decided. How strong could it be?

It occurred to me that my interest in Matt's activities bordered on obsession.

That isn't true, my rational self insisted. *You don't trust Annora. The company Matt keeps makes him suspect. And Matt is the man you've been confiding in.*

I needed to know who my real friends were. Certainly not Annora laughing with Matt as they moved through the sale. Not Patti because of the morning's unpleasantness over Dan Byron, and never again Gwendolyn, after her brazen attempt to take possession of my series book.

But Matt... I thought we'd made a connection. I believed I knew him. It was a disappointment to realize that I might be wrong.

THE SOUNDS OF the estate sale followed me home, all the way to the back porch, my cherished, quiet retreat. I sank into a chair with the booklet in my lap and listened to Kady's voice narrating the story behind an antique merry-go-round toy, Linda yelling at Aleta to turn the hot dogs over, the shrill cries of excited children and a revving motor. Through all the noise, the wind chimes tinkled a merry Stephen Foster tune.

No…they couldn't do that. I was hearing the ice cream truck.

Casting off a twinge of sadness, I watched the fountain water sparkle with rainbow colors as it crossed a sunbeam's path. If I were capturing the memorable elements of my life in some form of time capsule, I'd include rocky road cones, the stately old Victorians on Beechnut Street and Matt, all in pictorial form.

Now *that* was a happy notion. I was about to turn back to the memory book when a little girl with copper-colored braids tottered across Kady's backyard. She came to a stop at the fountain's rim and stood motionless, like a statue herself, smiling up at the satyr.

She's too close to it! Too near that beckoning hand!

Letting the book fall to the floor, I rushed to the screen door, just as an older girl sprinted across the grass. She swept the child up, holding her in a tight embrace.

"Janie!" The girl's voice rose high over a childish wail of protest. "Don't ever, *ever* go near that fountain!"

She hurried away with the child still in her arms, and I sat down again. Libby's backyard was peaceful once more, or as peaceful as it could be with its memories of what had happened to Libby here. What might have happened just now if no one had been watching?

Pepper stepped out onto the porch and padded over to me. She set her paw on my lap and stared at me, as if she knew my thoughts and cared that I'd been momentarily unhappy.

I fluffed the long fur on her neck. "Everything is all mixed up, but it's going to be all right," I told her.

With a sigh, I opened the memory book to find more pictures of girls and a few boys taken at a lakeside picnic. One of the girls had long dark hair.

Could she be Minta Bransford?

I looked more carefully, moving closer to the screen where the light was better.

No, two of the girls had long dark hair. Both wore blue shorts and white sleeveless blouses. How strange that they would dress alike. I should show this book to Allyson Camden. With luck, she might remember their names. She might even recognize the clue that kept eluding me.

A rap on the screen door broke into my speculation. Dalton stood outside, looking official and powerful in his uniform with his gun belt strapped on.

"Are you busy, Cressa?" he asked.

"Just looking through an estate sale find. Come on in."

He did, avoiding Pepper's exuberant lunge, and sat down at the table.

"Did you check out the tree house?" I asked.

"Just now. Whatever you saw, it's gone, except for the kids' furniture. What did you say was there again?"

I described each article, reminding him of the cloaked figure I'd seen on the night of Libby's death. "Do you believe me?" I asked.

"Is there some reason I shouldn't?"

"None at all, but there's no proof."

"I'll take your word for it. Some vagrant saw you and moved to another location, with his possessions such as they were."

"Like Ruby, the homeless woman who appears wherever there's free food?"

"Or someone similar."

"Those balloons were an eerie touch," I said.

"I can't argue with that. There was no trace of them at the site."

"Will you reopen the investigation into Libby's death?" I asked.

"I'll look around and check the tree house for fingerprints. Annora May needs to know that somebody's been camping in her woods."

I should have told her, but keeping the memory book away from her had been my primary objective. Anyway, it would be best for Dalton to deal with Annora in his capacity as a police officer.

"That's where we stand as of this minute," he said. "Tell me. Do you like barbecued ribs?"

The abrupt subject change left me floundering. "I guess so."

"Smothered in the tangy sauce with a touch of cherry flavor? Made from an old family recipe?"

"What a tempting description."

"Temptation is my game. How about joining me for dinner next Wednesday at the Smoking Rib? We can take in a movie, too, if you'd like."

"Well…" After our last date, I'd decided that Dalton wasn't the man for me, but that didn't mean we couldn't enjoy another evening together. I needed a friend, and where could I find a more trustworthy one than Lieutenant Dalton Gray of the MCPD? "I'd love to go."

His cornflower eyes had a wicked sparkle the satyr might envy. "You won't be sorry," he said.

BETWEEN VISIONS OF barbecued ribs and the prospect of a second date with Dalton—perhaps a star-spangled one—I was having difficulty concentrating on *Elizabeth's Book of Memories*. When I'd told Annora that it was an album, I had no idea this would prove to be true.

The memory book would have a certain appeal for Elizabeth's and Minta's contemporaries, but from my perspective, nothing was less relevant than old photographs of unknown people. Idly I flipped through the book, letting the smell of hot dogs cooking on the grill override my waning curiosity. This trip down somebody else's memory lane was a waste of time and, incidentally, of money. There was nothing here to find.

I turned another page. Nothing to find…except a white envelope with a four-cent stamp that felt warm in my hand, as if someone had recently handled it. An impossibility, of course. Addressed to the chief of police and sealed, somehow it had ended up in the memory book.

This might be anything, from a forgotten check for parking tickets to an invitation to a school function, I told myself. But I sensed that I was about to make an important discovery.

I ripped it open and drew out a thin sheet of stationary.

Dear Captain Demmer: I know what happened to Minta Bransford. She was murdered. Look for the body close to her home. Look for the killer among her friends. I'm sorry for not speaking out sooner, but I was afraid.

The letter was signed "Elizabeth Dorset"; the date at the top was June 13, 1976.

I read the paragraph again. Then again. Elizabeth Dorset? My neighbor, Libby? I couldn't reconcile the gentle woman I'd known with the writer of this accusatory letter.

If it was legitimate and not someone's idea of a twisted prank, then Libby had taken a grim secret to her grave. Had she intended to mail the letter, then changed her mind and stashed it in a place she'd be unlikely to look again? Like the memory book.

But why hadn't she simply thrown it away?

How could anyone know her reasons? In any event, I couldn't hand this cold case evidence over to the police without first showing it to Kady who should have looked through her aunt's papers more carefully before tossing them together in the seventy-five cents box.

Slipping Libby's confession into my pocket, I headed back to the estate sale, suspecting that every step was bringing me closer to the truth.

In the short time that I'd been on my porch, many of Libby's possessions had been sold. The balloons still turned in the wind, but the crowd was gone, and the carnival atmosphere had dissipated, giving the white Victorian a dejected coming-apart-at-the-seams look. Gwendolyn was right. Estate sales were sad.

I found Kady carrying delicate figurines back into the house. She moved more slowly than she had this morning, and wrinkles had stolen the crispness from her red sundress.

"Are you winding down?" I asked.

"Until tomorrow morning. We sold roughly half of our stuff, but it's been a long, long day."

I handed her the envelope. "You should see this. I found it in that old album I bought."

"Oh, no…" As she read the letter, she seemed to wilt. Quickly she refolded it. "Please don't tell anybody about this, Cressa."

"You don't seem surprised," I said.

She glanced at the grill where Linda and Aleta were arranging hot dogs on a platter. "Come inside for a moment."

I followed her into the living room that was crammed with

small tables, bric-a-brac and books. Inside the air was still and warm, and dust motes floated in the light. I took a deep breath, wishing myself back outside.

"My aunt wrote a letter similar to this one a week before she died," Kady said. "I don't know if she intended to send it. There was no envelope. I'm not sure what to do about it."

"These letters are important," I said. "Maybe there's a connection between the two murders."

"I never believed that Aunt Libby was killed," Kady said. "It was a terrible accident."

"But if it wasn't…"

"My aunt is still dead." Kady bit her lower lip. "Whatever happened was over a long time ago."

I wanted to tell Kady that it wasn't over at all, that fallout from the tragedy still haunted her house and mine, even that something of Minta Bransford lived on. But she didn't need to know that.

"When someone dies unexpectedly, there's so much left undone," she said. "Her new composition, a dress she was making. Now this. I wish I knew what she wants me to do about the letters."

"Finish what she didn't have a chance to do and maybe catch a killer."

"I guess so, but I need a few days to think this through. Promise that you won't say anything to anybody yet."

"I don't think we should wait."

"Just until Monday," she said. "This information has been in a holding pattern for over three decades. Another forty-eight hours can't possibly make a difference."

TWENTY-NINE

A LONG-HAIRED GIRL IN a green dress stood at my bedside looking down at me. Her eyes were the color of spring grass. The left side of her face from her temple to her jaw was broken and bleeding. Drops of blood fell on my outstretched arm and ran down onto the sheet.

She laid her hand on my forehead. Her touch was like a frozen weight, encompassing the cold of the deep earth—of all dead and decomposing things.

I tried to cry out but couldn't utter a sound, and I couldn't move. The bed held me in an icy grip.

"Come with me," she said.

I awoke, shivering in the hot room. My hand trembled as I turned on the lamp.

Nobody was there. Of course not. I'd been dreaming. The ceiling fan turned and hummed, circulating warm air. From the hallway, Pepper opened her eyes and promptly closed them again. Everything seemed normal.

Still, I felt that a Presence lingered in the shadows. It wanted something. Me.

Curb your out-of-control imagination, I told myself.

A late supper of hot dogs and brownies, combined with wild speculation about Libby's letter, had spawned the nightmare. One line in particular haunted me: "Look for her body close to her home." My house.

Now wide awake, I came back to Libby's revelations. Had she meant the woods?

Under the red canoe?

That was where Minta had first appeared, perched on top of

the canoe as if it were a garden bench. The owner, Annora's uncle, was long dead, and after decades of neglect, the canoe had become a part of the scenery, too heavy to move easily. Only a few people knew it was there.

When my promise to Kady expired in forty-eight hours, I'd contact Dalton. Nightmares, feelings, and ghosts weren't evidence. Libby's written statement was.

Fortunately I'd kept the old letter instead leaving it with Kady. I turned out the light and closed my eyes, remembering Minta's words. "Come with me." What could she possibly want except for me to bring her killer to justice?

Go back to sleep, I told myself. *You're not going to solve a murder mystery tonight.* But my thoughts were loud and insistent, demanding to be considered.

Look for the killer among her friends.

I could name three of them: Patti, Annora and the mysterious Dan Byron. Maybe Gwendolyn. I'd have to find out where she was in the mid-seventies. Not Matt, he was too young. Besides, he'd had to look up the Bransford story in the *Tribune* archives.

What of the other dozen or more young people in Minta's pictures? Who were they? And what had kept Libby silent for over three decades?

I was afraid, she'd written. Of the killer or of involving herself in the disappearance-turned-murder? Had she intended to send the second letter or hide it in a dusty obscure volume? And why hadn't she mailed the first one?

If only you could tell me, Libby, I thought, *and if only you'd been more specific. And when did your conscience overcome your fear?*

I was afraid, too, not of a nightmare but of the ghost from the woods and her agenda.

Turning on the bed again, I let images of summer flowers float through my mind. Pink mallows, black-eyed susans and purple coneflowers blowing in the breeze. That helped a little. My last thought before drifting off to sleep was to say a prayer for the soul of the murdered girl.

It no longer mattered that at one time, when she'd ruined my flowers, I had disliked her.

SUNDAY MORNINGS WERE invariably quiet on Beechnut Street. This one was different. From my living room window, I'd watched Kady set up the estate sale on a smaller scale. Aleta stationed herself on the porch to sell hot chocolate and doughnuts, and the early bargain seekers appeared to be buying rather than browsing.

I ate a light breakfast of cinnamon toast and hot tea and considered ways to mend the breach with Patti. We'd have to be on speaking terms if I hoped to question her about Minta again. Also I didn't care to be locked in a feud with a woman who lived across the street from me.

My opportunity came when I wandered over to the white Victorian for a cup of hot chocolate and a final look at Kady's wares. Patti, already there, waved to me and smiled brightly. Her pink lipstick matched the streak of sunburn across her nose. "Hi, Cressa," she said. "Isn't this a beautiful morning?"

"Gorgeous," I said. "Maybe too warm."

"You mean sweltering. I wonder if anybody bought that little fan." She ran her hand over the collection of small appliances jammed together in a wooden crate. "Here it is. Just two dollars. Great!"

"Where are you going to use it?" I asked.

"Oh—somewhere. It won't take up much room. So—I hear you beat Gwendolyn to a super bargain yesterday."

"How did I do that?"

"That old Beverly Gray book could be worth over a thousand dollars."

"I don't believe it."

"The way Gwendolyn tells the story, another publisher reprinted all the books in the series except that one, so there aren't many copies around. Just the originals. You found a collector's dream. Check the Net for prices."

"I wonder if Kady knows," I said.

"Obviously not or she wouldn't have sold it for pennies. Buyers keepers, sellers beware. Something like that. What are you going to do with it?"

"Just read it."

"Ha! That'll drive Gwendolyn crazy. She'd sell it on eBay and turn a nice profit."

I glanced toward the porch. "I think I'll have some hot chocolate," I said.

"Me, too."

We walked toward the makeshift doughnut stand together, looking like the congenial neighbors we'd been before the specter of an unknown man came between us.

"I'm sorry for snapping at you yesterday," she said. "You caught me off guard. But where did you hear about Dan Byron?"

"From Minta Bransford's cousin, Allyson. Matt Emmerton and I had lunch with her."

"Why was she talking about him?"

"She mentioned that he was on the police force when Minta vanished. Matt is writing another story about Minta for the *Tribune*. That's why we went to see her."

"Matt should leave that old case alone," Patti said. "Dan didn't know anything about the disappearance. I mean, naturally he knew the facts. What the other cops did. That's all."

"How can you be sure?" I asked.

"He's my ex, but I don't like to talk about him. We weren't married long, and it didn't end well."

That personal trivia, however surprising, didn't answer my question. I tried again with another one.

"Was he your boyfriend when you were in high school?"

"No, not then. Dan was older, in his late twenties. We didn't get together until 1985."

"Then how can you say what he knew ten years earlier?"

"Because nobody knows anything about Minta Bransford," she said. "Why are you so fascinated by her anyway?"

"Because she lived in my house, I guess."

"Well, she isn't there now."

We'd reached the porch where the doughnuts lay in their white bakery boxes, crisp and irresistible. But I'd already had four slices of cinnamon toast. Thin slices.

"What'll it be?" Aleta asked.

"Two maple-iced dunkers and whatever you'd like, Cressa. It's my treat."

"Thanks. Just hot chocolate for me," I said.

She handed Aleta a five dollar bill. "Keep the change, honey."

I took a sip of the beverage. "This is so good."

"It's just the instant kind," Aleta said.

"I'd better pay for that fan before someone else nabs it. Good luck finding another bargain."

I watched Patti walk back to the crate. She moved briskly like someone who couldn't get away fast enough. For satisfying her curiosity about Dan Byron, she'd rewarded me with chocolate. Patti didn't want to talk about him, but she'd been quick to defend him. From what?

Every modest tidbit of information only led to another question. Deciding that I'd made some progress, I turned my attention to the sale, intending to look over Libby's possessions before they were all gone. Perhaps I'd find another treasure-in-disguise or a clue.

But after a quick sweep through the yard, I realized that nothing else appealed to me. I finished my drink and started walking slowly back toward the curb, surveying the items and their price tags. Kady was just going into the house. Annora, alone today, was looking through Libby's sheet music. Ruby had stationed herself an arm's distance from the doughnuts. Impossible to miss in a peasant skirt with alternating layers of red, pink and orange and a flowery straw hat that tied under her chin, she cast furtive glances at Aleta who was measuring chocolate powder into cups.

Here was another opportunity, too promising to pass up. I'd offer to buy her a crueler or lunch stick and start a conversation about tree houses or cloaks.

Before I'd fully formed the thought, she seized two cinnamon buns, one in each hand, and sprinted around the wraparound to the far side of the white Victorian. Aleta shouted, "Come back here. Those aren't free!"

Pepper set up an angry warning bark from my porch. Without thinking, I followed Ruby, threading my way through an uneven aisle of end tables. Rounding the corner, I rushed to the back. Too late.

There wasn't a sign of Ruby, or anyone else. Only green grass, dipped in shade, Libby's forsaken flowers and the satyr gleaming in the sunlight, his eyes so sharp and mocking that he seemed almost alive.

As he always did.

I looked away. Ruby must have escaped into the woods. Even if I caught up with her, she wouldn't be in a mood for a casual chat. She'd probably think I had pursued her to demand payment for the stolen cinnamon buns.

If cornered, who knew how she'd react? This wasn't the time to confront her. Besides the weather was too oppressive for a chase.

I stood still, wondering where my sudden intense discomfort had come from. The temperature seemed to have climbed ten degrees in ten minutes. Definitely, it was warmer in the backyard than it had been in front, even with the maple tree and the nearness of the water.

It's because of drinking hot chocolate, I thought. Cold juice would have been a better choice.

I recalled Annora's lighthearted remark about jumping in the fountain. Had anyone ever done that? Stepped across the rocky border on a hot day to cool off under the gushing spray? Only water could wash away the heat and the pain and the guilt…

That's the idea, Cressa. Only the water can save you.

The satyr's hand beckoned. His talon fingers were curved. Sunrays danced off his long, pointed nails as he reached out for me.

No!

"Hey, Cressa."

I felt a strong arm around my waist.

"What are you doing back here by yourself?" Matt asked. Then, "Are you all right?" He waited. His blue-green eyes demanded an answer.

"I—I'm fine. You startled me. I came to see where Ruby went."

"You're pale. Are you sure nothing's wrong?"

"It's just the heat," I said. "Ruby stole some cinnamon buns from Aleta."

"Forget about her. I'll pay Aleta for them."

He had a box in his hand, wrapped in glittering white paper, tied with matching ribbon.

"Are you going to a birthday party?" I asked.

"It's a present for you," he said. "A little trinket from the sale. I thought you'd like it."

I stared at the package, trying to hide my pleasure. "How sweet of you, Matt. Thanks."

"Let's get out of this heat. You can open it on the porch."

He kept his arm around me as we walked across the grass, past the satyr, away from the fountain. Then we were on my property, going through the door to the back porch. Once again, I was home and safe.

THIRTY

THE PORCH WAS MY safe place. It kept the burning sun and the satyr at bay. With Pepper on guard and Matt sitting beside me, I felt protected and a little foolish for overreacting to elements in the environment. After all, Texas summers were hotter, and the statue had never been anything more than a hunk of stone.

"You still look pale." Matt took a step toward the kitchen door. "Let me get you a glass of water."

Carefully removing the bow on the package, I said, "I'm fine. Now what's in the box?"

"One of Libby's souvenirs from up north." He stepped over Pepper and settled in the wicker rocker. "Kady says she bought it in the fifties, so it qualifies as an antique."

Matt's gift was an oval tray decorated with seashells and tiny dried bouquets on an aqua background. I lifted it by the woven straw handles and ran my hand over the glass top. "This is beautiful, Matt."

He glanced at my pendant and half moon earrings. "One of them looks like a star."

"If I'd seen this yesterday, I would have bought it for myself in an instant."

"I'm glad you like it. Did you find any good buys at the sale?" he asked.

"Some genuine treasures. A rare Beverly Gray edition that could be worth a thousand dollars and another scrapbook from the past." I described Minta's picture collection and summarized the old letter that had practically fallen into my lap. "Kady told me that Libby wrote another one a few days before she died but never mailed it. I think she meant to but didn't have the chance."

"Could be. Then Minta might have been murdered and buried secretly. Close to home could be anywhere in Maple Creek, even Wyndemere Park."

"Parks have people wandering around in them. If I had a body to get rid of, I'd bury it in the woods. Besides, the girl in green keeps turning up here."

"Good point."

"Also I learned that Patti Graham and Dan Byron were married in the eighties."

He nodded. "Interesting, but I don't see how that ties in to our mystery."

"Patti insisted that he didn't know anything about Minta, but they weren't together at the time."

"She might be covering up for him," he said. "Let's go check out the canoe. You coming, pup?"

Pepper thumped her tail on the floor but didn't get up.

"She doesn't like the heat," I said. "Besides, something back here spooks her."

"I wonder what."

"Something we can't see."

We walked slowly to the woods' edge. The wild ferns that grew along the property line lay close to the ground. It looked as if a creature had used them as a nest or trampled on them. Some wild animal or Ruby fleeing with her stolen cinnamon buns.

"Darn," I said. "I'll have to cut them now."

"They tend to fall over and dry up anyway," Matt said. "Let's see what's under this old tub."

He lifted one end and moved it as far as the rusty chains allowed, exposing the hard-packed dirt underneath to the light. We looked down at a colony of scattering beetles and crumbled brown leaves laced with cobwebs.

"Oh, for X-ray vision." I slapped at a tiny insect that flew in front of my face. "This place is creepy."

"And dark."

"Like a cemetery," I said.

It was easy to imagine Minta emerging from the ground for

a bittersweet look at her lost world. Unseen from the shadows, she'd watched as I moved the bones of her dog to the back of the yard. On another visit to the surface, she'd tossed pink petals on Sunny's grave.

That would explain her flower shredding behavior, except, afterward, she had gone into the woods, not the ground.

Well, she was a ghost. Her remains lay under the earth; her spirit could roam at will.

Whenever I thought about Minta, my imagination went galloping off into frightening realms. No wonder I had appalling nightmares and intuitions. In fact, it seemed as if someone were watching me now.

Not the satyr. He faced in the other direction. Possibly Rube, spying on the people who lived in houses, seething with envy. Someone… Minta?

I didn't see anything and couldn't hear a single alien sound. Still, a prickling sensation raced up my arms. I folded them and watched Matt.

Oblivious of undercurrents, he punched the canoe's rotting underside. A chunk of wood broke loose, and red paint chips drifted to the ground. "She'll never sail a lake again," he said.

"Annora was supposed to have it hauled away."

"She probably forgot. Ask her again."

"In the meantime, we could do some minor excavating, just a little way down."

"Not without notifying Annora first." He moved the canoe back in place. "I'm sure she'll cooperate if you show her the letter."

"Maybe," I said, knowing I wouldn't do that. "On Monday I'm calling Dalton."

"Dalton?"

"Lieutenant Gray," I said. "The police."

Matt laid his hand on my shoulder, a firm, warm touch. Once again it seemed to me that I'd known him in my past and would know him forever.

"Like I told you, Cressa, we're in this together," he said.

I wanted to believe him and felt certain that I could. *But,* an inner voice whispered, *What about Annora?*